RODENT

LISA J. LAWRENCE

ORCA BOOK PUBLISHERS

Library and Archives Canada Cataloguing in Publication

Lawrence, Lisa J., 1975–, author
Rodent / Lisa J. Lawrence.

Issued in print and electronic formats.
ISBN 978-1-4598-0976-5 (paperback).—ISBN 978-1-4598-0977-2 (pdf).—
ISBN 978-1-4598-0978-9 (epub)

I. Title.
PS8623.A9266R63 2016   jc813'.6   C2015-904506-1
C2015-904507-X

First published in the United States, 2016
Library of Congress Control Number: 2015946330

Summary: In this novel for teens, Isabelle knows all about shouldering responsibility:
she looks after her younger siblings because their mother is often drunk or absent. School is
a nightmare, but one teacher seems to understand that Isabelle has talent to spare.

*Orca Book Publishers is dedicated to preserving the environment and has
printed this book on Forest Stewardship Council® certified paper.*

Orca Book Publishers gratefully acknowledges the support for its publishing
programs provided by the following agencies: the Government of Canada through
the Canada Book Fund and the Canada Council for the Arts, and the Province of British
Columbia through the BC Arts Council and the Book Publishing Tax Credit.

Cover design by Teresa Bubela
Cover images by iStock.com, Dreamstime.com and Shutterstock.com
Author photo by Michael Lawrence

ORCA BOOK PUBLISHERS
www.orcabook.com

Printed and bound in Canada.

19 18 17 16 • 4 3 2 1

*To Mike: expert bug disposer,
computer fixer and fellow daydreamer*

ONE

"I'm wet," a voice whimpers in my ear.

My eyelids snap open as my head jerks from the pillow. Evan stands beside my bed, hair disheveled, naked from the waist down. Chicken legs shivering.

"What?" I blink, trying to clear my head.

"I'm wet." Now the tears come.

"Evan!" I grab his wrist and drag him, wailing, toward his bedroom. "Not again!"

In the early-morning sun filtering through the blinds, Maisie is still asleep in her bed next to his, curled up with a matted lamb. I strip the blankets and sheets from the mattress, cursing under my breath. I fling everything in a pile at his feet.

"Disgusting," I say, eyeing the foul wet circle. Rounding on him, I bring my finger right up to his pale face. "Tonight, you're wearing a pull-up."

"No! No diaper!" He sobs harder now.

"Yes, diaper!" I snap. "If you act like a baby, you have to wear a diaper." Maisie stirs in her bed, makes a chirping sound and rolls over.

Evan gives up arguing now and shivers, tears running down his cheeks. He scratches at his peed-on legs. He looks so pathetic, I start to feel sorry for him. I check the clock for the first time. Mickey Mouse's hands tell me it's 6:15 AM. I was cheated out of an extra fifteen minutes of sleep.

"C'mon," I say, taking his hand and pulling him to the bathroom. I mop him up and find a clean pair of underwear. The plastic garbage bag I always put under his sheet has slipped to one side in the night, so I scrub his wet mattress for a minute before giving up. What's one more stain at this point? He waits on the sofa in his Batman underwear while I wake up Maisie and get started.

Breakfast. Shower for me while they're eating. Lunches. I lay their clothes on the sofa and let them watch some alphabet cartoon while they dress themselves. That gives me ten minutes to get myself ready. Right before we leave, I try to wrestle a brush through Maisie's straggly mess of cinnamon curls.

She shrieks, trying to writhe away. I clamp my hands on her shoulders and push her back down. "Sit still! You want to look like a hobo on your first day at a new school?"

She gives me a dirty look but gets her shoes on when I tell her to. I help Evan into his.

"All ready?" I say, trying to sound more cheerful. Evan nods slowly, and Maisie just stares. "Okay then."

I lock the door behind me, and we shuffle to the end of the hall. The elevator smells like piss again. I blame the loser on the floor below us, who roams the halls in his bathrobe half the time.

"Don't touch anything," I tell Evan and Maisie, making them stand on either side of me. This place is even more of a dump than the last, and that's saying a lot. In the lobby we follow a worn path across the dirt-colored carpet to the main door and step into the bright September sun. Once outside, Maisie perks up and starts to tell me about her dream, which involves a farm.

"I got to ride the pony as much as I wanted," she says, skipping over the cracks in the sidewalk.

I pick up the pace. Evan almost runs to keep up, two fingers gripping my belt loop. We follow the sidewalk to a strip mall half a block away, stopping in front of a rainbow-striped sign: *Little Treasures Day Care*. Someone has thrown a rock through the corner of the sign, so the *r* in *Care* doesn't line up anymore.

Mrs. Carrigan, the owner, smiles at me as I push through the streaked door. I nod at her and crouch to help Evan take off his shoes and sweater, which I drop into his cubby. Then I corner Elaine, who runs the three-to-five-year-old room. She reminds me of a donkey, with her flat, tawny hair and the way she brays at the kids. Evan's only been coming here a week, and I already know Elaine's useless. Government subsidy covers most of the day-care fee, but it still feels like we pay too much for this place.

I get straight to the point. "Can you make sure Evan comes home in the right socks today?"

"Those *were* his socks." She frowns and pulls her head back, which gives her about four chins.

"My Little Pony?" I say, eyebrows raised. "I don't think so." Without waiting for a reply, I turn and herd Maisie out the door with me.

We have about thirty seconds to make it to the bus stop on the corner, so we cover the rest of the block at a full-out run. Maisie's backpack thumps up and down with every step, and I hear her puffing behind me. I turn and take her hand, slowing my pace a bit.

We make it with ten seconds to spare. The bus is packed. I finally find one seat near the back door and point for Maisie to sit down. Holding the bar above my head, I sway as the city slides by: cop cars, dogs, old people raking leaves, pawn shops, parking meters.

Maisie unpacks her backpack in her lap and shows me where she wrote her name on all of her school supplies. "I like this one," she says, pulling the cap off a glue stick. "The glue is pink."

After ten minutes, I ring the bell. The bus slides to a stop in front of Sir John A. Macdonald Elementary School, where we squeeze out with a few others. The bell has already rung, and the hallway's a solid wall of children. Two boys wrestle each other, swinging backpacks and laughing. When they trample on my feet, I give them a good shove and say, "Watch it."

We weave our way to the grade-two classrooms and scan the class list outside the door for *Maisie Bennett*. This is it. Her teacher, Mrs. Williams, strikes me as the cookie-baking-grandma sort. Silver hair pulled back in a hippie ponytail. Laugh lines around her eyes. She extends her hand to me as I leave Maisie at the door.

"Isabelle," I say, shaking it. "I'll be back to pick up Maisie after school." I give Maisie a pat on the head and push my way through the swarming hallway.

Back out on the sidewalk, I look up and see my final destination across the street—Glenn Eastbeck High School—where I'm about to begin my first day of grade eleven.

TWO

One of the women in the office assigns me a locker. Mine's a sickly blue and looks like it's been attacked by a battering ram. I look around as I unload my empty binders and loose-leaf paper. An emo couple is making out three lockers down. A group of girls talks at a decibel level that could shatter glass. Everyone else pretends not to be texting when a teacher walks by. This all looks pretty normal. And I consider myself somewhat of an expert on what's normal in high schools (and schools in general).

There have been five schools in the past three years, not to mention all the ones I passed through before I even hit junior high. I've seen it all. If I keep my head down, after two more years of this I'll be free. Then it won't matter if Mom has a good day or two when she finds a new job, drags us off to some other hellhole, then brings the whole thing crashing down. I won't be a puppet in this stupid game anymore.

I don't realize how hard I slam my locker until the girl next to me jumps. I give her a look like, *What?* and march off. Then I have to pull out a map of the school because I have no idea where I'm going. English. Room 102. Okay.

When I find it, I make a beeline for the back row, which is already taken by other students trying to be invisible or goof off. I end up sitting in front of a tall guy with a mop of dark hair and glasses that look like they belong in the sixties. He's reading a thesaurus. To my left, a chubby girl with stringy hair picks at her split ends. I think I've found my corner.

While the teacher, Mr. Drummond, goes through the course outline, some tool in the back row starts throwing paper balls.

"Hey, Will!" he whispers. I hear the whoosh of a ball land right on the desk behind me—the tall guy's desk. As far as I can tell without turning around, Will does nothing.

Then things get quiet. Mr. Drummond strolls down the aisle between us, his scuffed leather loafers not making a sound. His belly hangs over a pair of crisp khakis, and I can't see his mouth under a bristly mustache. Thick graying hair sticks up on his head, like he just walked through a windstorm. For some reason, we all look straight ahead as he gets closer, even those of us who haven't done anything.

I glance up at him for a split second as he pauses beside my desk. With that flicker of a look, square in his eyes, I see he's a man who can silence a room with a stare. I look away, but he doesn't move from beside my desk. He slowly scans the back row. Not a sound. Across the street, bus brakes hiss.

"That's quite enough," he says, his eyes moving from desk to desk. There's some foot shuffling and squirming, but nobody speaks.

After an eternity, he turns and walks back to the front of the class. He picks up where he left off, telling us that we're reading *Hamlet* this year. At least it isn't *Romeo and Juliet*, which I've read at my last three schools and didn't like the first time.

No one acts up again. When Mr. Drummond dismisses us, Will drops the paper ball in the garbage on the way out.

Social Studies. I check my map again before leaving English. Second floor. I elbow some girl out of the way for the last free desk at the back. The teacher, Mrs. Clarke, hands out a course outline. It's quiet for a minute before she starts reading it aloud. Then the whispers start. A guy gets up to sharpen his pencil. Pretty soon people turn in their desks and talk to friends beside them. Out come the phones. Mrs. Clarke keeps going, the paper an inch from her face. I follow along with her because I have nothing else to do. I feel kind of sorry for her. She lets us go fifteen minutes early.

At lunchtime I find the cafeteria by following the flow of bodies. Standing near the door, I survey the long tables—a rippling ocean of heads, arms and mouths. It seems everyone except me has made Best Friends Forever and can't stop talking, teasing and touching each other for even one second. I haven't had a chance to find the library yet, so I have no book to hide behind.

Off to the left, a line snakes from the cafeteria counter. People leave with stacks of French fries, piles of chicken nuggets and cans of soda tucked under their arms. I can see that one of those meals costs the same as two loaves of bread and a gallon of milk, so buying lunch isn't an option.

I find a bench along the wall rather than a table—there's no awkward stranger to avoid making eye contact with. I wolf down my bologna sandwich and banana at record speed and go looking for a garbage can. There's one near the door, conveniently close to my escape route.

In front of me, balancing a tray of empty wrappers and an apple core, is a girl with bright-red hair. Blunt bangs and long wavy curls down her back. Translucent white skin. She just stands there, not moving. How long is this going to take? I glance over her shoulder.

Three girls block the garbage can, smiling. I'd know that sort of smile anywhere, in any grade, in any school. The kind of smile that makes my stomach clench up.

The blond in the middle has thick, round shoulders. Stocky build, like an ox. Her shiny hair falls in a curtain over her shoulders. Small squinty eyes that look like a pig's when she smiles. The brunette on her right is tall, athletic. She'd be gorgeous except her makeup is so thick she looks like a pole dancer. I recognize her from my Social Studies class. On the other side stands a black girl with an impressive afro and shimmery eye shadow. Silver bangles and purple-painted nails.

"Pick it up," the blond says, still smiling, nodding to a crushed milk container and ketchup-covered napkin on the floor.

"It's not mine," the redhead says, all breathy.

"It is now, so pick it up."

"No." She sounds a bit edgier now, like she's either going to stand her ground or start to cry. "I don't want to."

I don't know if it's the blond's smug expression or her petty show of authority, but I feel like jamming that milk container right down her throat. When she takes a step forward and opens her mouth to speak again, my words fly out all by themselves.

"Pick it up yourself," I say in a quiet voice that somehow echoes through the entire cafeteria. Every table within twenty feet falls silent. My heart starts to pound.

The ugly smile slides from the blond's face as she glances past the redhead to the stranger behind her. She looks me over. Probably doesn't think much of what she sees: wiry, on the small side, long brown hair and hard, hard blue eyes. I don't blink.

"What did you say?" she whispers. Her two friends start to shift, looking around.

"Pick it up yourself," I say again, louder. Something grinds inside me. The redhead flees.

It happens in an instant. The blond narrows her eyes and moves to take a step toward me. Between the eye-narrowing and when she lifts her foot, I form a fist. I know how to make a decent fist. My cousin Jacquie taught me—thumb on the outside, knuckles not too tight. It has served me well, especially at these ghetto schools I usually end up in.

The blond opens her mouth to say something, shoulders squared for a fight. Before she can get the word out, I slam her in the face. She staggers back into the arms of her friends. Grabs her nose to stop the gush of blood spraying down her turquoise tank top. Shock is all I see on the face of every single person, including her. They weren't expecting this. Ice floods my gut. Tears form in her squinty eyes. Then something else, something I recognize instantly: rage.

She twists herself away from her friends' arms and straightens up. Eyes locked on mine, face on fire. Here it comes. As she's about to spring, a woman in a hairnet shows up beside me, gripping my arm. "You, come with me," she barks, dragging me through the door. "Take her to the nurse!" she calls over her shoulder to the blond's friends.

She marches me through the half-empty hallway, every person turning to gawk. I feel like I'm being dragged to a public hanging. Hairnet woman is still squeezing my arm in her bony fingers, so I yank myself free. She turns like she wants to grab me again but sees the expression on my face and lowers her hand. Maybe she's afraid I'll slug her too.

"I'm capable of walking by myself, thank you," I say in my coldest voice.

She purses her lips and marches ahead of me. I consider making a break for it, but to where? I still have to pick up Maisie at three thirty. Don't exactly want to hang out in a locker or bathroom stall for three hours. No, better to face these things kicking and screaming.

We round a corner, and we're back at the office again. The admin assistant who assigned me the locker looks up and stops typing as we parade by.

"Sit." Hairnet points to a punishingly hard wooden chair outside an inner office. A black plaque on the door reads

Andrew Talmage, Principal. Hairnet knocks and slips through, giving me one last evil eye before she shuts the door behind her. I sit for an eternity. The phone rings endlessly, and the admin assistant answers a long list of the most boring questions and requests imaginable. "He won't go on the bus today then? Okay, I'll let him know to meet you out front…" "The students are dismissed at 3:25…" "If you paid your fees, we have no record of them. You'll have to send another check…" My knuckles throb.

Why am I sitting here? How easy would it be to just get up and leave? I could walk a few blocks down, to where no one would see. Get on a bus to anywhere. Disappear. Never come back to this stupid office and this hard-as-a-rock chair, never listen again to people go on and on about the trivial crap in their silly little lives. No one would even notice.

Then I picture Maisie standing at the door of her second-grade classroom as all the other moms come with soccer uniforms and homemade muffins and whisk their precious babies away. And Evan, stuck with the Donkey until Child and Family Services is called. Shipped off to some foster home where they keep him in the basement and feed him Wonder bread and water three times a day. Or worse. My cousin Jacquie spent six months in a foster home a few years back and said the wife couldn't keep her hands off her, beating her black and blue. The husband couldn't either. No way I'll let that happen.

The heat starts rising in my gut again, so when Mr. Talmage opens the door and peers down at me, I'm ready to scratch out his eyes too.

THREE

In his office, he gestures for me to sit on another rock-hard chair, then settles behind his desk in a cushy leather one. Reclines. Stares. I know this trick well—the I'm-just-going-to-stare-at-you-for-a-while technique, used to arouse shame and discomfort. *Sorry, buddy, but have you got the wrong girl.* Two can play this game. I lean back in my wooden chair and try to appear as comfortable as possible. Which is a feat. I smile and look around, like I've never been in a nicer place. I even manage to work in a sigh of contentment.

Mr. Talmage raises two beefy fingers to his lips and continues his contemplation. He looks like an ex-NFL player gone to seed. His hulking body barely fits in the chair. Square jaw beneath the jowls. Wisps of gray in his sideburns. A comb-over that's downright embarrassing.

"Do you want to tell me what happened?" he says. Ah, the kind-counselor approach, waiting to pounce on an admission of guilt.

"I defended myself," I say, staring straight into his eyes.

"From what I heard, you were the only one doing the punching."

"She came at me to hit me." My voice is a little edgy now.

He stops and does some more staring, which is starting to unnerve me more than I'd like to admit. "Is it possible she was just going to say something to you?"

As he says the words, I'm forced to admit the truth that comes bubbling to the surface. Something akin to guilt starts to dampen my anger. I push it away. If she wasn't going to hit me at that moment, she would at another. That look doesn't just fade away to nothing. I'd pay sooner or later.

"It didn't look that way from where I was standing," I say.

Mr. Talmage takes a deep breath. "Miss Bennett," he begins, and I know this is where kind counselor turns into parole officer, "I don't know how things were at your last school"—when he says *last school*, his lip curls slightly—"but here at Glenn Eastbeck, we don't just *whack* someone when they look at us in a way we don't like." He pauses, either for effect or to let me respond. Which I don't.

"I've tried to reach your mother," he continues, examining my face. "Any idea where she is?"

"Sleeping it off," I say. I can tell by his scowl that he doesn't believe me. Which is why I said it.

"You want to try that again?" Still the parole officer.

Well, he didn't believe the truth, so I try a lie. "At work." The standard answer for what most adults do during the day. No one seems to question that one. When he asks me where she works, I tell him it's a sports bar, and I don't know the name or phone number because it's a new job. Ironically, the more honest I am with this man, the more I seem to annoy him.

"You don't know the name?" he says. I shake my head. "Well, Isabelle, I will be talking to your mother personally. And you"—he takes a breath to make sure he has my attention—"you have a two-day suspension to think about your actions." He runs his tongue over his fat lips. "Consider this your final warning. If we meet again under these circumstances, it will be to discuss your expulsion." He raises his bushy eyebrows, nodding slowly to give me time to digest his words.

I try not to smile. He threatens me with my mother—who's nearly impossible to catch both awake and sober at the same time—and gives me two days off school. I don't want to push things at this point though. I nod back—slow, serious.

"Wait outside my office until I can reach her," he says, gesturing to the door. He turns back to his computer before I've even left.

This is the real punishment, having to sit around listening to everyone else's stupid conversations while my butt goes numb. The admin assistant talks to the custodian about her nephew's new baby boy, who is just so extremely precious, as though people don't have babies every day.

"Can I collect my stuff from my locker?" I ask her. She's done an excellent job of ignoring me up to this point. She gives a furtive look toward Mr. Talmage's closed door.

When she doesn't answer, I tell her, "I'll come right back." Trying to sound as innocuous as possible. She nods.

I get my books and jacket from my locker and return to my jail chair in the office. At least I have some reading material now, in the form of my English textbook. I spend the rest of the third block—supposed to be Biology—reading about some fool getting buried alive, one brick at a time, behind a cellar wall.

Mr. Talmage sticks his head out the door right before the last bell and tells me to get my mother to call him. I take it he couldn't get her out of bed to answer the phone. "You won't be returning to school until I have that conversation," he says, as if that's a threat. Like there aren't a hundred other crappy schools in this city to choose from. He starts to say something else, but the bell cuts him off mid-word. I get up and walk away before he can repeat himself.

Across the street, Maisie's waiting in her classroom like I told her to. She hops up from a circle mat and runs to my side. She shows me a craft she made with cotton balls and pipe cleaners. I have no idea what it is but tell her, "That's really nice! Now get your sweater. Evan's waiting." She waves goodbye to Mrs. Williams, who's lost behind an enormous stack of papers on her desk.

On the bus to day care, I ask her about her first day of grade two.

"I made a friend. She's called Emily, and she has a loose tooth." Maisie raises her hand absently to her own very intact teeth. "But I had to sit by another boy who was pokey."

"What do you mean, *pokey?*"

"He poked me in the arm with his finger," she says. "I didn't like it."

"Well, if he ever does it again, give him a smack and tell him to cut it out." I know I should be giving her some motherly advice about talking through conflict, using words to express her feelings, or telling a grown-up. But I give her the advice she'll actually need to survive eleven more years in this jungle. "And if he doesn't," I add, "tell him your big sister's coming after him."

Maisie considers this and nods.

Evan brightens at the sight of us in the doorway. It seems that he and his buddy, Patrick, are in the middle of a squabble over the best truck in the room, and we're his reinforcements. As usual, Elaine hasn't helped at all. Too busy cutting out apples from construction paper in the corner.

"C'mon, Evan," I call. "I've got to get to work."

Evan lowers his chin and stands his ground. He knows that to leave now is to concede and lose it all.

"Now!"

He comes slowly, dragging his feet across the carpet. "I bet you can play with the truck first tomorrow," I say as we head down the hallway to his cubby. He doesn't believe me and makes me put on his shoes and sweater without lifting his arms and feet to help.

I half-drag Evan and Maisie, one in each hand, down the block to our apartment, through the lobby, into the elevator.

They start fighting over who gets to press the button for our floor, so I do it myself. Which makes them both sulk.

I pause outside our apartment door. What I'll find on the other side is like a choose-your own-adventure story. I turn the key and push the door open, standing in front of Maisie and Evan.

Mom's in the kitchen, drying her damp hair with a towel, a ratty bathrobe stretched across her generous hips and chest. She smiles. I exhale.

Maisie and Evan run to her. "My teacher let us use the paints!" Maisie says.

"Patrick took the best truck." Evan tugs on her terrycloth belt.

As she starts to ask them about their day, I say, "You'll make them supper?" She nods. I grab a piece of bread and dash for the door. She calls me back.

"What?" I say, sounding like a cat getting stepped on.

She pushes her face close to mine—coffee breath this time. The skin around her light blue eyes is puffy, creased by crow's-feet. She finger-combs her damp platinum hair, a shock of mousy regrowth at the roots.

"Well," she says, "how was your first day?"

"Oh, fine. I got the classes I wanted."

"Good." She brightens and shifts away. I feel a twinge of guilt. Just for one second.

I say goodbye to Maisie and Evan and jog down to the convenience store right beside our apartment building. I started working there three weeks ago, just a few days a week.

Two hours after school, during rush hour, before Mom leaves for her shift. I stock the shelves and clean up. They've started training me on the till too, except for lotto and cigarettes.

Rupa's at the counter. Her husband, Arif, is nowhere to be seen. Rupa's all right, but Arif constantly scrutinizes me, peeking around chip displays. Like he expects to catch me shoplifting any second. Their son, Hasan, works there too sometimes. He's eighteen and way too good-looking to be trusted. He smiles at me and volunteers for "training," which usually prompts me to rearrange the cooler or reclean the bathroom. Something about his white teeth and dimples makes me start dropping things and tripping over my own feet.

In a lull between customers, Rupa asks me about my first day of school. I smile, shrug and tell her it was good—everything oh-so-normal. I'd rather die than look this woman in the eye—her warm, open face—and tell her I'm one step away from foster care, homelessness or prison. Those kinds of conversations don't exactly build employer-employee relationships. There's something else about her too. Like, I could picture bringing her a test where I got an A and waving it around, like Maisie does with me and her drawings.

Rupa has me stock the cooler and then asks me to find Arif to see what he wants done. I'm not surprised at all when he hands me a toilet brush and a pair of gloves and sends me to clean the bathroom. They must save this for me. I hang the Closed sign on the doorknob and get to work.

I grit my teeth and scrub at the urinal. It looks like half the city passed through today and took turns missing.

I consider putting a Cheerio in the bottom for aim, like I do for Evan. The toilet is even worse. By the time I finish it and haul out the garbage, which has a nasty diaper or two, I'm sweaty and in no mood for Hasan's winning smiles. I barely say hello to him and ask Rupa if I can work the till for a while. She stands next to me, in case I get stuck. At the end of my shift, I buy a box of cereal to take home and a few five-cent sour candies for Maisie and Evan.

I know as soon as I open the apartment door and see that Evan and Maisie have pulled out a box of crackers for supper, leaving a trail of crumbs between the kitchen and living room. The television is blaring.

I don't even know why I ask, "Where's Mom?"

"She's sleeping," Evan says slowly, knowing that for some reason this answer always makes me mad. Maisie just looks at me and waits.

I storm into the kitchen and toss the bag with the cereal on the counter, tipping over a coffee mug, which smashes on the floor. I pick up one of the large pieces and hurl it into the sink, where it shatters into tiny shards. Evan begins to cry. Maisie stands still, watching me.

Charging down the hall, I throw open the door and flick on the light. There she is, half dressed for work, on her belly, snoring. One empty bottle is tipped over on the dresser, and there's another one on the floor by the bed.

"Get up!" I shriek. "Your shift starts in less than an hour!"

She doesn't even stir. And in her stillness, I want to pick up an empty bottle and beat her senseless with it. Shake her, slap her, scream. I want to sink my nails into her limp arm to the point of drawing blood and make her respond to me.

Instead I turn off the light, shut the door and find Evan. Holding him in my lap, I stroke his hair and tell him it will be okay. I smile at Maisie and tell her I'll make supper soon. When my voice is steady enough, I find my mom's new work number on the fridge and call, telling them she's deathly ill with food poisoning and won't make it in tonight. They're still too new to know that this will happen again. And again. And again. Until someone catches on and, in a humiliating scene, fires her. Then we'll pack what little we have and move to some other dump or shelter or friend's basement to start it all over again.

I know one thing tonight, with Evan's hair against my cheek and Maisie waiting for me to feed her: I've had enough of the wooden chairs, concrete floors, suitcases and bedbugs. The lying, laundry, excuses, hunger, dirt and piss. My fingers tremble as I touch Evan's hair. I've had enough, and I'm getting out.

FOUR

Every time I start to drift off on their bedroom floor, Maisie scratches at her legs, like she always does in her sleep. Evan hasn't even stirred. I let them stay up late to watch a rerun of *The Wizard of Oz* on TV. Cable is a recent luxury, and we only have it now because it's a rental incentive for the apartment. Our television's not pretty, but it works. And it's tough. Uncle Richie, Jacquie's dad, once chucked an empty vodka bottle at the screen, offended by the weather forecast. It didn't even chip.

I could get up and move to my own bed or sleep on the sofa. I'm supposed to share a room with Mom. I have a camping cot set up next to her bed. Most nights, though, especially lately, I can't even stand to hear her breathing next to me. On those nights, I pull the cushions off the sofa instead and drop them on Maisie and Evan's floor. Something about watching them sleep makes me feel less like beating Mom with a tire iron.

On nights like this, I pull out my notebook. It isn't a journal, exactly—more for writing stories, poems, things I don't want to say out loud. I'd rather douse this entire building with gasoline and light a match than have this discovered and read by another living soul. I've found a pretty good hiding spot for it too—inside my suitcase. I slip it in where the lining is ripped and maneuver it to a place near the base, where it's not visible. Not that anyone's looking.

I drag my suitcase off the shelf in their closet and start to root around for it. It has slipped past the spot I usually leave it. There's a moment of panic while I grope around, imagining that Evan has found the notebook and covered it in crayon. Or worse, that Mom has. My poetry would trigger a binge for sure. There, I've found its hard corner. I work it out through the frayed lining, the pen tucked tight in the coil binding. Then I tiptoe into Mom's room—she's still out cold—and grab my flashlight from under my cot. She doesn't even twitch.

With a pen in one hand and the flashlight in the other, I wait for the words to come. After a minute I flip to a story near the back and pick up where I left off. Abby, my protagonist, is making a suicide pact with her twin sister. If their mother goes ahead and marries her abusive boyfriend, they'll drink poisoned Kool-Aid. Her mother has just announced the wedding date. I'm not sure if I'll off Abby or not, but I'm pretty sure the sister will at least become a heroin addict. I only scribble another paragraph, though, before the heaviness of the day creeps back. I try to push it away, but it nags at me and blocks my words. I lay my cheek on the pillow, pushing the notebook aside.

It's been a bad week. Mom hasn't come out and said it, but I know this is the one-year anniversary of when Claude—Maisie's and Evan's dad—left. I did a happy dance myself, but I hear her crying at night sometimes. And the way he did it: empty apartment, kids' piggy banks cleaned out, not even a note. What a douche.

I drift off this way and have restless dreams about the tinkling of bottles like tiny bells. Being closed up in muffled darkness, one brick at a time. Small voices whimpering somewhere I can't reach.

I wake to Maisie crouching over me, her hair dangling down and tickling my eyebrow. "What's that?" she asks. My eyes snap open. My notebook has fallen to the floor beside me, its pages splayed.

I snatch it up and tell her, "Homework." I tuck it on their high shelf, behind a box of winter clothes.

Evan is already mucking around in the kitchen, having pulled a chair over to the counter to reach the loaf of bread. I take the bread from his hand after he's had a bite or two. "Do you want me to toast this for you?" He nods. I must have really been out of it to miss all of this. It's 9:23 AM. Bus left. Bell rung. Class started. There's no way I can pull it off this morning. I call Maisie's school and tell an ancient-sounding admin assistant that Maisie is sick and won't be in today.

Evan, standing at my elbow, says, "We're not going to school today?"

"There is no school today, Evan. School's closed." He seems to accept this, since often things he's interested in are closed—the toy store, the swimming pool, sometimes the park. "You'll be home with me today, okay?" I say.

"And Mom?"

I pause. "Maybe. We'll see. I guess so." I mean, technically she'll be in the apartment, right?

She stumbles out around noon, just as I'm getting out of the shower. The kids are watching TV. Her hair is puffed up on one side; she must have passed out while it was still damp. "Why didn't you wake me up last night?" she says, reaching for the water jug in the fridge.

I give her the look.

"I was just having a bit of a nap before you got home." She rubs her temple. "You should've woken me."

"I had to call in for you again." I can't even look her in the eye.

"Why, Isabelle? You should've woken me," she says, pouring a tall glass. I've started down the hall to grab my notebook and take off when the phone rings.

I know exactly who it is. I dash for it as she takes a few lazy steps, clamping my hand over the receiver the second before she reaches it.

"Isabelle, what on earth?"

"Sit down, Mom." Then I tell her about punching the blond, making it out like she was a bloodthirsty maniac who tried to kill me. All while the phone rings endlessly behind us.

It finally stops as I get around to mentioning my totally unjust suspension.

She still manages to look shocked every time I get in trouble at school.

"Isabelle." She opens her pale mouth, struggling with the words, "I didn't raise you…"

"No, you didn't raise me!" I holler, banging both fists against the table. Knocking over a salt shaker.

My words seem to suck the air out of her. That's how I leave her as I break for the door and head down the hall, small voices trailing behind me. I lose them at the elevator, ignoring the pull in my stomach as the doors slide closed before they reach me.

I've forgotten my jacket. Low clouds dampen a gray skyline, making goose bumps prickle my arms. I walk for an hour, the wind scratching my cheeks red.

When I get back, Mom is sitting at the table with the phone in front of her. She gives me a pointed stare. I gather Mr. Talmage has given her the your-daughter-beats-up-inno-cent-children-and-fluffy-kittens talk.

I stare straight back. *Just bring it up, Mom. Just try.*

She chooses each word carefully. "Your principal called." Takes a breath. "He said you can go back on Monday, but he wants to see you in his office before your first class."

"Okay." I can tell she wants to say more.

"Isabelle." She clears her croaky throat. I know what's coming. I don't want to hear any apologies today about her being a bad mother or not giving us what we deserve.

As she continues to be a bad mother and not give us what we deserve. Not today.

"Don't, *Mother*," I say, marching past her.

She lays her head on the table.

The moment I slam the bedroom door, that guilt bubbles up. I have the impulse to rush back and hug her, like I did when I was Maisie's age. Can't remember the last time I was hugged by anyone other than Maisie and Evan. Or that drunk guy at Jacquie's birthday party, who I had to knee in the balls to get away from.

No. She made this bed. This bed of vomit and piss and dirty sheets. Let her lie in it.

A minute later I hear the shower run.

* * *

Over the weekend, I stay glued to Mom.

"Stop it, Isabelle," she says during dinner on Saturday, watching my eyes follow the beer bottle to her mouth. "I'm allowed to have a drink."

Later, when she's taking too long in the bathroom, I burst in without knocking. She's on the toilet, reading a mystery novel, and scrambles to cover herself. Like I haven't seen it all a million times.

"Cut it out!" She shoves me from the bathroom, pants still around her ankles. The lock clicks behind her.

Still, she makes it to work both nights.

* * *

On Monday morning, my stomach flutters as I wind through the hallway on my way to Mr. Talmage's office. Because of the weekend after my two-day suspension, it feels like I've been away a while.

I keep my eyes peeled for the squinty blond and her friends but don't see anyone I recognize. Might as well get the bowing and scraping over with so I can get on with this year and get the hell out.

Mr. Talmage's door is shut, muffled voices inside. Who's with him? I knock. His hulking frame fills the doorway. He looks down at me like I'm a used Band-Aid on his breakfast plate.

"Miss Bennett," he says. "Come in."

As he pushes the door open wider, I see her in one of the wooden chairs. The blond. And she has an impressive bruise. I don't know whether to be proud or ashamed. She looks up at me. I look away.

Mr. Talmage gestures to an empty chair beside her. We both stare straight ahead, although I'm close enough to smell her fruity shampoo.

"Miss Bennett and I have discussed the inappropriateness of her actions," Mr. Talmage says, leaning toward the blond, "but I think she should know more about her victim."

Victim? He makes me sound like a serial killer.

He looks me in the eye and gestures toward her. "Ainsley is an honors student and an active member of our students' union. She has participated in fundraising for the food bank, after-school programs and jerseys for our sports teams." The man has actually made a list. He inhales slowly to give me time to admire the wonder that is Ainsley.

"She plays on the volleyball team and is president of the Art Club." Is this winding up anytime soon? "She is an asset to our school." And another word I can think of beginning with *a*. "Is there something you would like to say to Ainsley?" he says. I bite my tongue. In the silence, he prompts, "I think you owe Ainsley an apology, Isabelle."

Ainsley, who's been sitting with her hands folded in her lap like a sainted nun up to this point, turns her pale face toward me, eyes open wide, and blinks.

I wonder how long we'll sit here if I say nothing at all. I mean, really, I have all day. That dark cloud of *what if* moves in my mind, always ending up at those two small faces. As much as this place is a dump, it's right across from Maisie's school. Being at another school wouldn't work as well.

I steel myself, look into her piggy eyes and say, "I'm sorry I hit you." Mr. Talmage nods, like we're just getting started. *What? What else?* "And I won't do it again." I feel about five years old. He keeps nodding, but I'm all out of words. He makes some kind of gesture for us to shake hands, which we don't.

Ainsley blinks again, gazing angelically at Mr. Talmage. I stare at a stapler on his desk.

"Now, no more of this nonsense," he says as the phone on his desk starts to ring. "There's no reason you girls can't be friends. Off to class." He shoos us toward the door.

We scrape our chairs back and try to maneuver around each other without touching or making eye contact. As we head for the door, I stop to let her step through first. Mr. Talmage laughs loudly into the receiver and swivels his back to us.

"You're dead," she whispers in my ear as she pushes past me.

FIVE

The black girl—Celeste is her name—is in my English class. How did I not notice her before? She sits near the front by a different blond with red lipstick. Between the two of them, there's constant whispering, giggling and sliding of bangles. She catches me watching her once and stares back. Not in a mean way—mostly curious. I disappear behind my paper.

We're starting with one of those stupid what-I-did-on-my-summer-vacation writing assignments, "to assess our writing abilities." To assess my lying abilities, more like. I fought a bedbug infestation in the last place—lost. Mom got fired, again. Packed and moved. Cleaned up pee (Evan's), puke (Mom's). Sat around picking my nose, watching Maisie and Evan at the park. Tried to keep Jacquie out of juvy. Who wants to hear about all of that?

Sometimes I think I feel eyes on me. I turn around and see Will, the tall guy, scribbling on his third sheet of paper.

Everyone else is messing around with their phones behind their dictionaries.

"Those phones are about to be mine," Mr. Drummond says from the front of the class, not even looking up. There's a mad scramble of hands in pockets and purses.

I was right about the tall girl, the pole dancer, being in my Social Studies class. Great. Two out of three now. She catches my eye on purpose and laughs, like my mere existence is a joke. Some stupid-looking football type sitting beside her laughs too. Without the courage to look me in the eye though.

Someone whispers, "It's Mike Tyson!" as I sit down. Good. Now they know to leave me alone.

Mrs. Clarke talks about a group project we're starting next week. Excellent. I already know how this is going to end up—me and the pole dancer cozied up to a poster on World War II.

Pole Dancer finds reasons to walk by my desk three times during class. Mrs. Clarke doesn't even notice people moving around. The last time she goes by, Pole Dancer drops a folded-up note on my desk, and I make a big show of getting up and throwing it straight in the garbage without opening it.

"What are you doing, dear?" Mrs. Clarke says, singling me out of at least ten kids who are wandering around the classroom. "No reason for you to be out of your desk now."

Pole Dancer and her football friend snigger. I'm the first one out the door when the bell rings.

Lunch. I need to find a safe place before everyone can regroup, talk, make a plan. I practically tackle the custodian as he weaves his cart through the sea of indifferent bodies.

"Where's the library?" I say.

He stares at me for a second. I'm guessing not a lot of kids talk to him. "Down the stairs and to your left." He motions with a finger.

I push through the hall, hawk eyes on everyone. My heart pounds as I round the stairwell. The stairs would be the worst place—hard to get away, hard to defend myself, trapped.

So far, so good. I notice some people staring or smiling as I walk by. I must have made quite an impression in the cafeteria. *Stupid, Isabelle.* I don't care about making friends, but it's the invisibility factor that usually gets me by.

Okay, down the stairs and to my left. There it is, like some kind of oasis. Something about a library instantly calms me. The sharp smell of pages, yellow and old, crisp and brand-new. The shuffling of paper, quiet clicking on a keyboard, the scratch of a pencil. Like nothing bad could ever happen in a library.

There is also a direct correlation between how cranky a librarian is and how well the library is run. The crankier the better. At my last school, the librarian was this sweet, soft lady who was always humming and letting kids listen to stuff on their iPhones. People dropped books wherever, always talking. It felt like desecration.

"Watch out there," the librarian says, looking up from her desk and gesturing to an open box of books near my feet.

She has a pointy nose and one of those beaded chains for her glasses. She's wearing a sweater the color of baby poop. I smile.

Her eyes stay fixed on me as I find the perfect table—a good view of the door but not backed into a corner. She seems appeased once I pull out my English and Social Studies textbooks. I'm supposed to read the first two scenes of *Hamlet* by tomorrow. I don't think I missed anything at all in Social Studies during my two-day holiday.

I stay the whole lunch hour, breaking off bits of my peanut-butter sandwich when the librarian turns her back or disappears behind a shelf. I'm careful not to leave any crumbs behind. I need this woman on my side. Little does she know I'm about to become her new best friend. I sign out a stack of books near the end of the lunch hour—my escape at home and school.

I wait until the bell rings before making a move to my next class—Biology—to let the halls fill with people. Easier to get lost in the shuffle, and there's safety in numbers.

Now that I have two of the three musketeers in my morning classes, I'm fully prepared for Saint Ainsley to bless either Biology or Spanish with her presence, but no. No squinty blond ox in either one. My shoulders unclench a bit.

In fact, in Spanish a brunette with buck teeth leans over to me and whispers, "I hear you punched Ainsley Peters."

"Yeah?" I say, more defensively than I intended.

"How'd that feel?" If I'm giving off a negative vibe, she's not catching it.

"Pretty good, actually."

"Yeah." She nods and smiles, turning back to her book. "Pretty good."

Apparently I'm not the only one who wants to punch Ainsley in the face. Happy to have been of service to losers everywhere.

By the end of the day, though, I'm tired of sneaking around like a criminal. I did apologize (insincerely), and this is my school too (unfortunately). As I head toward my locker, I throw my shoulders back and stare down any looks that come my way. No more tiptoeing.

As I turn the corner to my locker, I see three ugly, smiling faces. My stomach drops. Mid-step, I think of ten different escape routes. No. I can't. Won't. Head up, shoulders back. March on.

My fingers tremble as I turn the combination on my lock and the voices start around me.

"Well, look who's back."

"Look who has a death wish."

They go round and round, a swirl of empty, stupid threats. I don't say anything, head down as I try to gather my jacket and books as quickly as I can. I can't have any more trouble at this school.

Out of the corner of my eye, I see that Ainsley and Pole Dancer are doing most of the talking. Celeste stands with her arms crossed, looking on. I balance my books and backpack in one arm and try to swing my locker shut. Pole Dancer sticks her foot inside while Ainsley elbows my books to the floor. They crash. Heads turn.

"Whoops! Let me help," Ainsley says, bending at the same time as me. Her hand touches mine, almost gently, as we reach for the same binder. We both stop. Quietly, even too quietly for her friends to hear, she whispers, "Your day is coming, princess. You've been warned." Then she stands and leaves me to my mess.

I think they'll leave now, but they watch me scrape the pile of papers off the floor and stack my textbooks again. My cheeks are on fire. I haven't said a single word. I manage to shut the locker this time, and they trail down the hall after me.

"Look who thinks she's something special." Again with the comments.

I feel panic rising on top of the broiling mess already churning in my gut. I have to pick up Maisie now. How can I possibly bring this freak show to her? They'll see where I'm going. They'll know I have a little sister. What could Maisie do against this, against their ugly words? Would they hurt her? My chest pulls tight. She'll be waiting by now, standing at the door with her backpack on. I'm already late.

"We'll see who's laughing when she's bleeding on the floor." Pole Dancer's voice behind me. *Idiot. Who's laughing now? Who ever laughed?*

Something comes to me at the end of the hall, as I head down the stairs to the main doors. I hold the railing, just in case I get a push from behind.

At the bottom of the stairs, instead of turning right to leave, I turn left toward the office. A few stragglers watch us move by, then turn away, pretending not to see.

"You can give it, but you can't take it, eh?" Ainsley says.

Then they realize where I'm headed.

"Running to tell Daddy?"

I walk on.

At the office door, I turn to see what they'll do. They stand a few feet away from me in the hall, waiting, watching. Celeste steps back and looks away, raising a nail to her mouth.

Mr. Talmage's door is shut—good thing. The admin assistant cradles the phone at her ear as she clicks across her keyboard. I sit in the wooden chair outside his door, *the* chair, like I'm waiting to see him.

They shift outside the office door, leaning together to whisper. If Mr. Talmage comes out, I'll have to say something to him, make something up. It beats getting jumped in the hallway. They stand around another minute before Ainsley motions with her hand and they leave.

The admin assistant finishes her call as I creep to the door and peek out. "Can I help you?" she says. I shake my head and give her a wave.

The second I hit the doorway, I break into a run. *Maisie, I'm coming.* My heart pounds with every stride. The school parking lot is mostly empty now. What will she think? Is she still waiting for me?

A car honks as I step into the street. I keep running. Up the walk. Through the main door. Past the custodian. Down, down, down the hallway to Mrs. Williams's classroom. The door is locked. A stab in my throat. I turn and lope back toward the main entrance, to the office. As I step through the door, the ancient admin assistant squints at her computer screen. Her pink scalp shows through her thinning hair.

There, on a chair in the corner. My six-year-old with the cinnamon tangles. I look down, blinking the water from my eyes.

"You're late," she says.

"I'm sorry, Maisie. Something happened at my school, but I'm here now."

"Nobody came to get me."

"I'm sorry."

She seems to see me for the first time now, sees how the past twenty minutes have played on my face. "Are you going to throw up?" she asks.

"I might." It's true. A thick, sour paste coats my mouth. Piercing pain in my chest. I fall into a chair next to her and drop my head into my hands. She watches.

After a long pause, I stand. "Maisie, I'll always come get you." I pull her up and wave to the old lady, who didn't seem to notice us coming or going. I get a long drink from a very short water fountain. "Now, let's go get Evan."

The bus is crowded, the beginning of rush hour now, which gives me an excuse to sit Maisie on my lap and hide my face in her tickly hair. She's getting heavy now. My right leg falls asleep, so I jiggle it. I don't want to say another word for the rest of the day.

"What happened at your school?" Maisie asks.

I don't answer immediately, choosing careful words. "I met a girl who was pokey."

Maisie perks up. She tries to turn her face toward me. "Did you smack her?"

I swallow. "I did, Maisie." The bus lurches to a stop, and someone crushes my baby toe. The press of people around us shifts toward the back of the bus as new bodies file on. "And she smacked back."

SIX

No sign of my three stalkers before class the next day. I'm jumpy, ready to tackle total strangers as they brush by me in the hall. I find a pink princess sticker on my locker. The kiss of death on the dented blue metal.

Celeste ignores me entirely in English, which is nothing but good news as far as I'm concerned. Doesn't turn her head in my direction even once.

Mr. Drummond gives us a pop quiz on the characters and events in the first two scenes of *Hamlet*. I started reading it in the library yesterday but didn't get too far, being mostly focused on not getting killed. I only know three out of the ten questions for sure. The rest I leave blank. When I hand it in, Mr. Drummond gives me a hard look. I pretend not to notice and retreat to my corner of misfit toys.

Heading back to my desk, I catch Will's eye for one second, so fast I'm not sure it happened. What has he heard about me? Is he on Team Ainsley or Team Loser? I'd guess

Team Loser, at a glance. Maybe he's a pacifist and loathes my barbaric ways, period.

Mr. Drummond assigns students to read out the parts in Scene 2. I sit a little lower in my desk, wishing myself invisible. At this point, I'd rather have a lunch date with Ainsley than read Shakespeare out loud to the class.

He ends up picking Celeste's blond friend, some dark-haired girl named Gabriela, and a handful of other people. Exhale. I tune out during most of the reading and discussion and think about Jacquie coming over this weekend. I have a lot to tell her. Outside the window, the bus rumbles to a stop. A hunched lady pushing a walker teeters off the bus and shuffles away. Going to a quiet place, I think, having already finished all of this. The bus chugs on.

Right before the end of class, Mr. Drummond assigns us a one-page monologue for tomorrow, written from the point of view of a character of our choice.

There's a lump in the pit of my stomach as I walk to Social Studies. I try a different strategy this time: sitting right under the teacher's nose. Pole Dancer and her friends have already secured a chunk in the middle of the classroom, and Mrs. Clarke doesn't seem to have any idea what goes on at the back. Safety at the front—whatever safety the old bat can offer.

"Okay, class, let's get started." She smiles, and four of us in the front actually listen.

She dims the lights and puts on a PowerPoint about the events leading up to World War II, reading through the whole thing—word for word—without looking up even once.

I could be attacked with a baseball bat, and she'd never know.

After a minute I feel a flick on the back of my head. Then another. I raise my hand to the spot and find spitty pellets of paper clinging to my hair. Disgusting. As I turn my head to see where they're coming from, another one flies at me and sticks to my eyebrow. I brush it to the floor. Pole Dancer and her friends burst out laughing, banging their hands against their desks with a hearty *thump, thump.*

Mrs. Clarke presses on, undaunted. Can't interrupt World War II now.

I'll give it to Pole Dancer—she's really starting to piss me off. I get up and move to an empty desk on my left, second from the front. It's slightly out of their direct spitting range.

As Mrs. Clarke wraps up her PowerPoint, the noise level rises to one decibel below deafening. She grabs a stack of handouts off her desk and gets ready to pass them out. Standing at the front of each row, she counts the number of students, licks her fingers and separates the right number of sheets. She watches them being passed back from student to student until the end of the row, then moves to the next. Torture.

While I'm waiting for her, something slams me right between the shoulder blades and falls to the floor. I gasp. A red apple ricochets between chair legs and rolls toward the open space at the front of the room. Guffaws explode from Pole Dancer and her friends. Others yelp at the apple bumping their feet. I swallow, stretching my eyes wide to stop the tears. My back throbs.

I will not wipe my eyes. Or sniffle. Or lower my head. That didn't hurt me at all. I think of something faraway— pushing Evan on the swing at the park. Taking Maisie to see the birds at the pet store.

Mrs. Clarke finally settles at her desk and asks, "Who would like to read for us?" Of course, no one volunteers. "Okay, I'll begin." She starts to slowly read the first page of the handout, word for word, without looking up at the class. I'm not sure which is more painful—being attacked with an apple or listening to Mrs. Clarke's version of teaching.

As she drones on, something light and feathery lands on my shoulder and slips down my arm. I sigh and look down. Someone's dirty gym sock.

Giggles erupt. *Enough.* I jump from my seat and stand to face them. Satisfaction on their faces like, *Here she comes now.* I want to make this girl hurt in a big way. But I won't. Won't give them what they want. *Deep breath, Isabelle. Keep it together.* I stroll down the aisle between us, toward her.

As I get closer, there are some titters around Pole Dancer, although the stupid grin starts to slide from her face. With each step, the bodies around her edge away. Good friends she has. Her eyes dart from side to side, like she's checking for reinforcements. She sneers, but I see the panic. She should be scared. Tall skinny bitch hasn't had to fight and claw through every day of her life like I have. I could have her on the floor in less than five seconds. As I look in her eyes, she knows it.

"Excuse me!" Mrs. Clarke has just noticed the disruption to her flawless lesson plan. It was probably the quiet room that told her something was wrong.

I stand in front of Pole Dancer's desk for a second and enjoy watching her squirm. Some idiot next to her starts to laugh again, then stops abruptly.

"Back to your seat, please!" Mrs. Clarke warbles.

In that moment of silence, I drop the dirty sock in the middle of Pole Dancer's open binder. Her nose wrinkles.

"I think this is yours," I say. "It smells like you."

Her cheeks flush an angry red. All ears are listening. I turn on my heel and strut back up the aisle, her whispered cursing behind me.

Mrs. Clarke's mouth hangs open, aghast at my rude behavior. In a flash, I pick up the apple—still whole—from underneath the whiteboard and polish it on my shirt. Placing it gently on the corner of her desk, I summon my most courteous voice. "So sorry—I have to go."

She's speechless.

All eyes are on me as I gather my books off my desk and pick my sweater off the back of my chair. At the door, I give a cheerful wave and shut it firmly behind me. The class erupts.

*　　*　　*

I close my eyes and breathe in the musty smell of the library. I had meant to catch up on reading for English but instead start writing a story about a girl who is bullied until she snaps and beats another girl into a coma. It's quiet now, the librarian having chased away the only other group working in here. (*Get your books and go! This isn't a frat house!*) *Ms. Hillary*, her name placard says. I consider asking her to whip Mrs. Clarke's class into shape.

When I open my eyes, a redheaded apparition stands in front of me. I blink. I had actually forgotten about this pale wisp, the catalyst for my current misery.

"I followed you in," she says, her voice falling to a whisper. "I hope that's okay."

I nod. Not sure what to say to this girl.

"I never had a chance to thank you for sticking up for me." She's found her voice now.

I shrug. "She had it coming."

"Well," she says, "no one's ever done that for me before." She looks down at the floor. I see Ms. Hillary eyeing her. We've run out of words.

I expect her to leave now, but instead she says, "Do you mind if I sit down?" She gestures to the empty chairs at my table.

"Be my guest." I slide my books to one side and tuck my story into a biology textbook. "You'd better do some work, though, or the librarian will kick you out."

"She's scary," she whispers.

"Even I wouldn't take her on," I say, and we try not to laugh.

"I'm Clara." She reaches out to shake my hand, which surprises me a bit. Clara, like some kind of porcelain character out of a Jane Austen novel.

I shake it back. "Isabelle."

"I know," she says, a little shy.

I snort. "Who doesn't by now?"

*　　*　　*

At the end of the lunch hour, I march up to the admin assistant in the office. "I need to drop a class."

She tears herself away from the computer screen, annoyed. "You'll have to see the guidance counselor before making any changes." She points to an office not far from Mr. Talmage's. "Miss Yee's in right now."

"Miss Yee." I throw open the door; the doorknob whacks the wall behind it, leaving a round circle in the paint. "I need to drop Social Studies."

"Call me Lily." She smiles, pretending not to notice the doorknob mark. She is one of those natural beauties—the kind who looks hot even when she's camping or running a marathon. High cheekbones, shiny black hair falling over her shoulders. She probably has half the staff sniffing around her like a pack of dogs. "Let's see your schedule then."

She looks it over and says, "You can drop it now and have a spare instead, but you'll have to take a full schedule next semester."

"That's fine." Then, as an afterthought, I ask, "Does anyone else teach Social Studies besides Mrs. Clarke?"

She gives me a searching look and doesn't answer right away. "There is one other teacher—Mr. Arjun—but he's full this semester." The kind voice kicks in. "Is there a problem in that class, Isabelle?"

"No." I shrug. She knows I'm lying, of course.

"Okay then." She hammers at her keyboard for a minute. "Done."

As I get up to leave, Miss Yee says, "Isabelle, you know you can talk to me anytime, right? About anything?"

"Sure." I give her a quick smile and head for the door. Poor Miss Yee. Bless her beautiful, clueless heart. Kind and lovely, like a benevolent queen looking down on her subjects when she's never actually scrubbed a floor or peeled a carrot. "Thanks."

My chest is a little lighter as I leave.

*　　*　　*

When the bell rings at the end of the day, after Spanish class, all I can think about is getting to higher ground, like there's a flood coming. I need some way to watch the three of them in the school—where they're going, what they're doing. That's nearly impossible, though, because I don't know where any of them are at the end of the day. Other than at lunch, I don't see Ainsley at all.

Outside would be easier. Most people go out the main door, get picked up, drive themselves or catch the bus.

If only I could scale the flagpole or hide in a strategically placed bush.

Then it comes to me. The Spanish classroom won't work for my idea. I slip out with the crowd but don't go to my locker. Instead, I go halfway down the hall, eyes peeled, and try one of the doors on the other side. This one would be perfect. *Chemistry*, it says on the door. It's locked. I try the next door over. The handle turns easily in my hand. I knock as I slip inside.

A young teacher with dark hair and thick glasses sits at her desk, looking up as I enter. Near the back of the class, a guy wrestles with an over-stuffed bag.

"Um, yes." I come right up to the teacher's desk, almost whispering, "My mom is picking me up after school, and I've forgotten my jacket." I point to the gray drizzle outside. "Do you mind if I watch for her from the window?"

"Not at all. Go ahead," she says and turns back to marking a stack of worksheets.

From the window, I have a perfect view of the mass of people leaving via the main doors and also of the bus stop in front of the school and the loading zone.

I pull up a chair and begin my vigil. Five minutes pass. Ten minutes. I can't wait much longer without worrying Maisie again.

There. Is it Celeste? I see a crazy afro break away from the crowd on the front lawn and stroll toward a white Lexus in the loading zone. Why am I not surprised? Then Ainsley, Pole Dancer and two other girls head for the bus stop. Pole Dancer wears a jacket but hasn't pulled up the hood.

Ainsley is in a T-shirt. Dark water stains creep down her shoulders. They drop their bags by the bench and keep talking. Okay, they're catching a bus.

After twelve minutes, the bus pulls up. Everyone piles on and leaves.

"Thanks so much," I say to the teacher on my way out. I may need her again.

I jog down the front path and across the street, checking for unwanted faces coming my way. Nobody.

I catch Maisie with Mrs. Williams as she locks her classroom door.

"Isabelle," she says. "I was just dropping Maisie at the office."

I try to catch my breath. "Sorry, something came up." I gesture toward the high school, shaking my head like it's too long and complicated to explain. Which it is. "Actually, I may be a few minutes late every day."

"Okay." Mrs. Williams hoists her bag over her shoulder and starts to walk down the hall with us. "I'll have Maisie wait in the office if I have to leave before you get here."

I thank her and pull Maisie toward the bus stop.

"Hurry now," I say. Outside, I take her hand and start to jog. "It's another fifteen minutes if we miss this bus, and I have to work today."

Maisie drags her feet, straining against my arm. "You were late again." Raindrops splatter her pink tights. The elastic has slipped from one ponytail and it hangs limply, lower than the one on the other side.

"Maisie, it was important." No soppy apology from me today. She may hate it, but I need to make sure I'm not leading three psychopaths straight to her. I'll take her anger. "Now move it."

As we cross the street, I see the bus coming at the end of the road. Just in time. We find two empty seats together.

I'm barely sitting down before Maisie asks, "Can Jasmin come to my birthday party?"

"I don't want to talk about birthday parties today, Maisie," I say, deflecting her question.

"She's my new friend. Can she come? I said she could."

"I don't know if we're having that kind of party, Maisie," I explain for the millionth time.

"Why not?" she asks for the millionth time.

Too poor. Ugly apartment. Drunk mother. She doesn't realize I'm saving her a lot of embarrassment. When I was in grade two, I knew which kids were poor, which had weird parents. I wonder if Maisie has figured out yet that we fall into both categories. "Our apartment is too small. There's only room for family."

"We could have it at The Party Place," she says. I actually looked into it once. You can rent a room for an hour. There are slides and ball pits—some kind of kiddie paradise. Costs a fortune. Everything that doesn't involve having people at our apartment is really expensive. Even if I did fix up our place, there's no promise that Mom wouldn't come staggering out of her room and wreck it all.

"Let me think about it," I tell her, just to end the conversation.

When we get to the day care, Evan's lying on a mat in the corner instead of tearing around the room with Patrick.

"What's wrong?" I ask Elaine.

She shrugs and keeps stapling artwork to a bulletin board. *Stupid cow.* His cheeks are hot under my hand. He whimpers.

"I want to go home," he says and starts to cry.

SEVEN

"Come here, little man." I scoop him up and struggle to my feet, then turn to Elaine. "He's sick. Did you call home?"

She shakes her head and picks up another picture to staple. I feel like ripping it from her hands and stapling it to her forehead. "Why not?" I say, trying not to shout.

"He seemed fine at lunch," she says. "He even asked for seconds."

"Does he look fine to you?" I march out of the room before I say something I'll regret, which has happened a lot lately. Maisie trots at my heels.

"Something wrong?" Mrs. Carrigan asks as I work Evan's hot arms into the sleeves of his sweater.

"Can someone please call home or my school if Evan gets sick." I say it like a statement, not a question. I'm trying really hard not to go postal on everyone here.

"Oh, he's sick?" she says. *Not a word, Isabelle. Just go.*

I leave before I curse out the entire staff of Little Treasures. Stupid dump. He'd have a better life if I stayed home with him myself. What am I learning at school anyway, besides how to sneak around like a secret agent? What exactly is the point?

Mom works late, but there's no reason she couldn't be with him in the afternoon. Just because government subsidy pays for it doesn't mean he should spend every waking hour with those morons. What kind of mother doesn't want to be with her own kid?

I head for the apartment like some kind of speed-walking champion, the rain still coming down in a steady drizzle. Maisie pants behind me.

Evan starts to whimper again once we hit the elevator. "I feel sick." His cheek is hot against my neck.

"Almost home, Evan," I say.

When we enter the apartment, there's no sign of Mom. The logical part of my brain says it's not fair to be mad at Elaine. Mom probably wouldn't have picked up if Elaine had called. Still.

I lower Evan to the sagging sofa, and he closes his eyes and curls into a ball. I rummage in the cupboard for the Children's Tylenol. Of course, there's none.

The bedroom and bathroom are both empty—bathrobe on the floor and the smell of perfume.

"Where the hell is she?" I slam my hand against the counter, looking at the clock.

"I got Evan a glass of water," Maisie says at my elbow.

My shift starts in ten minutes. I'll have to call them and say I'm not coming. And screw up my job too? I've only been there for three weeks. In that time, I've had money to buy bread when we've needed it and coins for the laundry. I can't remember how many times I've had to scrub underwear in the bathroom sink when the money ran out.

I'll tell them I'm sick. No, they probably just watched me walk by with Evan and Maisie. I could kill Mom.

"Maisie, listen to me." I take her thin shoulders in my hands. "I've got to go now. Do you think you could be a big girl and look after Evan for a bit? Mom should be back soon." Lies.

"By myself?" she asks, eyes wide.

I nod. "Sit next to him on the sofa and help him like you just did. You brought water, right?"

She looks up at me. "Are you coming back soon?"

"I'll be right back." More lies. "I'm going to get Evan some medicine."

"Okay," she says, a tremor in her voice.

I tuck them both under a blanket on the sofa and find some sitcom on TV—probably too old for them, but it beats the news.

"Don't answer the door or the phone," I say before locking the door behind me.

* * *

"Isabelle." Rupa looks up from the counter as the bells jingle over the door.

I can't imagine how I must look right now: wet, limp hair, red face, stomach churning. I've been at a full-out run for almost an hour. As mad as hell.

"I'm sorry," I say. "My bus schedule changed. It's a bit of a rush."

"Well, you're here now." She smiles down at me. I wait for her to give me a job to do.

"Can you do the glass, please?" She motions to the tall windows running the length of the store. "Inside tonight."

I collect the bucket and squeegee from the back. Somewhere behind the boxes, I hear Arif rummaging and stacking. No sign of Hasan yet.

Things pick up by the time I've finished two large panes. Arif brings me a mop and bucket from the back and points to the trail of muck between the door and the counter.

"Keep an eye on this," he says. Whenever there's a lull between customers, which isn't very often, I drop down the sloppy string mop and scrub. More like spreading it around, if you ask me. Arif joins Rupa at the other till to keep the line moving.

I turn back to the windows. I don't know if it's from carrying Evan or washing or mopping, but I feel weary to the bone. I raise the squeegee above my head, and my whole arm trembles. I steady myself against the glass.

Right now Maisie's up in the apartment, watching the door for my return. Unless Mom has come home—then who knows what's going on? At this very moment the fire alarm could be ringing. Evan could be having a seizure. Maisie could be choking on a cracker.

I left a six-year-old to watch a four-year-old. What have I done? And the thing I hate the most, what makes me squat to catch my breath, is that I've just done to Maisie what Mom does to me. The floor lurches.

"Isabelle." Rupa's at my side, touching my shoulder. "What is it?"

I take her hand to pull myself up. I realize I haven't eaten anything since breakfast. "Sorry, I'm feeling sick. I have to go."

She nods, worry in her eyes. "Yes, go home." As she guides me toward the door, I suddenly remember.

"Rupa, can I buy some Tylenol for my brother?"

"Of course." She grabs the small pink box from the shelf and puts it in my hand. "Just take it to Arif. He'll ring it through."

"Only"—I hate these words out loud—"I can't pay for it now." I gave Mom my last twenty to catch a taxi to work the other day. Payday isn't for another five days.

Rupa's face falls, like I've just told her a sad story. She doesn't answer.

"You can take it straight off my check," I offer, "and I'll pay you back double." Who am I to ask her these things? It hasn't even been a month.

"No, no. Not double." Her eyes flick toward Arif, who has just turned his back to pick out a carton of cigarettes. "Go now. Just take it. We'll work it out later."

I tuck the box close to my body as I head for the door, like we've just done an illicit drug deal. As I pass by the counter, Rupa breaks away and calls to Arif. He turns his head in her direction and doesn't see me leave. There is no urinal I wouldn't scrub for this woman.

Outside, I take a deep breath in the damp, then break into a run. *Let them be okay. I'll never leave them alone again. Never.*

I bump some old lady out of the way getting onto the elevator and bang the tenth-floor button again and again. The doors pull shut in slow motion. A few creaks and groans as it creeps from floor to floor. Piece of junk. The stairs would be faster.

"'Scuse me," I say, pushing past a mom with a stroller who's blocking the way off, jamming her wheels into the wall. I run away from her indignant cry toward our chipped peach door. My mouth so dry I can't swallow.

I fumble with the lock and dive through the door. Maisie's right there in my face.

"What, Maisie? What is it?"

"Evan." She points to him on the sofa. "He threw up." Her lip droops as she says it. There are tear tracks on her cheeks. "I tried to take him to the bathroom, but he said he couldn't." She chokes up. "He wouldn't go."

I look to the sofa and see Evan, who has shifted away from the brown, lumpy mess dripping down onto the carpet. The sour smell hits me now. His eyes are closed.

"Maisie"—I pick her up in a bear hug—"you did such a good job looking after Evan. Now I'm here, and you don't have to anymore."

She nods and wipes her cheeks. "Okay."

"Go make yourself a peanut-butter sandwich while I clean this up." She pads to the kitchen, freed from her unpleasant duties. "And wash your hands first!"

I haul Evan to the other side of the sofa, away from the mess. Clean his face with a wet cloth and pull the soiled shirt off of him. His ribs burn under my fingers.

"Maisie, bring me Evan's blanket." Once he's settled, falling in and out of sleep, I turn to the vomit. I'm practically an expert at this. Still makes me gag every time.

The shifting mess seeps through the paper towel, making my stomach twist. I clear away the big stuff and then pull out my bucket and rag. At least it won't stain. You could hide a world of bodily fluids in this rust-colored shag. I do my best with it, then turn back to Evan.

Maisie watches me pour the thick pink liquid into a spoon. "Is that Evan's medicine?" she asks.

"Yup." Shame I didn't bargain for a bottle of ginger ale as well. I wake him up enough to swallow it and offer a sip of water. "Don't gulp," I say, pulling back. "You'll throw up again."

"More," he cries.

"Wait and see if your tummy holds it down."

He whimpers and falls back asleep, his head resting on the arm of the sofa.

Maisie brings me a peanut-butter sandwich too. It sticks in my throat, my stomach still queasy. "Did Mom come home at all?" I ask. Maisie shakes her head. "Did anyone call?" She shakes her head again.

I pick Mom's work number off the fridge and dial it. Some rough-sounding guy answers.

"Hi, this is Isabelle Bennett, Marnie's daughter."

Silence on the other end.

"Marnie had a bit of a family emergency today. I was wondering if she made it to work tonight?"

"She's not here." He sounds pissed.

"Okay, I'm sure she'll be back again tomorrow," I say.

There's some kind of grunting sound on the other end. I can't tell if that was actually a word.

"Sorry for the inconvenience." I hang up.

As I put down the receiver, the weight of every lie I've told today comes crashing down on me. Was it every word? Every conversation? All to protect *this*—this reality show gone bad.

I read Maisie an extra chapter of *Alice in Wonderland* to make up for being a jerk today. Still haunted by what I did, and she's too young to even know it.

"I think we'll have a home day tomorrow, Maisie," I say, tucking her in.

"No! Tomorrow I'm the helper!"

"Well, you'll be the helper again another time."

"No, tomorrow's my first turn. I've been waiting a long time." The whole five days of school so far. Her lip trembles.

I sigh. "What about Evan? He's sick."

"Mom can look after him," she says. Is she talking about someone else's mother? Ours took off sometime today and hasn't come back yet. Still, it's not a good time for me to miss school either, given my shaky standing with Mr. Talmage.

"We'll see, okay?"

She smiles and rolls over, tucking her blankets under her feet. "Okay." In less than a minute her breaths are long and slow. I so envy that.

I pull Evan from the sofa, where he's been sleeping for over an hour, and arrange him in Mom's bed. I need to be close to him tonight. Towel over the pillow. Bowl by his side. I climb into bed next to him and lay the back of my hand against his cheeks. They're flushed pink but not as hot as before. *Thank you, Rupa.* He doesn't stir at my fingers in his matted hair.

With his eyes closed, he's a mini Claude—nut-brown hair, narrow nose, high eyebrows. I might be tempted to hate him for that, except that Evan always has a wide-eyed look of surprise, like he just got a puff of air in the face. That soft bewilderment is so different from Claude's unpredictable rages. Evan cries when he accidentally steps on an ant.

When Evan gasps next to me, I jerk awake and grapple for the bowl. I must have drifted off. Evan sobs, and vomit gushes from his mouth. I lunge to get the bowl in place; there's a warm splash on my hand before getting it right.

"It's okay." I pat his back as his body shudders. Tears leak from his eyes as he continues to heave when there's nothing left. "Deep breath now."

When the retching subsides, he falls back onto the pillow, eyes closed. His face a sloppy mess. I wipe him off and mop up the parts that missed the bowl. We have no extra blankets.

"Drink," he whispers to me, starting to cry when I only give him a sip. I lay my palm on his forehead and then on the small of his back. Hot again. I must have been out for a few hours. Not sure he'll keep down any medicine at this point.

I hope he'll sleep again, but he wakes up every half hour to dry-heave. My eyes are two balls boring into my head. Opening and closing my eyelids is a strain. I somehow propel myself to go through the motions: the wiping, the patting, the holding. I could sleep on the kitchen lino at this point.

I hear a key in the lock. A jolt of electricity shoots through me. I find myself in the hallway, carefully pulling the door shut behind me. I reach over and shut Maisie's door as well. The kitchen stove blinks 4:10. My head is a balloon floating above a leaden body.

A dark shadow stumbles in the entryway. I wait.

She jumps as she turns and sees me in the living room, outlined in the dim light coming through the window from the street.

"Isabelle," she says, "you scared me half to death! Did I wake you?" I can smell her from a few feet away—perfume and rum.

"Where were you?"

"I was out with Ingrid," she says. Ingrid is another drunk she met a few bar jobs ago. They've (unfortunately) kept in touch.

"We got a little carried away, lost track of the time." She starts to laugh, struggling to take off her strappy heels.

"What's wrong with you?" I say it so quietly that she barely hears.

"What?" She stands up.

"I had to leave my job early and phone your job. Evan's been puking all night."

"Oh, poor lamb." She clucks. "Is he awake now?"

I take a step toward her. "What kind of a mother does that?" I know my words will hurt, but I also want to know. I actually want her to answer the question.

"Isabelle," she says, "don't overreact. Even moms need a night out now and again." Like she's every other mom. Like this only happens now and again.

It's the way she brushes it all away, like a fly on her arm. "Don't!" I'm right in her face now. "Don't you dare pretend you've done nothing wrong!"

She tries to take my hands in hers. I recoil. Then she reaches for me, to hug, console, say it will be okay. I don't want her touching me. Don't want to hear her lies. I twist and step away while her hands keep coming, along with her sad words of comfort.

"I'm sorry, I'm sorry," she says again and again, reaching.

My hand flies, palm open, across her cheek. A sickening smack, and she staggers backward. My palm stings. Leaning against the wall, she raises a slow hand to her cheek, eyes looking at nothing.

While she's there, buckled, stunned, I deliver the final blow. "You never should've had kids."

Before I can think, before the horror of what I've done can touch me, I bang into our bedroom—Evan finally asleep—and grab the blanket and pillow from my cot. I fly back out to the living room and toss them toward her.

A low sobbing noise rises from the shadow in the entryway.

I run back down the hall, slam the bedroom door, leap across the bed. I reach Evan's bowl as it all comes up.

EIGHT

"Isabelle," next to my ear.

"Hmmm."

"Isabelle."

"What?" I sit bolt upright, take in Evan next to me, the pattern of the towel pressed into his cheek. Maisie is beside me, waiting.

"What time is it?" I twist the clock toward me. "Maisie, the alarm hasn't even gone off yet. What are you doing?"

"I'm ready." She points at her clothes—she's fully dressed. She even has her shoes on. "I packed my lunch too." That should be interesting.

"Maisie, this isn't a good day."

"Please." She says it like a statement. "Please take me to school." The tears from yesterday are gone, and she's prepped for some hard-core bargaining. "I'll run to the bus stop the whole way."

I consider telling her to ask Mom, but that would just be cruel.

"Okay. I'll be up in a minute."

"It's stinky in here," she says on her way out.

I lie back on the pillow and close my eyes. Concentrate on the sour taste in my mouth, my heavy limbs. I don't want to think, remember.

I've said some cruel things over the years—meant every word—but I've never hit her before. Once, when Claude slapped her, I tried to kill him. Literally. Mom had to lie across my body while Claude pried the paring knife from my fingers. Then she kept lying there to shield me from him, her pregnant belly crushing me. When she wouldn't move, he turned to grab something—a kitchen chair maybe—to swing.

Out the front! I had whispered, pushing her off me. As he turned back, I snatched the nearest thing—a white coffee mug—and flung it at him. Caught him above the eyebrow, a red gash. Mom pulled Maisie from under the kitchen table and headed for the front. Me, out the back door, the devil at my heels. Over the garbage bags and into the alley. I found Mom, and we ran. It was November. I only had socks on my feet.

He'd stopped at the door, watching us go down the street, but didn't follow. Too many witnesses. We spent a couple of weeks squatting in someone's basement, then went back home sweet home. We picked up where we'd left off with Claude—nothing changed.

Maisie was three. I hope she doesn't remember.

Now I've done the same as him. I swallow. One foot in front of the other—that's how I'll get through this day. *Don't think about anything.*

Maisie reappears at my door. "Are you coming?"

Evan's fever seems to be gone. He doesn't stir at my hands on his cheeks and the back of his neck.

I skip the shower and opt for a ponytail today. Lunches. I check Maisie's—not bad. A peanut-butter sandwich and a package of instant oatmeal. I switch the oatmeal for a banana. Maisie waits at the table, coloring something in her school notebook while I get dressed. I try not to look at the disheveled heap on the sofa, blond tips poking out of the blanket.

Right before we head for the bus, I scoop Evan from our bed. He makes a squeaking noise and rubs his eyes. I lay him at the end of the sofa by Mom's feet, his head on the arm of the sofa. Pull the blanket over him and put a glass of water and the barf bowl beside him on the floor.

"Mom." I shake the lumpy blanket and pull my hand away. "Mom," I say a little louder. She stirs. I feel every heartbeat in my chest. "I've put Evan out here with you. Take care of him today."

No response. Maisie comes to stand beside me, regarding the two lumps on the sofa. I don't have the courage to apologize, to say what I'm sorry for. Not in front of Maisie and Evan. Maybe not even to myself. The nausea washes through me again.

"Let's go," I say, and we head for the bus stop.

*　　*　　*

If anyone is stalking me today, I don't notice. My world has become very small—the size of my desk in English. Words around me sound hollow, tinny. I jump at the thump of a textbook on the floor, the scrape of a chair.

As soon as class starts, Mr. Drummond asks us to pass our *Hamlet* monologues to the front. *Hamlet* monologues. As if, in the middle of all that, I was able to write a monologue.

A tap on my shoulder, and a sheet of paper appears with Will's chicken scratch in black pen. I turn around to see if more are coming, but that's it. I send it on up the line. Mr. Drummond collects them all in a neat pile and drops them on his desk. He's looking for readers again.

"*Hamlet. Act 1. Scene 3.* Isabelle, will you be our Ophelia?"

I feel a jolt at hearing my name—a small burst of terror. It's quiet. I can't look up, can't look him in the eye. Why can't the tall guy sit in front of me?

"No, thank you," I say, barely above a whisper.

If he's looking at me, I don't know. Will he try to force me?

A pause. "Very well. Rachael, will you give it a try?" Out of the corner of my eye, I see Rachael's hand waving; she's dying to be Ophelia. Twit. He assigns the other parts as well. I can tell some of the guys aren't too thrilled about it, but no one else says no.

To stay awake, I doodle a maze of squares in the margins of my paper, trying to keep my eyes open. Every time my thoughts creep back to the moment I hit Mom, I jerk away. Can't. Won't. It's too much right now.

When the bell rings, I'm the first out of my desk and heading for the door.

"Isabelle," Mr. Drummond says in that voice that somehow echoes in every corner, "can I see you for a minute, please?" As he says it, I'm poised mid-step in front of the entire class. They file out past me, some turning to stare. I catch Celeste's eye as she walks by, still unreadable.

Once they've all left, he settles in the chair behind his desk, buttons stretching across his hard belly. He regards me, not unkindly, as I stand stiffly in front of him.

"Isabelle, I saw your test score yesterday. And today, no monologue from you," he says.

I say nothing, not helping him out at all.

"It's clear to me," he continues, "that you're not doing the reading or the work for this course." Still nothing. "Are you expecting this to be easy? I see you on a dangerous path here."

Dangerous. I'm trying not to get killed at school or let my brother and sister die at home, dodging hunger, fists, homelessness, foster care. I'm pretty sure *Hamlet* is the least dangerous thing in my life.

It must be clear on my face, because he straightens in his chair. "You'll have to catch up on missed work after school today, if you intend to stay in this class."

"I can't," I say instantly.

"Can't? I think it's time for you to prioritize. The decision is yours."

Heat creeps from my gut upward. I feel like driving an elbow right into that round paunch. *Prioritize?* What the hell does he know? And I just dropped Social Studies too. I don't think I can lose another course.

"I pick up"—I swallow hard, trying to drive down the lump in my throat—"I pick up my sister after school, across the street."

"Can she come here and wait with you?"

"No, she—" I shake my head and look away. How can I explain the whole sequence, how it all comes down to me? Picking up Evan, my job, babysitting Mom and getting her off to work. A careful line of dominoes, all depending on my push to carry it through. Even half an hour late, and none of it will work.

Voices float past in the hall. I wait for them to fade before trying again.

"I look after my brother and sister when my mom…" I can't continue. I feel the hot tears now. Hate him. I hate him. "When my mom…" I can't push out that final word, beat one more lie out of that sentence. When my mom what? Checks out on a daily basis? I turn and watch the yellow leaves tumble across the sidewalk.

Mr. Drummond leans in and tries to finish it for me. "Goes to work?"

A laugh catches in my throat, like a bark. I sniff and wipe my face with my sleeve. I think the tears will stop now, but they keep spilling from the corners of my eyes. "Mostly drinks. Sometimes works." I give a bitter laugh. How strange on my lips, the truth. I focus on his feet, scuffed loafers poking out from under the desk. I should run. Lock myself in the bathroom. Switch schools. But here I am, in front of this walrus, coming unglued. Something about my confession knocks me off-kilter, like the beams have fallen and the ceiling's caving in.

I turn from him now, walk to the window and cry. Now I feel it too, that awful, stinging shame from last night. I completely crumble. I have no idea what Mr. Drummond does while I blubber. I hear a scuffle of feet in the hallway, and Mr. Drummond crosses the floor and closes the door. The clock hums on the wall.

Mr. Drummond drops a box of Kleenex onto the desk beside me and wedges himself into one of the chairs. "Look, Isabelle," he says, "you're not the first person to come from a crap family. At least you're still here, in school. I didn't finish high school until I was twenty-one."

Is he saying what I think he's saying? I reach for a tissue and try to mop up, eyes stinging.

"Are you able to do the reading and finish the assignment this weekend?" he asks. I nod. *Don't ask me to say anything else.* Those four words—*mostly drinks, sometimes works*—are more than I've ever said. To anyone. "Okay, fair enough," he says.

I drop into a chair, my legs suddenly weak. Exhausted in every bone.

"Didn't get much sleep last night, did you?" he says. Clearly I'm not as good at faking it as I thought. I shake my head. "Go to the infirmary now," he says. "Get some rest."

I think I've lost the capacity to speak. I hear him calling the office as I leave.

*　　*　　*

The admin assistant waves me toward her as I enter. "Mr. Drummond called down. He said you were sick." I see her examining my face, which feels swollen to three times its normal size. It's probably not a tough sell.

She leads me by the elbow to a room behind the main office area, like I'm about to collapse at any second. "Here you go." She points to a sterile-looking bed pushed against the wall of a small room. A few cabinets run along the other wall, painted an austere white. "Do you want a glass of water?" she asks.

"Yes, please." I clear my throat.

She brings the water and returns to her desk, the door hanging ajar between us. I close it, twisting the knob so it shuts silently. Pull the blinds closed, take off my shoes, lie down on the crinkly bed.

Out in the office, I hear snatches of the most boring conversations imaginable. The click of fingers on a keyboard. On the other side of the window, the crunch of gravel under tires in the parking lot.

Maisie is safe in her class, being the helper. Evan is with Mom. She won't leave while he's there. My head spins in a dizzy circle when I close my eyes. I sleep without dreaming.

NINE

Jacquie stops by before lunch on Saturday, all cleavage in a little tank top.

"What *are* you wearing?" I ask.

"Hey, you got it, flaunt it."

Jacquie once tried on one of Maisie's shirts and said, *Not bad*. Her belly-button ring was peeking out the bottom and her boobs bursting out the top.

Not bad for a stripper, I had said.

"Wassup, pup?" She bends down to Maisie, tickling her. Maisie screeches and runs for the sofa. Evan tackles Jacquie's legs, sitting on her foot and wrapping himself around a calf. She drags him around the room—her thin dark hair swaying—before asking, "Where's your mom?"

"Still sleeping," I say.

"Hard night?" Jacquie winks.

"I don't think so. She had to work late."

It's weird. The day after the "incident," I had come home to Mom and Evan sitting on the sofa, coloring. Crayons spread out on a cushion. Mom was drawing pictures on lined paper and giving them to Evan to color in. I didn't know she could draw a frog.

"I ate some toast!" Evan said. Maisie squeezed in to join them.

Mom smiled at us, not meeting my eye. A slight red blotch marked her left cheekbone. She got up to have a shower once I was in the door. I gave her space.

When she was in the bedroom, I went in, shutting the door behind me. "Mom." Not sure what to say next. She turned away from me, almost shyly, and kept getting dressed. "Mom, I'm sorry for...what happened." Still couldn't say those words out loud.

She stopped, one leg in a pair of tights, her back to me. "Isabelle, do you really believe"—she pushed the words out—"that I never should've had children?"

That was what upset her the most? "No, Mom. I don't really believe that." Don't I? "I just get really mad at you sometimes."

She nodded and wiped her eyes on the back of her hand. "I'll do better," she said.

"Don't say that."

"I'll do better."

I had left before the anger could take root and rise up again. But she has been sober the past two days and even helped make school lunches before she left for work.

"Do you think we could leave the brats here for a while?" Jacquie reaches down and pinches Evan's nose.

"I want to come!" they howl in unison.

"If you stay here, I'll bring you back a surprise," she says. Howling stops. She sees my face and says, "What? I've got a bit of money."

"Wake Mom up if you need help," I tell Maisie.

We take a bus to Goodwill to check things out. We wander around, looking at all the stuff we would need to move out together. We do this at least once a month, talk big.

"Look, a lamp for five bucks," Jacquie says.

"Ugly."

"So what? It gives light, right?"

"Look, this teapot has a cat on it." I hold it up to show her.

"And that's better than the lamp?"

We test out the reclining chairs and shake the bookshelves for sturdiness. I find an area rug that matches one of the chairs.

"It wouldn't take that much," I say, "now that I'm working. We could have everything we need in a couple of paychecks."

"I could pay the rent if I left school." Jacquie tries on a pair of ski boots discarded near the shelves.

"You want to be a dishwasher all your life?"

"Look at you, Little Miss Ambitious."

The truth is, I haven't thought a day past my high-school graduation. I picture the school doors opening and me running away as fast as I can. A quiet apartment. A job in a coffee shop, maybe. Jacquie tells me about the parties we'll have, and maybe that will be okay. I don't think much about that part.

We wander through the kids' clothes and toys. I keep my eyes peeled for something for Maisie's birthday. All the dolls look sad. Matted hair, felt marker on their legs. Lots of baby toys—blocks and rattles and stuff.

I'm flipping through a rack of size 8 girls' clothes when I see a pink sleeve. I pull it all the way out to have a look. A light pink dress with embroidered flowers on the bodice and a ribbon around the waist. It would be the prettiest thing she owned. The hem is unraveling in one spot near the back, but I could fix that easy.

"Jacquie, lend me eight bucks?"

With Jacquie's help, I also dig around the toy section and find a plastic truck and ramp for Evan. He has hardly any toys. We stored some stuff with a friend of Mom's during the last move, and then she took off and abandoned the place. I guess the landlord ended up with it.

After we take a bus back, Jacquie remembers her promise to Maisie and Evan. I take her to my store to buy some candy, saving the other stuff for Maisie's birthday.

Hasan is at the counter, and the only other customer is at the ATM by the bathroom. Hasan's eyes light at Jacquie's toothy smile and skin-tight shirt.

"Hasan, this is my cousin, Jacquie," I say. He's probably wondering why he got stuck with the boring cousin.

She shakes his hand, charm cranked to one hundred percent. "Pleasure."

"We're getting some candy for my brother and sister," I say.

He comes around the counter to help, like it's a really tough job. "You could try this one—a little bit spicy." He shakes a box and winks at Jacquie.

She bends down, giving him a good eyeful, and grabs the Sweet Tarts off the bottom shelf. "Or this—sweet and tart." She smiles. They go on for another minute, hands brushing, making a big show. I think I'm going to puke.

"Smarties it is," I say, pulling three boxes off the shelf. They both wilt like a kid who's just lost his helium balloon.

"See you Monday." I wave to Hasan on our way out. We settle on the curb outside and crack open one of the boxes.

"I'd like to corrupt that one," Jacquie says.

"I think he's already been corrupted, Jacquie."

It's a warm day. I take off my sweater and tie it around my waist. Jacquie holds out her arms, willing the sun to shine on them. While she picks out the blue Smarties, I tell her about Ainsley and Co. and getting suspended.

"Do you want me to take care of them?" she asks, eyes flinty. She would too. Jacquie's a ripple of lean muscle that moves like a flash. She's only six months older than I am, but taller and fuller. She takes after Uncle Richie.

"No. I can't mess things up at that school. It's right by Maisie's."

"They don't have to know we're related."

"They'll figure it out when they do the police report," I say.

She laughs and pops a handful of Smarties into her mouth. "Think about it."

I almost tell her about hitting Mom and talking to Mr. Drummond—whatever that was about—but the words don't come. We watch cars and trucks move in and out of the parking lot for a while before heading home.

*   *   *

When I hand in my monologue to Mr. Drummond on Monday, he gives me a wink. Like we're two peas in the same crappy-mother pod.

"I'm looking forward to reading this, Miss Bennett," he says.

I'm actually a little nervous about it. Mom didn't have to work on Saturday night, so she sat with Maisie and Evan while I was holed up in my room, scribbling away. I noticed that most people's papers were done on a computer. So what?

As I turn back to my desk, I catch Will watching me. For sure, this time. He looks away a little too quickly and makes a big deal of digging around in his bag for a pen. I'm tempted to give him the finger, but there's something about him I recognize. Like he too wishes he could go through this entire year without saying a word to anyone. Like if he could live on a desert island and communicate by messenger pigeon and smoke signals, that would be fine. Whatever this staring is about, I don't think it has anything to do with Ainsley.

It must be my day for freaks, because Clara comes and finds me in the library during the lunch hour. I thought her last visit was a one-off, that she had done her duty to God and country and moved on.

"Hi, Isabelle." She sits down next to me without asking this time.

"Hey."

She starts to pull out books to make it look like she's working on something. "How was your weekend?"

"Hmm. My cousin came over on Saturday, and I finished an English assignment." Yawn. Just another day in the tranquil life of Isabelle Bennett. "How about you?"

"A lot of homework. And I have riding lessons on Saturdays."

Riding lessons. Of course.

Ms. Hillary gives us a warning look. We lower our heads over our books and get back to work. I'm grateful, actually, because I don't have anything else to say to her. I try to finish my reading for English. Who knows if I'll get a chance tonight.

A burst of voices and the *bang* of books dropped on a nearby table. My gut freezes. They've found my hiding hole. I don't look up. Don't need to.

"Look, it's master and slave!" That will be Pole Dancer. I wonder which of us is the master and which is the slave?

More giggling and banging around.

Ms. Hillary is all over them. "Are you girls here to work or not?"

As she turns away, one of them mimics her. "*Are you girls here to work or not?*" I suck in my breath. They're more stupid than I thought. Ms. Hillary seems to let it go and returns to her desk. I'm not fooled.

Celeste pulls out her phone, and they whisper with their heads together. After more giggling, I hear a click, and a light flashes in my direction. Did they just take my picture? I gauge for damage control. I'm in a library. Fully clothed. Studying. How bad could it be?

Next to me, Clara's pale cheeks flush pink. She hasn't turned the page of her math text since they sat down.

It's Ainsley's own suicide when she pulls out a soda can and takes a long swig, not even trying to hide it.

"You lot, out!" Ms. Hillary barks from the desk.

"I was just taking some medication," Ainsley says.

"Out!"

There's a round of cursing. Pole Dancer knocks over a chair behind her and leaves it tipped, legs in the air. Ms. Hillary mutters and tidies up behind them.

Clara and I wait for a minute after the bell rings before leaving. I go out first, just in case they're waiting. No one. I head to my locker, take out my jacket and load all my books into my backpack. It strains at the zipper and bends my back at an unnatural angle. I feel like the old lady with the walker.

I'm a few minutes late for Biology. It's the one class where I feel totally anonymous. No Ainsley, Celeste or Pole Dancer. No one stares or even says hello. Miss Dennhart nods at me but doesn't stop talking about photosynthesis. My empty seat at the back is ready and waiting.

In Spanish, the bucktoothed girl asks if we can be partners when it's time to practice introducing ourselves. I wonder if I've become a magnet for all the school freaks. She's nice though.

"*Me llamo Daniela*," she tells me in a way that makes it sound like she's a llama.

At the end of Spanish, I approach Mr. Dent. "Can I wait here for a minute? I could help you, if you need it."

"*Claro que sí!*" he says, which I take as a yes. He gets me to erase the board and gather up loose sheets of paper for recycling.

"What are you waiting for, Isabelle?" he asks.

I'm about to tell him I'm waiting for my mom to come, but I'm tired of lying to people. It's getting harder to say the words. "It's just better for me," I say.

He looks at me oddly but doesn't press. When I'm done with the recycling, he asks me to take down students' old posters from a bulletin board. After ten minutes I tell him "*adiós*" and head for the main doors of the school. I have everything with me and don't need to stop at my locker. It's a sure fixed point where they know to find me. Might as well strap a blinking red light to my head. I won't be visiting the Blue Beast for a while.

From the main doors, I see a group of stragglers waiting at the shelter. No sign of Ainsley and Co. I bolt to pick up Maisie, bracing myself for her reproach.

* * *

The next morning in English, I decide I'll be brave if Mr. Drummond asks me to read. I'll be totally expressionless, with no sound effects and hand movements like that Rachael chick, but I won't say no.

He doesn't ask me, but I try to pay attention for once. Someone named Brittany gets the part of Ophelia, and Brandon is chosen to be Reynaldo, a servant.

Then Mr. Drummond scans the room for a new voice to play Ophelia's father, Polonius. "Will," he says. "You'll make a fine Polonius."

Silence behind me. I imagine Will crawling under his desk—all six feet four inches of him.

He doesn't say yes or no but starts reading a flat, "Give him this money and these notes, Reynaldo."

"I will, my lord," Brandon says, with about as much enthusiasm as Will.

"Marry, sir, here's my drift; And I believe, it is a fetch of wit: You laying these slight sullies on my son…" He presses on, with giggling behind him. Will is the worst Polonius ever, like he's reading a menu. I kind of respect him, though, for doing it anyway.

"Very good, my lord."

Brittany eventually joins in, reading in this sort of high falsetto which gets really annoying, "O, my lord, my lord, I have been so affrighted!"

Will manages to make it through to the end of the scene, where Polonius leaves to see the king about Hamlet's madness. He sighs and falls back in his chair, the marathon of humiliation finished.

"Very good," Mr. Drummond says. "Now I'd like to share something with you." We all watch as he walks to his desk and picks up a stack of papers.

"For the sake of privacy, I will not share the names of the authors," he continues, "but I'd like to read some excerpts from the best monologues I received last week."

A nervous hum in my stomach. Will he read mine? I don't want him to. Do I? I trace and retrace the lines on the bottom of my paper.

He lifts the first paper and starts, "*My father, where art thou now?*" My heart sinks—relieved and disappointed. Definitely not mine. It's written from Hamlet's point of view, about missing his father, in attempted Shakespearian language. Which I definitely didn't do. From all the giggling in the corner, I'm guessing that Celeste's blond friend wrote it. Possibly less stupid than she looks. Polite applause at the end.

Mr. Drummond finishes reading and shuffles the papers in his hands. It's there. The only handwritten monologue in the pile. Was there someone else? Will, maybe. I can't see the color of pen from here. I lean my head closer to my desk.

He pulls it to the top. "*Every day, I put on my mask,*" he begins. The blood rushes to my head, drowning out the next few lines. Can they tell it's mine? I don't look up to see heads turning around, looking for the telltale laughter and blushing that would give away who wrote it. *Perfectly still, Isabelle. Don't even breathe.*

Mr. Drummond presses on, clearly unaware of my agony. I wrote my monologue from the point of view of Hamlet's mother, the fear and isolation she must feel. That she senses her son's coldness and anger. That she misses her dead husband but didn't feel like she could reject his brother's marriage proposal. She's still queen and needs to carry on, alone. Applause at the end.

"Who wrote that one?" Brittany asks, scanning the room.

Mr. Drummond makes a lips-locked gesture and shrugs. I telepathically thank him. He reads two more after that, both from the point of view of the ghost of Hamlet's father.

At the end of class, I slip out before he can see me smiling. Mine was one of the best.

TEN

I go through the next week waiting for that moment when all of this peace will explode, like a blender without the lid on. The calm makes me jumpy, but something else too—a bit slow. An early spring fly, bumbling against a pane of glass. Crawling stupidly, taking in the warmth. The kind of fly you feel like putting out of its misery, it's so disoriented.

Still. The warmth.

When Mr. Drummond passes back our monologues, a phantom voice behind me says, "I thought that one was yours."

I jerk my head around and stuff the paper in my binder at the same time. No one looks at me, but I know who said it. I look him straight in the face. Enough of this sneaky staring and creeping around.

"How'd you know?" I ask.

He meets my eyes now, floppy hair below one eyebrow. Pushes up his glasses over his brown eyes. "I could tell."

I roll my eyes and turn around. Was that a compliment? So hard to tell with that one.

*   *   *

Clara still finds me at lunch sometimes. When she's not with me, I also see her in the cafeteria with this other short girl named Emma. So what? Normal people have more than one friend, right? I thought for a second that the three of us could be friends. But once, when I said hi to them together, Emma looked like she was about to wet herself. So that's not going to work.

When Clara does find me, though, I feel like maybe I don't exist in an entirely different dimension after all.

I let her do most of the talking. She likes this guy in her math class named Chad. Wish I could offer her some kind of advice. Running, hiding and acting invisible are my specialty. If she wanted never to be noticed, then I'm her girl.

In Spanish, that Daniela girl keeps talking to me, even when I try to ignore her. Her friend Damien, who has pink streaks in his hair, has started joining in. Mr. Dent even called us out once for talking when we weren't supposed to, and that doesn't happen to me.

Damien flipped through his dictionary until he found the right words. "*Lo siento, Señor Dent.*" He lowered his head.

Mr. Dent seemed to accept his apology and didn't separate us.

Damien looked back at me, eyebrows raised, like, *Phew*.

* * *

Mom tells me on Wednesday that she'll pick up Evan from day care, not to worry about it. I swing by with Maisie anyway on our way home, just in case. He's gone.

"Mrs. Bennett already came," Mrs. Carrigan says. She always calls Mom that, even though there has never been a Mr.

I speed-walk to the apartment, dragging Maisie and her backpack. What if she's been drinking and has taken him somewhere? They could be on some random bus on the other side of the city, Mom passed out in her seat while Evan takes candy from strangers.

I find them curled up on the sofa, reading one of Maisie's take-home reading books. Relief—and a mental note to get a public library card.

* * *

My after-school routine doesn't give me any warm fuzzies, but it seems to be working. I hang out for ten minutes after the bell—in the Spanish classroom, the library, the bathroom—until that first bus leaves. There was one day when they must have missed it, and Ainsley and Pole Dancer were still standing on the front lawn when I tried to leave.

I had to sneak out a side door and walk the long way around to Maisie's school. When I stood on the front step of the elementary school, they were too busy wrestling with some guys, getting leaves stuffed down their shirts, to notice me.

Pole Dancer's friend, that blond guy from Social Studies, follows her around like a magpie after a leaky garbage bag.

They're the ones who make me feel like the fly swatter is looming. They're too quiet. Too still. I caught a full-on mean smile from one of them as I passed through the cafeteria the other day. It hit me like a kick in the ribs. They've stopped following me though. Celeste looks away any time our eyes meet, an odd expression on her face. Like a bad memory.

I bumble along through the week, waiting for the ax to fall. I wonder if it's fallen when Mr. Drummond stands by my desk during English on Friday and says, as softly as a gravel truck, that he'd like to see me after class. Haven't I been keeping up okay? Is he going to ask me about Mom?

The girl who picks at her split ends meets my eye and cringes sympathetically. I'm starting to wonder if she's mute. She hasn't spoken once this term.

There's a nervous hum in my chest for the rest of the class and afterward, as I stand in front of his desk, arms crossed.

He wears a ratty gray sweater that matches his wiry hair and mustache. "Isabelle," he says, clearing away a stack of books on his desk, "pull up a chair."

I wish people wouldn't say that. As though difficult things are made easier while sitting down. I prefer to stand, myself. Easier to run. Still, I grab a chair from a nearby desk and arrange it across from him, like a job interview.

Once I'm sitting, he says, "Isabelle, I've been thinking about Words on the Wall."

I blink. *What?*

"Do you know what that is?" he asks.

I shake my head. Sounds like a trendy coffee shop.

"It's an event we have near the beginning of every school year, one of our welcome-back activities." I nod for him to continue. What does this have to do with me? "We cover an entire wall of the cafeteria with paper. Then we supply pens, pencils, crayons, you name it. A theme is chosen, and students come and write whatever they like on it—barring obscenities and hate speech—and it stays up for the week. Kind of a legal graffiti."

Okay. So he doesn't want me writing my disturbing troubled-home stuff on it?

"Ms. Furbank and I—she's the other English teacher— we're putting together a committee of grade-eleven students to organize and run it," he says. "Would you be interested in representing our class?"

I open my mouth, but no sound comes out. Represent the class? For a school event?

"You would be our class leader, but I'll ask for other student volunteers to help. You wouldn't be doing it alone." He waits for me to respond.

I open my mouth again and eventually choke out, "Are you sure?" After minutes of silence, that's the best I can do. *Great show of confidence, Isabelle.* Still, what is the man thinking? "I've never done anything like that," I say in a rumble of panic.

"No problem. The other class leader volunteered with set-up last year. You'll be in good hands." He leans back in his chair and smiles, like it's all settled.

"But—" I don't know what else to say to him. I should say no—no time, barely keeping up with homework, my job. The crazy, drunk mother. I should say all these things, but I can't stop staring at him with my mouth hanging open.

"Isabelle," he says, "you'll be good at this. You just don't know it yet."

I close my mouth. No one has ever said those words—*you'll be good at this*—to me before. "Okay."

He gives a firm nod and starts to shuffle things around on his desk again. We're done here. As I wander toward the library for my spare, a watery dread seeps through me—that familiar "run and hide." But then something overpowers it, dries it up: a slow, creeping warmth.

* * *

At the beginning of English on Monday, Mr. Drummond announces that I'll be the class leader for Words on the Wall. Twenty-five heads swivel and stare at me, like some kind of horror movie. I was hoping he'd be a bit more subtle about it, maybe printing it in a newsletter that nobody reads.

"If anyone else is interested in volunteering for the committee, please stay after class today," he says. A rush of relief. I was afraid he was going to ask for a show of hands right then. What if nobody else volunteered? It would be like that dream where you go to school naked and everyone stares.

It's hard for me to concentrate during class. At the end I take a long time gathering my stuff, reloading my bag.

Examining the end of my pen. I don't want to be standing at the front of the room as the entire class files out past me. The last kid picked for dodgeball.

When I finally swing my bag onto my back and look up, I exhale. Two bodies are beside Mr. Drummond's desk. Will (*Will?*) and that split-end girl. Mr. Drummond and his delegation of freaks.

As I walk toward the front of the class, Celeste shifts in the doorway. I turn to stare before I can stop myself. She looks at me—not Mr. Drummond—and opens her mouth to say something. No mean smile. She takes a step toward me, then sees Mr. Drummond join his (sad) group of volunteers and turns away. She's gone.

I don't know why, but I have the impulse to follow her and ask what she was going to say. Then my brain kicks in. Am I stupid? Follow Celeste to Ainsley and Pole Dancer?

Mr. Drummond waves us over. "Ah, the stout in heart! Isabelle, I trust you know Will and Amanda." Amanda, that's her name. I attempt a smile. "There's a meeting at lunchtime today with the volunteers from Ms. Furbank's class. Do you know where her room is?"

Will nods, and Amanda and I shake our heads.

"Just three doors that way." He points. "Let me know tomorrow what you decide for theme and materials and such." We all nod. I guess we're done. Will and Amanda wander off to their next classes. I go to my hiding hole in the library and finish my story about the bullied girl who loses it, trying to get my mind off the butterflies in my stomach.

When the lunch bell rings, I find Ms. Furbank's classroom. A few bodies are already gathered around her desk.

"You must be Isabelle," Ms. Furbank says, her reddish hair in a messy bun. Are those real chopsticks stuck through it? Light freckles dust her cheeks. "Come and meet everybody." She steers me by the elbow to a group of three. Damien! I feel a burst of relief at seeing his pink streaks, stupid grin.

"Isabelle! We already know each other," he says to Ms. Furbank.

"Oh, good. Isabelle, this is Zara, our class leader." Small upturned nose. Dark hair pulled away from her face. Wire-framed glasses. Everything about her is small and tidy. She gives me a tight smile and nods.

"Hey," I say.

The other member of the group is Nimra, who wears a light-green hijab and black-framed glasses. Shy smile.

"I'll leave you kids to it," Ms. Furbank says, gesturing to the empty classroom. "You're welcome to use this space for meetings, if you like."

As she heads for the door, Will and Amanda squeak through at the same time, in mid-conversation. Something twinges in me. I should have been part of that conversation too, instead of standing here like a wart, wanting to disappear.

The minute Ms. Furbank's heels *clip-clop* out the door, Zara announces, "We only have two weeks to put this together."

In the same breath, Damien says, "It's boring here. Let's go somewhere else." We all turn to stare.

"What?" Zara says.

"I know a better place we can meet."

"Does it really—" Zara begins, but Damien's already out the door, his hairy legs zipping by in a pair of striped shorts. We trail after him, Zara sighing behind us.

The hallway crowd has thinned out. Everyone's in the cafeteria or has left for lunch. Damien's blond-and-pink head bobs ahead of us. We pass into a part of the school where I've never been, near the band and cosmetology rooms. Never had a reason to come down here before, scurrying between my classrooms and the library.

He pauses in front of a light-blue door—the same color as my locker—and knocks lightly before trying the knob. As I go in, I see the placard on the door: *Drama*. Damien flicks on the lights, and a high ceiling appears. There's a low wooden stage against the far wall, and chairs scattered in small clusters around the room.

"What—" Zara begins.

"No, not here." Damien beckons us through a door off to the side of the drama room. "*Here!*"

We shuffle through and find ourselves in some kind of a large closet lined with musty clothes, old shoes, flamboyant hats. It smells like twenty years of sweaty polyester.

"We're meeting in the closet?" Nimra beats Zara to it this time.

"No, not a closet. It's a *prop room*," Damien corrects. "It's the perfect spot."

Zara looks as if someone just picked their nose and wiped it on her. "No way. I'm not working in here."

"Think about it," he says. "It's perfectly secluded, creative. Who would find us here? We could be totally focused."

He had me at *Who would find us here?* "Looks good to me!" I say. Damien perks up.

Will shifts next to me, ducking his head away from the overhanging wigs and boxes spilling from the high shelves. Amanda looks like she's trying not to laugh.

"Fine. But I pick the meeting place next time," Zara sniffs. No one objects.

With no room for chairs, we sit cross-legged in a circle on the floor, Will on my right and Nimra on my left. Will's leg presses against mine, warm through his jeans. Should I move away? I notice that his other knee touches Amanda's, though, and Nimra's knee bumps me on the other side. I stay put.

"Okay." Zara pulls out a clipboard and clicks her pen into action.

On cue, Damien jumps up and flits around the room. "Props! We need props."

Zara drops the clipboard into her lap and throws back her head, en route to a full-scale temper tantrum. I'm starting to wonder if this meeting is like one of those dreams where you start out for Disneyland and end up trying to find a pair of matching socks and eventually follow a firefly down a long tunnel instead.

Damien picks out a gray Stetson for Will, which actually kind of suits him. Tall cowboy type. He drops a moldy-looking boa in Zara's lap.

"Ew! Get that thing away from me!" she squeals, flinging it over her shoulder.

Amanda gets a checkered gingham apron, which she pulls over her head and ties around her thick waist. Damien pins a sheriff's badge on Nimra. He hands me a pair of Coke-bottle-thick old-man glasses with brown frames the size of my entire face. They still have the lenses. I try them on and look around the group, everything blurry and smeared. My eyes sting.

Next to me, a deep laugh erupts. I snatch off the glasses and turn. Will is smiling, head back, laughing right from the gut. First time I ever heard him laugh.

"You should wear those all the time," he tells me.

"Did anyone else come here for a meeting?" Zara says. We turn to her, smiles smothered, like we just shared a dirty joke. "Okay, last year they chose a Back to Our Roots theme and had sections on the wall like 'Louis Riel' and 'Laura Secord.'"

"Didn't they make the paper in the shape of Canada too?" Nimra asks.

"That was confusing," Damien says. "I wanted to write in Manitoba but couldn't think of anything to say about Louis Riel." He winks at me and keeps rummaging for his own prop.

Zara ignores him. "We want to do something totally different this year—make our own mark. I was thinking of a poet theme." We wait for her to continue. "Poets like Frost and Dickinson were born in the 1800s. We could do something like Two Centuries of Poetry and feature some main poets on a timeline?"

Damien chooses some tacky bling and hangs it around his neck. "How about Get Your Funk On?" he says, doing some bad hip-hop moves.

"Get the Funk Outta Here?" I say.

"Funk Off?" Damien again, and Will gives that deep, throaty laugh. His arm brushes mine, tickling me.

"Hilarious." Zara pouts and shoots me an accusatory look, like, *Aren't you supposed to be the class leader?* To be honest, I'm not sure what's wrong with me. We seem to be floating in an alternate universe that resembles a prop closet. Maybe this is what other people feel like all the time.

"I like the poet idea," Nimra says, and Amanda nods at her and Zara.

"It's a little"—Damien hesitates—"dull. You wanted something different, right?"

"Let's hear your great idea then," Zara says. Damien shrugs and examines the clutter around us.

"What about Get Your Poet On? Put both ideas together," I say. Nobody speaks for a second, and then Nimra nods.

"Get-Your-Poet-On," Damien says slowly.

"Does that make sense?" Nimra says. "I guess it does."

Zara's not throwing me a scrap. "*I* don't think it makes sense. But *some* might like it."

"That's good," Will says. "I like it."

"I like it too." From Damien. "All those in favor?"

Everyone raises their hand except Zara, and Damien gives a hearty "Aye." We spend the next ten minutes trying to work out other details, like what kind of materials we should use. Will mostly listens, nodding from time to time. Zara still pushes for the timeline idea, and Amanda suggests we supply finger paints.

"Too gross. Too messy," Nimra says. "It would take a long time to write a poem in finger paint."

"When was a timeline ever interesting? Think. In your entire life," Damien says to Zara.

"*I* know." Zara's voice gets all squeaky. "Why don't we just put on stupid costumes and wander around saying things that don't make sense? There, all settled." She snaps her clipboard shut and leaves, slamming the door behind her.

"Don't worry about her," Damien says to me, like I'm taking this personally. "She just likes to be in charge." *Hey, not my problem if Zara's got her panties in a knot.* He reaches out to collect our props. "We'll meet again tomorrow."

Nimra asks if she can wear the sheriff's pin for the rest of the afternoon, but I gladly hand back my old-man glasses. My head's still floating, disconnected. We wander together toward the cafeteria for the last few minutes of the lunch hour, to the other side of the looking glass where rabbits can't talk.

ELEVEN

I sit Maisie down as soon as we get home and finally level with her. I've been putting off the birthday conversation for a week.

"I'm sorry, Maisie," I say. "It'll just have to be a family party this year."

She blinks and bites down on her lip—the face she makes when she's trying to be brave. "Why?"

"We just don't have the money for anything else, and this apartment isn't right for a party with friends."

She nods, one tear trickling down her cheek. My chest collapses. I pull her into my lap and hug her tightly. "Don't worry. It'll be really nice. Maybe I can make some cupcakes to send to your school?" Like Mom never did for me.

Maisie nods and rubs her eyes. "Okay."

If I have to steal the ingredients and stay up until 2 AM, I'm making the damn cupcakes. "I already got your present," I whisper, giving her a big smile. Her face brightens. "Now go blow your nose."

She skips away, placated by my crappy compromise. Is she really asking that much? Some stupid party games with her school friends, candles on a cake. Presents in gift bags with colored tissue paper. Someone to take her picture.

I will make her next birthday different. I swear it. I'll save a few dollars from every paycheck and hide the money in the suitcase with my notebook. Her birthdays will be different than mine. Different memories. Different than all of this.

I barge into our bedroom without knocking. "Maisie's birthday is this weekend," I say to Mom. "Have you got her anything?"

She looks up from a book and marks her place with a finger. "Not yet."

"You mean not at all."

"Isabelle, I still have a few days!"

"Have you even thought about"—I hear my voice rising—"what she would like?"

"Of course I have," she says. "I already invited Richie and Jacquie over on Saturday." Because every little girl wants her drunk uncle and delinquent cousin to celebrate her special day. Might as well invite Mom and Uncle Richie's estranged sister, Laina, as well. One big happy family.

"She wanted a party with her school friends," I hiss. "You know, party hats and balloons and all of that."

"Well, she can have a party with friends." She's bewildered by this—no idea what I'm talking about. "What's the problem?"

I slam the door behind me before I tell her she's the reason we can't have a party, that she'll wreck it all. That she'll forget the party, or burn the cake. Throw up. Fall down. Promise Maisie a gift "later" that never comes. That she'll hook up with some drunk who will lock her daughter in the basement on her special day for being a pissant. It'll all be one big mess. And that girl will cry.

I run to the bathroom and lock the door. Run the tap. I stay in there until Evan's small fingers poke under the crack at the bottom of the door. "Isabelle?"

Deep breath. A kiss for Maisie and Evan before I leave for work.

"It'll be different, Maisie," I say to the top of her tangled cinnamon head. She sits at the table, drawing a picture of a cat, no idea what I'm talking about. Then I'm out the door and down the hall. Fire nipping at my heels.

* * *

All through English and my spare the next morning, I feel a sort of hum running through me. But it's sweet. Is it possible I'm excited about a meeting in a prop closet?

Will smiled at me as I sat down this morning, and my insides flipped. Stupid. I don't know exactly what I think of him, except it felt nice to sit by him yesterday. And, well, touch him. That great laugh hiding under all that hair. Now I want to get back there. Damien's insanity. Amanda and Nimra, the way I feel almost human sitting there with them. If I can have all of that, I don't mind putting up with Zara.

As I wait outside Ms. Furbank's room, Damien claws his way to the front of the line leaving class and pulls me aside.

"Just go there now!" he whispers.

"But Zara—"

"You, Will and Amanda go straight there, and I'll tell Zara that half the group is already waiting down there."

"She'll be pissed."

"What else is new?" He shrugs, slipping back inside to distract Zara.

I have to admit, meeting in a regular classroom doesn't hold the same appeal after yesterday. When Will and Amanda appear at the end of the hall, I grab them and drag them along with me.

Amanda flicks on the light in the prop room, and we discover new treasures for today in a tidy pile. Damien has been busy. Will claims a woman's hideous curly wig. It's almost the same color as his real hair, so it's hard to tell where his own hair ends and the wig begins. I howl. He makes a seriously ugly woman.

Amanda pulls on a leather biker vest. I offer her the matching bustier with silver spikes, but she declines. I opt for a string of pearls and a silk fan.

"Too pretty," Amanda says. She holds up a flea-bitten fur hat for me instead.

"I think I'll pass on the head lice today," I say, and Will rewards me with a big laugh that fills this space.

We're standing there—the rejects time forgot—when Damien, Zara and Nimra walk in. We freeze. I almost forgot why we were here in the first place.

Zara takes in the whole scene and flushes red. "I thought I was choosing the location today."

"Bustier?" Will offers her the studded leather thing. At that moment I truly love him. I can't believe he did that.

Nimra—diverting disaster—raises an eyebrow. "Damien, who exactly were you hoping would wear that?"

He shrugs and smiles. Everyone ignores Zara and settles on the floor again, sifting through the gaudy pile. Zara eventually joins the circle and pretends to have nothing to do with what's going on around her.

"I have an idea for writing implements," she says, pulling out the infamous clipboard.

"Okay." Damien snaps on a pirate patch. "Let's hear it."

"A symbol for a poet or writer is sometimes an inkpot with a quill pen." She pauses to make sure we're all listening. "We could buy or make ballpoint pens with feathers and keep them in jars that look like inkpots."

"Arr! Me likes, young lassie!" Damien growls in pirate-speak with a bad Scottish accent.

Zara clenches her jaw and turns to face Nimra, on her other side.

"If we wanted some color, we could also do the same with markers, right?" I say. Poor girl. I'll try to keep her from having kittens right here in the prop room. "I think it's a good idea."

Will nods. If I suggested we use human blood, he would probably do the same. He sits on my right side again, Amanda on my left. She stretches out her short legs in front of her, toward the middle of the circle, her scuffed black flats poking up. I'm about to do the same when I realize I'll lose that warm circle where Will's knee rests against mine. *Pathetic, Isabelle. Move.* I can't.

Zara looks less likely to claw out my eyes now. "I'll look into that then. I could probably get feathers at any craft store."

"I'm still against the timeline," Damien says.

"Okay." Zara swallows, all strained civility. "Other ideas then?"

We hum and haw for a minute and get distracted by playing around with a pair of handcuffs. After Damien finishes cuffing his ankles together, Will motions for him to throw them over. He snaps my wrist in one side and loops the other through the leg of a coffee table tucked beneath the rack of clothes.

"There, that'll keep you out of trouble," Will says.

I look up and catch Damien's raised eyebrow. My cheeks flush.

Damien crawls over to us, takes one end of the cuffs off the table leg and puts it on Will's wrist instead, so we're cuffed together. "That's more like it, I think," he says.

Face on fire, I can't look at either one of them. Jacquie has told me how bad I am at flirting. She's right. I never know the right words. Can't even catch a smile from Hasan without running for the toilet brush.

Silence. Have they stopped talking because of us? Can't look up. I press the release button and wriggle my wrist out, dropping my side to the floor with a *clank*. Stretch out my legs in front of me. Deep breath. Head up.

"We could still use poetry but in a different way," I say, all business now. Bubble popped. Nimra. Yes, I'll look at Nimra.

"What are you thinking?" she asks. She must have felt 100 percent of my attention hitting her all at once.

"We-ll…" I draw it out, since I don't exactly know what I'm thinking. I look around and see Amanda in the leather vest. Damien in an eye patch, now trying on the bustier over his T-shirt. Nimra in a flower lei. Can't bear to look at Will, but the wig. That repulsive wig. "What if we all pick a favorite poem and put up samples? Beat poetry, haikus, sonnets—anything, really."

Nimra nods, then Amanda. Damien's too busy wrestling with the clasp on the bustier to respond. I see Will's head bobbing out of the corner of my eye. Zara looks up, examining the ceiling, and makes a duck face.

"And we could make the paper in the shape of a scroll," I say, on a roll now, "to go with the feather pens."

Well, now that you mention the feather pens… "Okay." Zara nods. "That might work." She looks to Damien, who looks at his chest in the bustier. "Well?" she says.

"That's better." I'm not sure if he's talking about my idea or the bustier. "I'm doing Jimi Hendrix."

Zara opens her mouth to protest—probably not Robert Frost-ish enough for her—but closes it after a look from all of us.

We take a few minutes to iron out supplies, who's getting what, and how we're going to make this work. Nimra, who's also a member of the Art Club, thinks she can make the paper into the shape of a scroll.

When she says *Art Club,* a cloud moves over me. It's been twenty-four hours since I thought about Ainsley at all. Saint Ainsley, president of the Art Club. I didn't even notice whether Celeste was in English today.

"Maybe I can get the Art Club to help me put up the paper and shape it," Nimra says.

"That would be great." Zara scribbles something on her clipboard.

"I'm sure the six of us could handle it," I say.

"The more hands, the better," Zara chirps, like some forty-year-old rounding up volunteers for a church fundraiser. Discussion closed.

Zara gives us some assignments for the next meeting, which isn't until Monday. Almost a week away. It's only been two days, but the thought of returning to the dusty library, Ms. Hillary shuffling around, falls flat. I want to do this every day for the rest of the year—hide in a prop closet with lunatics. Zara can come and bark orders if she must.

As soon as we have things sorted, Zara and Nimra get up and leave. Damien, Amanda, Will and I stay back.

"Just like a little poodle," Damien says about Zara, "yipping in your ear."

We all sit with our legs stretched to the center of the circle, a lopsided star. Damien makes a halfhearted attempt to throw more props in our direction, but we're lazy now. Tossing words back and forth. Amanda's giggles ring over everything. A sad sinking feeling when the bell goes.

*   *   *

"What's with you and that Will guy?" Damien asks me in Spanish class.

Daniela leans in, looking back and forth between Damien and me. Every part of me shuts down.

"What do you mean?" I say.

"He obviously likes you."

Over the ringing in my ears, I hear Daniela's voice. "Will who? Which Will?"

Mercifully, Damien left out *and you like him*.

"He just sits by me in English," I say.

"Well"—he gives me that raised-eyebrow look again— "he 'just sits by you' in our meetings too." When I don't respond, he adds, "Try sitting in a different spot next time. You'll see who follows." Smug smile.

Mr. Dent stops conjugating the verb *hablar* on the board and stares at us, thin-lipped.

"*Lo siento, Señor Dent,*" Damien says, and Mr. Dent turns back to the board.

I feel like wiping that stupid smile off Damien's face. But I feel something else too. Through the window, sunshine trickles in.

TWELVE

Uncle Richie shows up to Maisie's birthday party with a twelve-pack of beer in one hand and a two-six of Jack Daniels in the other. Jacquie juggles coolers and an enormous gift bag.

"Good thing we aren't celebrating a kid's birthday or anything," I say to Jacquie, eyeing the haul.

"Are you kidding?" she says. "Wasn't this every birthday party you ever had?" I can't argue with that. "As traditional as candles on the cake in this family," she adds. Actually, more traditional.

"Where's the birthday girl?" Uncle Richie roars, scooping Maisie up by the armpits and swinging her. He must have come straight from work—a monkey with long hairy arms wearing a suit, a brown stain on his tie.

Mom pads out in a black dress, laughing. The dress has gray pearl buttons down the front and ends just above her knees. I call it her weddings-and-funerals dress—the only thing she owns that isn't high here and low there and lets it all hang out.

She leans in to kiss Uncle Richie on his stubbly cheek. She looks pretty tonight—hair done up, less makeup. Little pearl earrings. Sometimes I forget she's only thirty-two, a lot younger than other people's moms. She was sixteen when she had me.

Maisie, Evan and I have decorated the whole apartment with balloons. I got a shiny *Happy Birthday* banner from the dollar store and made Maisie wait in her room while I hung it.

"Happy Birthday. For me!" She hopped on the spot when she saw it.

"I want one too," Evan said.

"You'll have one when it's *your* birthday, Evan," she told him. "Today is *my* birthday."

I sent cupcakes to school on Friday, after getting a mix and a can of icing from my store. Rupa tried to give it to me for free when she found out it was for Maisie's birthday, but I insisted on paying. Have to keep things on the up-and-up there. Maisie came home with an empty container that day. "Even Mrs. Williams ate one," she said.

Mom took the bus to the grocery store this morning and came back with bags bursting. I'm worried she spent too much of her check at once, but I'll think about that tomorrow. Tonight I watch a newly-turned-seven-year-old skip around the apartment, face like a glow stick.

Mom tugged me into the bathroom as soon as she got home from shopping. "Look what I got Maisie," she said, pulling a plush pink koala from the plastic bag and shutting off the light. "The tag says it glows in the dark. See?"

Never mind that every pair of socks Maisie owns has holes, or that she needs a new backpack for school. She'll love it.

Mom also got everything to make lasagna, which is what she usually throws together when the weddings-and-funerals dress comes out. "Did you see the little cake I picked up?" she said, pointing to the fridge. She must've taken my birthday lecture seriously.

The smell of the lasagna fills the whole apartment now and makes my stomach growl.

"We're ten minutes from eating," Mom says, cracking open a cooler.

Maisie and Evan hover around the gift bag and snoop through the tissue paper. "Hey, hands off until after cake!" I tell them, waving them away. They chase each other down the hall.

Mom and Uncle Richie chat in the kitchen while Mom chops tomatoes for the salad. They pretend not to notice when Jacquie sneaks a cooler from the counter and settles next to me on the sofa.

"I hooked up with this guy from my phys ed class." Jacquie leans in.

"You mean, like, a boyfriend?"

"Hell, no." She pulls back her chin like I spit on her. "This is too much woman for one man to handle." Wicked laugh. "I'm going to see him again this weekend though."

Words leap to the front of my mouth—my own confessions. I swallow them. She'll make fun of Will, or ask me if he has a big dick or something. Make fun of me. *Your legs touched. Ooooooooh.*

"I'm the class leader for this school event. It's called Words on the Wall." That sounded even more lame out loud.

"Living on the edge, Isabelle!" she says, poking me in the side. She must see my face, though, and adds, "That's cool. Congratulations."

I consider telling her about them—Damien, Nimra, the lot. She'll probably make them sound boring, and the only one I wouldn't mind her dumping on is Zara. I don't say anything else, and she doesn't ask.

"So, when are you going to get a boyfriend?" Jacquie says. My favorite topic of conversation with her. Mom saves me by calling everyone to the table.

Ironically, Uncle Richie spends half of dinner teasing Maisie about how many boyfriends she'll have this year. It's probably true, Maisie having a boyfriend before I do. So what? Where has there been room for a boyfriend in this slummy carnival act? The guys from Jacquie's parties are all hands and loud mouths, like they're doing me a favor by hitting on me. Any guy I'd look at for more than a second—like Will—would see all of this and run screaming.

I put my fork down on my plate and push it away, appetite gone.

Mom gets up to grab another beer. She and Uncle Richie have worked their way through a few now but are still holding together okay. She whispers in my ear as she comes back, "You can have a cooler if you want." Like how I offer Maisie and Evan candy for being good. "But just one."

"No, thanks, Mom," I say. Too weird to be drinking with her. I have only drunk once before, at Jacquie's last birthday party. I ended up puking the next morning, Maisie standing there watching me hug the toilet.

Are you sick like Mom? she'd asked. A wave of revulsion had made me retch a second time. Never again will I give her reason to say that. After everything that's happened, even the sight of empty bottles makes me angry.

The second Maisie finishes her lasagna and pushes most of the salad off her plate, she starts in again. "Now can I open presents?"

"After cake," I tell her.

"Oh, go on," Mom says. "Let her open them now."

Maisie squirms in the middle of the living-room floor, and we gather around.

"Start with mine," I say, handing over a squishy package in wrapping paper that Evan and I made with lined paper and crayons.

"I drew the dog." Evan points to a lumpy oval with lines coming from its head.

She tears at the wrapping paper, embroidered pink fabric spilling into her lap. "A princess dress!" She holds it up and makes the bottom twirl around. It only took me two minutes to fix the hem in the back. Good as new.

"Remember your thank-yous," Mom says. Maisie gives me a giant hug that almost hurts.

She loves the koala from Mom, still wrapped in the plastic bag, and insists on trying it out in the dark bathroom right then. Evan tags along, tripping over her feet.

"It works! It's glowing." His voice floats from under the door.

They tumble back out to the living room for the biggest present, from Uncle Richie and Jacquie.

"I picked this out, kid," Jacquie tells her.

"And I paid for it," Uncle Richie says, chuckling.

Tissue paper flies, then silence. Maisie lifts a giant blue dollhouse from the bag, with a little verandah and four separate rooms—living room, bathroom, bedroom and study.

"Wait, there's more," Jacquie says, pulling a box from the bottom of the bag. It's filled with perfect wooden furniture, a family of four with painted smiles, tiny food.

Maisie blinks. She's never had anything this perfect before. Mom bites her lip. I look up at Jacquie. How can I repay this? Why did I think Maisie needed more than these people?

Maisie finds her voice. "Oh! Look at the little mom! And the baby—he fits in the bed." She forgets to say thank you. No one cares. "A toilet! There's a toilet!"

I hug Uncle Richie and Jacquie, no words.

"Wow," I say to Jacquie after Mom and Uncle Richie go to the kitchen to pull the cake from the fridge.

"Nice, eh?" she says. "I caught him on payday. Good thing too. He's going out tomorrow."

When she says "going out," she means going to the casino. Uncle Richie makes good money running his own computer business, but he drinks and gambles. Jacquie's life isn't much different than mine except for bursts of money between the periods of being flat broke. And no little people to look after.

"This'll wake you up, Marnie." Uncle Richie's voice from the kitchen. I look up to see him pouring her a shot of Jack Daniels. She flicks her head back to swallow and then bangs the empty glass down on the counter. For a while all I can hear are quiet voices and the clink of shot glasses.

Jacquie curls up next to me on the sofa and tucks her feet in. "So, any thought of when?" she asks.

"When what?"

"You know, moving out," she says. "Safeway is hiring. I could apply." Jacquie in an apron, stacking produce?

I watch Maisie trying to slide a tiny shower curtain onto a rod, her light eyebrows knit together. Evan cranes his neck to supervise. When he reaches out to try, she twists her back to him and holds the wooden bits to her chest.

"I don't know," I say, my eyes on Maisie and Evan. Her determined fingers. His high forehead as he leans in.

"Well, I hope that means soon. I'm not sticking around much longer." She juts her chin toward the two in the kitchen. Mom stumbles into Uncle Richie's chest, and he reaches to steady her. Pours another shot. Heads go back. Glasses bang on the counter. She giggles, wiping her mouth on the back of her hand.

After fifteen minutes, Mom tries to pull Maisie away from her dollhouse for cake.

"I don't want cake," Maisie says, arranging a miniature bathtub inside the bathroom. Evan examines the tiny food in his palm.

"Then just come and blow out the candles. We'll eat the cake!" Mom laughs, waving the knife. Uncle Richie ducks to avoid it.

I remember the truck and ramp for Evan, still up in my closet. If I pull them out now, it'll be another hour before I can get him in bed.

Mom points to the lopsided candles. "You'd better intervene, Richie," she says, clutching his arm and laughing.

I want Maisie and Evan in bed right now. There's a chance they'll be asleep, off in another room, if things go sideways.

"Let's sing now," I tell them. "You can eat the cake tomorrow."

"I want cake now," Evan cries, rubbing his eyes.

"Let the boy have cake, Isabelle," Mom says. "We don't have birthday parties every day." She licks the icing from her fingers.

I look at Jacquie. She shrugs.

"Maisie, *now*," I say. "The dollhouse isn't going anywhere."

She shoots me a look and drags herself over to the table, like we're torturing her with cake. Once Mom and Uncle Richie finally manage to light the candles, Maisie smiles again, freckles stretching across her cheeks as she blows. We sing, clap. Two candles left. Two boyfriends. Ha-ha.

"Just a little piece for them," I whisper to Mom in the kitchen. "It's right before bed."

"Isabelle, you're such an old soul," she says, kissing my cheek. Her breath is sharp with booze. "Let Maisie enjoy her moment. And go ask your uncle what he'd like to drink," she adds. Like I'm going to offer anyone more drinks at this point. I carry out pieces of cake instead, giving the smaller ones to Maisie and Evan.

"Eat up! It's bedtime," I tell them, which is a cue for them to take mouthfuls the size a fruit fly would.

Jacquie comes to stand by me. I know she wants to talk more. I can't sit still now, settle. I gather dirty dishes instead, fill the sink and start to scrub.

"Mom, come help me." I try to draw her in, distract her from drinking more. But that is exactly what she does. As she pulls another two beers from the pack, I put my hand on her wrist. "Mom, I think you've had enough."

Her soft cheeks fall, sparkle gone. "You're not the adult here," she says, her voice dropping low, "as much as you think you are." She pulls her hand away and joins Uncle Richie at the table, passing him a beer.

"Put your feet up, Richie," she says. "Long day?"

He starts complaining about work. I hover, pushing.

"Let's go, Maisie. Evan. Pajama time." No, if we have to leave, pajamas won't work. I look at them. Maisie's in a skirt and short-sleeved shirt. But she's wearing tights, and her sweater is by the door. Evan is in cords and a sweatshirt. Okay. "Never mind pajamas tonight. Just go to the bathroom," I say.

A chorus of howling from both of them. Evan clutches his unfinished cake, and Maisie makes a break for the dollhouse.

A chill runs through me as Uncle Richie's voice climbs. "The incompetence…" I hear, then "…bunch of liars." Mom gets sad when she drinks. Uncle Richie gets mad. He's never hit Jacquie (at least, not that I know of), but she has been caught in the crossfire. Once she had to go to Emergency when he kicked over a table and it fell on her arm. *Tell them you fell down*, he told her, spitting drunk, *or they'll take you away*. That was right after her mom left.

He goes on about an employee who's been dipping into the till. "I know it was him. I know it!" He swings his arm, knocking over a beer. It rolls across the table and falls to the floor. Mom flinches but doesn't move. His voice rises to a shout. "And when I confronted him, you know what he said?"

"Let's move this to your bedroom," I say to Maisie, lifting the house off the floor. She squeals and clings to the base of it. "You don't have to go to bed yet. Just play in there!" Panic creeping in. I try to twist it from her hands.

Jacquie knows. From the corner of my eye, I see her pick up Evan from his chair at the table. Over-excited. Past bedtime. He writhes in her arms, twisting back toward his cake.

Uncle Richie rises from his chair and gets in Mom's face, like she's the one who stole from him. "He says I can't prove anything and can't fire him or he'll sue for wrongful dismissal!

That son of a…" He slams a fist on the table. Mom blinks and mutters something.

She gets out of her chair but seems to forget where she's going. The kitchen? The bathroom? Then she notices the screaming kid in each corner. "Isabelle. Jacquie. Leave them be." She steadies herself on the back of a kitchen chair. "I will be—I will say when they have to go to bed." Her tongue works to form the words, thick in her mouth.

Then, to Uncle Richie, she says, "Didn't we take good care of Laina all those years?"

Oh hell.

Uncle Richie jumps from his chair, knocking it to the floor, yelling at no one and everyone. "And what for? What thanks?" He starts in on a tirade about Laina, who "thinks she's too good for everybody." Laina, who "lives in a fantasy world." That "backstabbing cow"—if she were here, the things he would say to her.

Laina is their younger sister who doesn't talk to them anymore. Owns a cushy house somewhere in the city. Lives her own sweet life. Any mention of Laina is gasoline on a bonfire.

Mom's face crumples. Uncle Richie raises an arm over his head and hurls a bottle against the living-room wall. The dollhouse falls from my arms as I curl over Maisie, shards of glass raining on my hair.

I straighten. Amber droplets of beer trickle down the wall where the bottle hit. Small arms limp in my hands now. Maisie doesn't struggle as I yank her to the door, Jacquie right behind me with Evan. Sweater, jacket, shoes in one swoop. We're down the hall, Evan bouncing on Jacquie's hip and Maisie trotting at my heels.

I push arms through sleeves, jam shoes on feet. Bang the elevator button. Jacquie's voice in my ear: "Happy birthday, eh?"

Out on the sidewalk, headlights whiz by. One car hits a puddle and showers our legs with muddy brown water.

Evan starts to cry. "That car got me wet. I'm wet now."

Maisie holds my hand, not speaking. Her tights are speckled with mud.

"Let's go to the park for a while," I say, squeezing her palm. "You get to go to the park instead of going to bed on your birthday!"

She doesn't move. "Why did Uncle Richie break that bottle?"

"He just got mad about something," I tell her. Maybe it's time I start being honest with her. She sees everything. "And he had too much to drink."

"Why did he have too much to drink?" she asks. *Question of the decade, Maisie.*

"I don't know." I zip up her sweater and pull her hood over her hair, then lace up Evan's shoes properly. Our breath balloons out around us, frosty. I rub my arms.

"You didn't bring a jacket," Jacquie says, watching me. I shake my head.

"Let's go." I motion toward the park, a few blocks away. Streetlights glare down on the still swings and chipped red monkey bars.

Evan runs ahead to the swings, sitting on the wet seat. "Push me!" he calls to anybody listening.

Maisie finds an empty swing and plants her toes in the damp sand, swaying from side to side.

"Should I start apartment hunting?" Jacquie stands close to me, her warm arm against mine.

"How can I leave them?" It always comes down to this.

"You can't be there forever," she says. "We had to learn to survive."

And look how good we turned out. I push Evan on the swing until he complains about being cold. Then an attempted game of hide-and-seek goes bad.

"It's scary in the park at night," Maisie says. *You think?* Some homeless guy with a shopping cart and gray clown hair wanders by. I'm checking for needles everywhere Maisie and Evan step.

"I have to pee," Evan says, and the park is done.

I take them to the store. Of course, it would be Arif at the counter.

"Do you mind if we use the bathroom?" I ask.

He shakes his head, eyes drilling into my head as I herd them to the back of the store. *Yes, Family of the Year, I know. Dragging under-dressed kids around at some ungodly hour.*

"Can you go check what's happening?" I say to Jacquie, wrestling with the button on Evan's pants, which are soaked from the knee down. "I'll wait here with them." She nods and disappears.

We stand inside the main door until she comes back, Evan's nose pressed against the glass. I feel like I should say something to Arif, but I don't know what. He stops watching after a while and restocks the cigarettes.

"Dad took off. Your mom's there—in a piss-poor state but okay," Jacquie says.

I thank Arif and drag the kids back to the apartment. Maisie's face is pale, her lips a thin line. Evan's a wreck. "I can't walk," he says, bursting into tears for the tenth time tonight. I hoist him up and carry him the rest of the way, my arms aching and wet where his pants press against me.

Adrenaline gone, just a heavy dread as I push open the apartment door. Maisie ducks behind me and sees it first, while I'm pulling off Evan's jacket.

"My house!" she gasps. I turn.

One side of the dollhouse is smashed, a bottle still embedded in its side. Smiling mother and tiny dishes are soaking in a pool of amber from another nearby bottle.

She opens her mouth and lets out a sob—a gulp of pain. I catch her as her thin legs buckle. I lie back as I cradle her and stroke her hair. "We'll fix it. We'll get another one. It's okay." Again and again. But it's not okay. I can't buy another one. I can't fix any of it.

Jacquie takes Evan and steps around us. After a few minutes, I hear the toilet flush and the tap running in the bathroom. Murmuring voices, then the click of his bedroom door.

"C'mon." I stand and pick up Maisie like a baby, straining to keep my balance. She clings to my neck, her cheeks wet.

As I turn to carry her to the bathroom, I see Mom at the table. Makeup smeared. Face red and puffy, nose running freely. Her head on the table, mouthing silent words. I turn Maisie so her back is to Mom. One more thing she doesn't need to see tonight.

A sound as I pass. "What more? What more could I do?"

The words reach me in fragments. I'm not even sure I heard them. Mom's eyes look past me, into the dark kitchen. Look through me.

For an instant I think she sees me, blinks. Then nothing. I keep walking. She—all of that —is something I can't touch tonight. Can't even say one word. Even a word will open up something horrific, something I can never undo.

I get Maisie undressed. Bathroom. Drink. Find the koala, some shred of comfort. I curl up in the bed with her and hold her in the curve of my body.

"Do you want to sleep here?" I whisper to Jacquie, standing over us.

She shakes her head. "I'll take a taxi home."

I mouth "thank you" to her, knowing it's not nearly enough.

"Same time next year?" She winks. I close my eyes, her words a bruise.

THIRTEEN

Monday morning, Will's eyes light up as I drop my backpack by my desk. He doesn't look away, waiting for me to give something back to him. A word, a smile. Something. I barely nod at him before sliding into my seat. *You don't want this, Romeo.* How could I think for an instant that he could be part of my world?

I picture Will sitting on the ugly sofa as Uncle Richie hurls beer bottles and we all scatter like cockroaches. Isn't that what every guy wants? *Congratulations, Will. You just won yourself a nice, dysfunctional family.* Even worse if he tried to help, to fix. The girlfriend who's also a project. It's for his own good that I walk away. He'll never know about the Molotov cocktail he just avoided. Still, the ache in my chest makes it hard for me to lift my head today.

It started that night and hasn't gone away. The worst was Sunday morning, as I tried to clean up Maisie's dollhouse with her behind me, sobbing. I straightened the cracked wall a bit, but it was still buckled and split. The dolls and furniture came out a little nicer—slightly stained but hardly noticeable.

"Look, Maisie. Good as new!" I held them up for her when they dried.

She looked at me, face flat, and wouldn't take them from my hand. Like they were contaminated. The ache washed over me then, and I had to hide my face from her.

The only time the aching stopped was when Mom came out hours later. Maisie ran to her and tugged on her arm, her plaintive voice running on and on. She pulled Mom over to the house and pointed at the disaster. Too young to see Mom's role in this, wanting her to set it right.

Mom raised a hand to her mouth, shocked. Anger like a fire engulfed every part of me. It radiated so strongly that when Mom turned her head to speak to me, she felt it—saw it—from across the room. Closed her mouth. She couldn't look away.

I haven't spoken to her since the night of Maisie's birthday, around the time we had cake. That is my only power.

"You can't stay silent forever, Isabelle," she told me Sunday evening. "You'll have to talk to me sooner or later." That's where she's wrong. Why didn't I see it before? My words only kept me tangled up with her, pulled into her mess. That endless back-and-forth tying us together. It's my silence that cuts her from my world. *You will find out, Mother, just how little I need you.*

*   *   *

Mr. Drummond's at the front, all wrapped up in *Hamlet* again. Enough bloody *Hamlet* already. He waves one hand as he talks, his voice carrying to every corner. He must like this part because he doesn't ask anyone else to read. "*How all occasions do inform against me, / And spur my dull revenge! What is a man, / If his chief good and market of his time / Be but to sleep and feed? a beast, no more…*"

I tune out until he gets to: "*How stand I then, / That have a father kill'd, a mother stain'd, / Excitements of my reason and my blood, / And let all sleep?…*" A mother stained, and let all sleep. The words scratch at me.

"What's Hamlet saying here?" Mr. Drummond asks. We all sit in silence, trying to avoid eye contact. After an awkward minute he answers his own question. "Hamlet has good reason to take action—his father murdered by his own brother, and his mother married to his father's murderer— yet he does nothing. Meanwhile, he watches thousands laying down their lives for a piece of land that isn't even sufficient to bury their dead."

He turns back to the play. "*O, from this time forth, / My thoughts be bloody, or be nothing worth!*" He looks up at us. "So what's Hamlet going to do?"

"Take action?" Rachael says.

"Take action." Mr. Drummond nods.

At the end of class, Mr. Drummond catches me as I dash for the door, waving Will and me over.

"Where are we at with Words on the Wall?" he asks.

I look at Will for the first time since class began. "Can you fill him in?" I say. I don't wait for a response. Out the door. Down the hall. Up the stairs two at a time, to the computer lab. It's not as quiet as the library, but it's easier to hide in. No Ms. Hillary pretending not to look over your shoulder.

I find a computer near the back corner, facing the door. Don't want any surprises creeping up behind me. I log in and bring up Google. Spend the next half hour trying to find information on becoming emancipated as a minor. Is there a legal process? Can I just leave? I find a jumble of information. Some sites say there's a legal process. Others say you can leave at sixteen if you can support yourself.

Who would know for sure? I think of sweet Miss Yee. She would try to help, but that's the problem. I don't need some naïve do-gooder messing around, trying to fix my broken life.

If the websites are right, I'll have to be able to support myself to move out. Choose between being free and being in school. I know what Jacquie would say. Still. I've seen what's out there for people who don't finish high school. Look at half of the people in my apartment building, shuffling around like they're in a zombie apocalypse. How could I ever do anything better for myself?

And all the old worries about Maisie and Evan surface. Could they dodge bottles in the middle of the night or make supper from a box of macaroni and a bottle of mustard? I could take them with me. I'm already doing all the work. No, someone would come after us for sure. Maybe when I'm eighteen I could sue Mom for custody. Spill my guts about all the crap. Or I could live nearby and visit every day, make sure they're okay. I could buy them a cell phone and teach them how to use it if they need me.

Thoughts swarm my head, possibilities heaped one on top of the other, cutting each other off. I close my eyes. Muddled. Tired. The room spins in a slow circle.

The lunch bell rings while I'm still mucking around, nothing accomplished. I don't feel like going to the meeting today. With Zara and her damn clipboard. Damien's props. Will's hopeful eyes. Do I have to? It all seems really pointless now. I end up hiding in the computer lab for the rest of the lunch hour, checking the doorway for a group of angry freaks in costumes.

In Spanish class Damien asks, "Hey, what happened to you today? We don't have a poem from you or Will. Zara almost had an aneurysm."

"There was something I had to do," I say. I know which poem I'll use.

* * *

When I open the apartment door, I can smell supper cooking. The living room is clean. There are a few coloring books on the table. Maisie and Evan run to them without even taking off their shoes.

"I saw these on sale today," Mom says to me, motioning toward the books. *Yes, coloring books. Those will fix everything.*

I drop my backpack on the floor and turn to leave for work. With this kind of routine, I can easily make it until the end of the year without saying a word to her.

"Early today!" Rupa says as I walk through the door. Arif, at the other till, watches me but doesn't say anything. Hasan's not in tonight, so I'm busy running around, stocking shelves and helping customers. There isn't even time for me to clean the bathrooms.

Five minutes before the end of my shift, Rupa waves me into the back room. I stand there, not wanting to come. She's going to sit me down and tell me that times are tough and they don't have any more hours for me. Or they have to slash my already pathetic wage. Or they don't want any funny business between their son and me.

She's smiling, though, so I follow her. Once I'm through the swinging door, she leads me over to a box filled with cereal and cans of soup.

"Arif and I noticed that you"—she pauses and looks away—"take good care of your brother and sister." She doesn't seem to know what to say next. I start to squirm. What do Maisie and Evan have to do with my job? "We wondered if you might like some extra food for your family?" She's actually blushing. "Better eat the cereal right away. It expires soon. I'm sorry for that."

I didn't see that coming. She nudges the box toward me and smiles. I look in it again—easily a week's worth of wages in food. I don't know how to thank her without sounding trite.

"Wow. Thanks" is the best I can do.

As I haul the food home, cans clanking, a warmth edges over the ache. There's even a box of Evan's favorite cereal.

*   *   *

"Shakespeare?" Zara says. "Really?"

I could have picked Justin Bieber. She should be happy. "Yes. That's what I choose." I stare her straight in the face.

"Sure." She shrugs.

Damien, across the circle, nods. He's wearing a seventies shirt with a butterfly collar. I humor him today and slip on an enormous pair of cowboy boots. They'd probably fit Will's big boats.

"And you?" Zara turns to Will now.

"Still don't know," he says. "I don't read a lot of poetry."

"Choose a song," Damien suggests, and all the others pipe up at the same time. Probably trying to keep Zara from keeling over dead. Amanda's bumblebee antennae wave above her head as she talks.

Will finds his way to my side again. I give up. Let him follow me around. He'll see what good comes of it. I find him a plate-sized belt buckle on a chewed leather belt and loop it around his skinny waist. Rescue the Stetson from a shelf. Don't look at Damien.

Today is our last meeting before setting up in the cafeteria. It's our last time in the prop room. Last time to wander through Wonderland and have this mad tea party. Today I don't want to think about anything else. I want to let myself sit close to somebody who wants to sit close to me. Because in thirty minutes it will all be over.

"Do you want to try these on?" I ask Will, pointing to my fancy boots.

He shakes his head. "No, they look good on you."

"Maybe I'll wear them to Words on the Wall."

"Let's move on," Zara says, giving us the evil eye. "The Art Club is coming to help us set up on Thursday afternoon during the third and fourth periods and after school."

Great. Two things that won't work for me. "I can't stay after school on Thursday," I say.

Zara sighs. Stuck with the worst class leader ever. "Why not?"

Too busy selling meth in the parking lot. Should I have to explain myself to her? "I babysit my brother and sister after school." *Babysit.* Such a normal word.

She rolls her eyes. Not good enough. "What about Thursday after lunch?"

"Yes, I'll be there." The thought of standing around with Ainsley flattens my buzz over finding Will's arm behind me. He leans back on his palms, long arms spread wide.

Zara runs through the list of supplies she assigned to Amanda and Nimra. Then she says, "We need someone to write the poems on the paper before it gets put up on the wall. The writing has to be big, so you can read it from far away."

She holds her hands wide to show "big," in case we didn't understand.

"I'll do it," I say. I am our class leader, after all. And I've seen Will's chicken scratch. I can do my job in a quiet corner and then disappear. "I have decent writing." If she asks to see a sample, I'm going to kick her in the teeth with these boots.

"Okay." She scribbles something on her clipboard. "That's the first thing on the agenda then. Get your poems to Isabelle right after lunch on Thursday. We'll all meet in the cafeteria."

She pulls out a sample inkpot, which is made from a spray-painted plastic vase. It looks pretty good, actually. She shows us a few quills, which she made by gluing bright plumes to ordinary pens and markers. As much as she's a pain in the butt, it's probably good we have someone in the group like this, who actually gets things done. I imagine asking Mom not to get drunk for a night so I could spray-paint vases, or dragging Maisie and Evan to fifty places on the bus to pick up craft supplies.

Zara wants to talk to Nimra about the Art Club and its plans. The minutes tick by. Yesterday's ache is gone, but there's a sinking in my chest as the minutes pass. I lean back until I feel Will's arm against me, my hair brushing him. I wait for him to shift away. He doesn't.

I don't want to say anything—just sit here and feel this, everything here in this circle. In a week, these people will get on with their lives. A few meetings in a closet will be nothing in their worlds of family, vacations, friends, parties. For me, though, it's been the best time of my life.

I sit, hardly breathing, until the bell rings out in the drama room. It's done. I give my boots to Damien and leave without looking back. *Goodbye, Will. Too bad we can only exist in Wonderland.*

FOURTEEN

I run into Clara in the library during lunch on Thursday.

"Here you are!" she says. "I just dropped in on a whim. You disappeared for a while."

Odd. In the last two weeks, I entirely forgot about Clara, my Jane Austen girl. I explain to her about Words on the Wall and the meetings.

"Oh, you're part of that?" she asks, surprised.

"Class leader." I can't help myself.

"Cool." She lingers another minute, tapping her fingers against the tabletop. Maybe this would be easier in the prop room, wearing overalls and a straw hat.

"I have to meet Emma now—my friend," Clara says. Yes, I know who Emma is: the one who almost wet her pants when I said hello.

"All right. See you later." I watch her go, knowing I won't see her later. Knowing that we never found two building blocks that fit together.

I wait for a minute after the bell goes to give the cafeteria time to clear out. I walk in to see Zara wiping down one of the long tables.

"We'll cut our paper on this one," she says. We stand together, hands on our hips, waiting for the rest of the group to show up. Damien's next, waving from the far door. Then Nimra, Amanda and Will all at the same time. Once we're all huddled up, Zara explains the process.

"The scroll will be made from five long sheets of paper attached together." She points to the fat roll of white paper on the table. "Our poems should be staggered throughout the scroll, so we'll put one on each sheet. One sheet will have two." Got it. "The Art Club will help shape the paper into the scroll, and they also made the banner for Get Your Poet On."

Nimra asks, "Are we putting our names with our poems?"

Amanda and Damien say yes at the same time Will, Nimra and I say no. We all look to Zara.

"This isn't about us being superstars," I say. As though posting large poems in public makes us superstars in any way. More honest would have been, *Let's not make ourselves targets more than we already are.*

Zara looks stunned—it's a question she hadn't thought of. "I don't think the organizers typically post their names," she says slowly. "Let's leave them off."

Zara and Nimra roll out the paper along the table, and Nimra uses a tape measure to figure out where to stop. Once they get the sheet cut to the right length, Zara waves me over.

"You're up," she says. Then, to the group, "Whose poem is first?" Funny, I thought it would be hers.

Damien lopes over. "Me, pick me!"

We discuss what kind of letters he would like, and I write with a dark-purple marker.

Purple haze, all in my brain,
Lately things just don't seem the same.

And into the next verse.

"At first I thought about"—he starts to sing—"*I'm goin' down to shoot my ol' lady, I caught her messin' 'round with another man*, but then I decided against it."

"Good call," I say.

On the next sheet, Zara's right next to me. I knew her poem would be close to the top of the scroll. "Here, this is mine." She hands me a piece of loose-leaf with an Emily Dickinson poem written on it. We pick a thick black marker, and she tells me she wants "elegant" writing. I do a few words in pencil first and get her go-ahead.

Nimra and Amanda agree to share the next sheet, so I put one poem at each end, leaving room in the middle for others to write.

What happens to a dream deferred?
Does it dry up
like a raisin in the sun?

No one's paying attention as I get the next sheet ready, so I write my own:

How all occasions do inform against me,
And spur my dull revenge! What is a man,
If his chief good and market of his time
Be but to sleep and feed? a beast, no more...
O, from this time forth,
My thoughts be bloody, or be nothing worth!

I know I probably should have chosen *To be or not to be...*, but I think that one's been beaten to death with a stick, resurrected and beaten again. Shakespeare definitely isn't my favorite, but something about the bloody thoughts resonates with me. Like Hamlet and I shared a moment.

Will lingers as I finish, watching me write in bold block letters. As I pull up another sheet, he shifts around, hands in his pockets. When it's smoothed into place, I turn to him. Last one.

He won't look me in the eye. Drops a folded paper on the table and mumbles, "It's a song by Tinderbox Stick Men. My mom listens to it all the time." He walks away, making himself busy with black vases with pens. Damien's there, right over my shoulder.

I unfold the frayed paper:

I see through the wall you've built:
cracked cinder block and mortar.
I stand waiting, waning,

at the end of your self-exile.
Take a step in my direction.

"Wow, he's more gone than I thought," Damien says. Of course he would be there. Of course. "I'm sure this was inspired by mommy." He cackles in my ear.

Face in flames. Static in my head. I can't even tell Damien to shut up. I read it again, trying to make sense of the words, the paper hot under my fingers. I go through the motions: pick a pen, pick a script, write it in pencil. I should really call Will over and ask him what he wants, but I have a feeling the earth would open up and swallow us both.

"Are you blushing?" Damien says.

"Would you shut up?" The more angry I get, the more he laughs. And he called *Zara* a yipping poodle?

I pick a dark red and make all the letters different sizes, like a ransom note. Zara wanders over. "Hey, that looks good. Last one?" They've been working on attaching all the sheets together, taping them at the back to make one giant rectangle that spills onto the cafeteria floor.

I hear Damien's voice, deliberately loud, a few tables away. "So, Will. What made you choose that song?" I can't hear Will's response. "So, no *particular* reason?" Damien draws out the word. I could kill him. Wrap my hands around his scrawny neck and choke him dead.

"Are you okay?" Zara says. She must have noticed my flushed face.

"Yes," I say too fast. "What else needs to be done?"

"Well"—she surveys the scene—"we're just waiting for the Art Club now. The paper's ready. Pens and vases are ready. Oh, here they are!"

Nimra walks over to greet them as they straggle into the cafeteria. In the middle, a blond head, thick shoulders. I can hear her voice from here.

I had steeled myself for this, but Will's poem knocked my legs out from under me. I feel like a kid getting off a roller coaster. A flutter of panic rises up. Too much. I can't do this right now. I snatch Zara's arm as she starts to walk toward them.

"I'm supposed to see Miss Yee as soon as I'm done here," I say. Clearly I'm a mixed-up teen who needs lots of counseling. "Do you think you could do without me now?"

She looks at me like I suggested we streak the cafeteria topless. "I guess so."

"See you at noon tomorrow," I call after her. That's when the principal will say a few words to officially open Words on the Wall.

I grab my jacket and bag without looking up. The last thing I need now is eye contact with Will. I'm just about to leave when I turn back. One more thing. I grab Will's poem off the table and stuff it in my back pocket. Flee, like redheaded Clara.

*   *   *

"I have a tuna casserole in the oven," Mom says, practically stepping on me as I walk in the door after school. Maisie and

Evan are loving this new mommy—always around, awake. Standing upright.

I nod. I'll give her that anyway. I should appreciate her efforts this week, but they just make me nervous. The higher the climb, the farther the fall, et cetera. Ignoring her has become a habit now. I'm not actually sure what she would have to do to make me speak.

Although the bottles disappear from the fridge and cupboard, she doesn't drink them in front of us. Ever. Maybe it's the lopsided dollhouse in the corner or the memory of my anger rolling across the floor to meet her.

After Mom leaves for work, I pull out a family tree for my Spanish class. I add Mom and then make up the rest of it. *Madre*—Marnie. *Padre*—Cliff. Well, that actually is my father's name, but he might as well be fictitious. I only have one picture of him, moving in the background, blurred. His slight hand on his hip. Dark hair. I'm my father's daughter. Mom doesn't say much about him, except that they weren't together long. I think she's too embarrassed to say it was just a hookup.

When I asked her once if he knew about me, she ducked her head and said, *Yes, he did. But we were so young, Isabelle.* Making excuses. I'm the same age as they were, and I'd want to know my own kid. *I don't know where he is now*, she'd added.

Whatever. I have enough on my plate without chasing down some deadbeat.

Abuelo. Abuela. The fiction continues. I only ever hear snatches about my grandparents—"Mom" and "Everett"—

usually said to a chorus of cursing and tipping bottles. When I was Maisie's age and figured out that other people have grandparents, I asked Mom where mine were. She said they lived far away, and she didn't see them anymore.

Why? I asked. *Why don't you see them?*

Ours wasn't a happy home, Isabelle, she said. I didn't ask again.

Tío. Richie. *Tía.* Better not put down Laina. Mom might see her name and go running for the nearest liquor store. As annoying as this Supermommy stuff is, I'll take it over her traditional swagger and stagger.

Claude. No way in hell I'm putting his name on anything. I add Maisie and Evan under Mom and Cliff and invent a pair of paternal grandparents. There.

I read a story with Maisie and Evan before bed. Maisie takes the book from my hands and reads the last pages herself. "*And the little star was happy with his new friends…*" I watch her eyes follow the words, her small, sure mouth. Evan climbs in my lap to see the pictures better, resting his head against my chin.

After they fall asleep, I pull down the suitcase from their room and tuck Will's song between the pages of my notebook. When I'm with Jacquie, and her ape friends close in with their sweaty hands, rubbing up against me—when my elbows come out—then I'll think of Will. *I stand waiting, waning, at the end of your self-exile. Take a step in my direction.*

And I'll know there's hope for the human race after all.

* * *

I settle in my camping cot to read for a bit, borrowing Mom's cheesy romance. One day, when I have a job and my own place, I'm going to buy a real bed. A cushy, soft one that doesn't make my hip go numb. And I'm going to sleep spread-eagled on it. Take up the whole thing.

A noise. I bolt upright. The book tumbles to the floor. "Mom," I say before I can stop myself. I must have fallen asleep—the light's still blazing. I lie down again, dizzy.

"Shh, it's just me," she says. Silly grin, slipping off her skirt and tights. She hums down the hall to the bathroom.

I knew it wouldn't last. Probably drinking with the bartender again. Just as well I didn't get too attached to this school. Her boss probably won't tolerate his employees getting hammered at work.

I must doze off again, because suddenly she's right over my face, breathing down. She doesn't smell like booze. Her hands tuck my blankets around me, quick and sure. I let her, something odd tickling at the back of my mind.

* * *

I wake to Evan beside me, shifting. Like he's not sure he should wake me but wants me to wake up anyway.

He beams as I crack open one eye. "I'm hungry."

I snatch the clock next to me. It says 8:43. Forgot to set the alarm. I guess that takes care of the issue of seeing

Will in English. Zara's probably having a fit right about now—the other class leader is MIA.

"Go, go, go." I shoo him out of the room ahead of me.

I take a quick shower. My hair's still dripping by the time we get to the day care, the wind whipping wet strands in my face.

I deliver Maisie to her school office. "Sorry we're late," I tell the admin assistant, who doesn't seem to hear me. "Just go to your classroom," I say to Maisie.

I've missed first period, and people are wandering in the halls on their way to their second-period classes. Not quite sure what to do with myself, I make my way to the cafeteria. That's where we'll all end up anyway.

A scroll stretches across the wall, about eight feet high and twelve feet wide. Instead of making the paper actually curl at the top and bottom, the Art Club drew and cut the edges to look like curling paper. I try to ignore the red letters leaping out across the bottom. They've put up a sign with *Get Your Poet On* in funky, lightning-bolt letters across the top. It looks great. I almost forget who made it.

While I'm standing there, gawking, there's a bump at my side, and tight fingers pinch my arm. "There you are," Zara says, cutting off my circulation. "Will said you weren't here today."

I blink at the mention of Will. "Just running late," I say.

"Are you ready for your speech?"

"Speech?"

"The two class leaders usually say a few words at the opening. I've made mine sound like a poem"—she sniffs—"fitting with the theme."

Run, Isabelle. Find a bathroom stall. Or go back home.
"No one mentioned a speech."

"They do it every year," Zara says. Like that means anything to me. "Help me bring some stools from the equipment room?"

After I help her haul out some stools and tables, I disappear into the bathroom, where I take a few deep breaths and finger-comb my hair. This *would* be the day I didn't have time for makeup. I find a tube of Chapstick in the bottom of my bag and put some on. Good enough.

I track down Zara a few minutes later, still hovering around the display, replacing tape and rearranging pens. "Why don't you sit down with me?" I say, pulling out two chairs at a nearby table. She wanders over, resigned.

We sit with our arms crossed, watching the scroll like it's about to come to life. She pulls out her speech, written on a recipe card, and starts to read it over. I close my eyes. The lunch bell rings. Deep breath.

I wave at Nimra and Amanda, who come and sit by us. Damien gives us a wave as he dodges past with friends. People to see, things to do. Mr. Drummond bustles in with a microphone and cable in hand. He hooks it up, taps to test it. When he's finished, he comes to stand by me and Zara.

"Ladies, you really outdid yourselves," he says. Zara beams. I think he might ask me about missing English, but he doesn't. "We'll just wait for Mr. Talmage now."

In the crowd forming around our scroll, I catch sight of a mop of dark hair. Wide glasses. A smile. Something in me calms. I smile back at him, for once.

Suddenly Mr. Talmage is testing the mic, getting started. "Ladies and gentlemen, I'd like to welcome you to an annual tradition here at Glenn Eastbeck." He signals for applause. "We've been in school together for just over a month now." Has it only been one month? "Words on the Wall is one of the ways we welcome each other to a new school year." He talks a bit about its origins, how it began with a group of students promoting freedom of speech and creativity. He goes over the rules—no profanity, no vulgarity, no hate speech, et cetera. No writing on top of or changing another student's work.

"I'd like to thank this year's committee," he says and runs through all of our names. "I'm going to turn this over to the class leaders now to say a few words." He holds the mic in our direction. Zara bolts out of her seat, lest her precious poem be missed.

"Creative spirit abounds in all," her voice booms through the cafeteria, "honoring that special call." I hear a cackle at the back that sounds a lot like Damien. "We will meet it where it stands, hold it in our youthful hands."

A murmur through the crowd as heads turn to each other. She continues, "When we write the words we feel, we will really know what's real." I feel like crawling under my chair on her behalf. Sniggers break out as she presses on, head high. A ripple through the crowd.

"So come, good friends. Come one and all. Write your words upon the wall." She pauses. Is that the end? "Thank you." Yes, that's the end. There's a scatter of confused applause.

She meets my eye as I rise to take her place, triumph on her face. It's possible that Zara is a species unto herself.

My heart bangs in my chest as I center myself in front of the scroll and look up. Will's steady eye. Pole Dancer's sneer. Deep breath. It's pin-drop quiet. They're probably waiting to see if I'm going to do an interpretive dance or something.

"Hi, everyone. I just want to say what a great experience it has been to be a part of this. I'd like to thank Mr. Drummond, Ms. Furbank and my other group members. A thank-you also to the Art Club for its work. Enjoy!" As I hand the mic back to Mr. Talmage, applause booms from every direction. It wasn't a great speech, but it was my first, and I didn't blow it.

The circle around us starts to dissolve as people make their way to the table for pens and then approach the scroll. Nimra and Amanda come over to hug Zara and me. I'm floating, giddy. I look up to see Will's face twisting through the crowd toward me. I start in his direction, ready to make some crack about forgetting the cowboy boots.

There's a tap on my shoulder. I turn. Celeste. I open my mouth but no sound comes out.

FIFTEEN

Celeste tugs on the sides of her jeans and looks past my head. "Can we talk for a second?" she says. She must think I'm a total idiot. I'd rather not volunteer for an ambush today, thanks. Reading my face, she adds, "Just you and me."

She follows my eyes to the center of the cafeteria, where I see Ainsley sitting with her crowd. Pole Dancer is leaning against the table behind her. They don't seem to notice us.

"We'll just stand right outside the door." She points to the main cafeteria doors.

"Okay." I follow her as she moves through the bodies. I have no idea what this is about. Out of the corner of my eye, I already see splashes of color across the scroll and the quiver of scribbling feathers.

Once we're outside the cafeteria, she pulls me away from the door and off to the side. We stand there, looking at each other. A thousand cutting comments rush to the tip of my tongue, but I'm too curious to say anything at all.

"I asked to talk to you"—she takes a deep breath and sighs—"to say sorry about…what's happened between…you and my friends." It's like the words have to climb out of her mouth by themselves. She doesn't talk that way in English class—she must really be bad at apologies.

"That's okay. Water under the bridge, right?" *That's it?* It seems like a good time for a clean start. I'm tired of worrying about those three. I turn to head back inside and she grabs my arm, pulling me back.

"Um, what I mean is"—she looks up at the ceiling—"we treated you badly. How…how do you feel about that?"

This is getting weird now. I look around for a spy camera from the Dr. Phil show. "Well, to be honest," I say, "I didn't think you were a big part of it." Relief on her face for an instant. "And I did punch your friend in the face." She chews on her lip and nods, her hoop earrings swaying.

"Yeah, I guess you did," she says, and we both break into a tight laugh. "You know, sometimes these things just snowball…" She goes on and on. My mind drifts back through the doors, where my friends are waiting and people are writing on a scroll I helped create. I don't want to miss it all. "…and people react irrationally. After all, Ainsley did say you apologized, right?"

While she talks, her eyes glance toward the cafeteria door, then back to my face. I'm starting to feel edgy, like someone might burst through those doors any second and drag me away. "…especially that one time at your locker.

That wasn't necessary. Three against one isn't even a fair fight…" Now I'm just getting bored.

I'm finally about to interrupt her when she stops herself mid-sentence and says, "I'm glad we talked. See you in English."

Hands down, the strangest conversation of my life. "Okay" is all I manage. She's at my shoulder as I reach the cafeteria door. I swing it open and hold it for her.

She opens her mouth to say something, then shakes her head. "Isabelle, I'm sorry." Afro bouncing, she turns and jogs down the hall. Disappears. And I thought she was the normal one.

Back inside the cafeteria, some of the crowd has dispersed, found tables and settled down. A clump still lingers around the scroll, packed close to it. I scan the room, looking for a familiar face. Off in the far corner, Will is standing with his hands stuffed in his pockets, his back to me. Nimra, Amanda and Zara are there too, laughing. Amanda waves to me. I wave back and start to make my way over, between tables and over feet. Will turns, meets my eye.

At that moment I hear my name from the other direction, by the scroll. More like a hiss or a whisper, so I'm not even sure I heard it. No, there it is again. I stop, turn. Heads turn in my direction, some bent low, eyes flickering. Others smirk, waving more friends over. I freeze. A steady trickle joins the group at the scroll. Some laughing. Others talking in an urgent stage whisper—the angry buzz of hornets.

I look back to where my friends stand, waiting. They read my expression and stop smiling, chins up like they smell something. Back at the scroll, the group grows and churns.

"Isabelle, I have a dollar!" some guy shouts. Whatever that means.

I turn and go back between tables, back over feet. One step at a time toward the scroll. A crowd blocks my way, some stepping aside as I get closer. Others step in front of me.

"No, you don't want to," one dark-haired girl tells me, blocking my path. "Come back later." I move around her, closer to the scroll. There's the blond guy from Social Studies, a grin splitting his stupid face. He steps aside, bowing, and points the way. I should turn back now. If he wants me to see it, I won't like it. But I can't stop now. I jostle shoulders, elbows out, to clear the rest of the way.

Will's red poem is in front of me, with scrawls to the left and right. Does this have something to do with Will? Did Damien say something?

I glance up, breath caught in my throat. There, beside my Shakespeare, *Isabelle* leaps out at me, written bigger and bolder than the words around it. A photograph is taped beside it. Once I see my name, my mind gathers all the words and forms them into sentences. In thick, black marker, for all the world to see:

My name's Isabelle,
I'll make your life hell.
My mom is a drunk,

I live in a dump.
I'll have a go
For a dollar or so,
If you can put up with the smell.

Beside it is the picture Ainsley took of Clara and me in the library. Someone has used a ballpoint pen to draw Clara as a pimp—goofy hat, cigar, bills in her hand. Me, bare boobs hanging over the table and stink lines coming up from beneath it. Speech bubble above my head: *I do it for free.*

Ice falls over me. I can't move. Can't speak. Can't even shift my eyes from the horror in front of me. *My Mom is a drunk, I live in a dump.* My agony for all these people to see, laugh at. I close my eyes, wishing for my heart to stop.

The crowd rolls behind me now. Voices feeding off voices and multiplying. Arms out—some pat, pull, hold. I shake them from me. Friend, enemy—I don't know the difference. That incessant buzzing in my ear. I hear myself yelling and push, wild to get away. The doors in my sight. I run.

In the hall, I scramble over books and outstretched legs. Trip over someone's bag, hear the cry behind me as I'm on my feet and off again. There's only one place, one safe place. My feet pound down the hall. Throat dry. Voices die behind me as I get closer—farther from everywhere else.

The door's unlocked. Through the dark and another door. I curl up in the corner, in the musty body-odor smell. Safe. I sob, head pressed to my knees, a searing pain in my chest. That didn't happen. Couldn't happen. I hold myself together by the strength of my own arms, my body in a tight ball to keep myself from falling to pieces, blowing away.

The door clicks as it opens and closes. From darkness to darkness. I hold my breath. Feet shuffle toward the center of the room, total blackness. Hands tug me upward. I know these hands, these feet I stumble over. I press my face into his T-shirt. Close my eyes and breathe in fabric softener. Cheek against his flat chest, I cry until my throat aches—hands holding me up. My arms, first limp at my sides, wrap around him now. His breath in and out under my fingers.

When I've cried myself out, he pulls me back to sit on the floor along the wall. I lean against his chest, my head under his chin. His long arm around me. I never want to move from here.

"I'm sorry," I say, tugging at the damp circle on his shirt where my face was for twenty minutes.

"Don't be silly," he says, which sounds strange coming from a guy.

"Where's a tissue when you need one?"

"You could probably use any shirt in here," he says, "and no one would know the difference." We laugh, jostling each other.

Then we are still again. I feel him twirling the ends of my hair between his fingers, his heartbeat against me.

"I can't go back," I say.

"You can."

"No, I really can't. You don't understand."

"What don't I understand?" he says.

Somehow the darkness makes the words easier. "My mother *is* a drunk." A lump rises up again. I swallow it down. "And I *do* live in a dump."

"I don't care about that stuff," he says.

"Well, I care," I say, pushing away from him. "Do you know what it's like having the whole school know that?"

"No."

"No. That's why I can't go back." He doesn't respond. I lean in again. Silence. "But I'm not a prostitute." *Better clear that one up.*

He laughs his deep laugh, and I worry someone outside will hear it. "Okay."

*   *   *

We sit through the bell at the end of lunch, not moving. Then the bell at the end of the first class. Then the second. Through two announcements over the intercom calling me to the office. The whole afternoon in the dark.

"How did you know I'd come here?" I ask him.

"Where else would you go?" he says. Like it's so obvious. "I don't know. I just knew."

When I want to forget, I ask him to talk. About anything. So he does. Star Wars, his mom's obsession with vampire books, being an only child, the probability of being struck by lightning, his dog.

In a lull, I say, "Will, you know I punched that girl, Ainsley, right?" I'm not sure why, but I need to know.

"Yeah, I know."

"And?"

"I figured you had your reasons."

That's it? If only Mom and Mr. Talmage would cut me that much slack.

When the last bell rings, I know my prop-room hiding with Will is over.

"Can you do something for me?" I feel his chin nod against my head. "Get my backpack and jacket from the cafeteria?"

When he brings them back, I'm standing just inside the prop-room door, waiting. I cringe away from the crack of light. He tries to shut the door behind us, but I swing it open.

"My sister's waiting now," I say.

He tugs on my arm and tries to pull me close again. Wants something more. But the door is open, the real world flooding in. Time to go.

"Thank you, Will." And I'm gone.

* * *

Maisie can't stop staring at my face. "Did you get hurt?" she asks. I nod. "Was it that girl again—the pokey one?"

I nod again. "I think so." Wish I'd had time to splash some water on my face.

I see her mouth opening, brow creased, about to ask how I don't know which girl hurt me.

"What did you do at school today?" I say.

That does it. "We got to play with the parachute in gym!" That'll keep her going for another ten minutes without me having to speak at all. I hear about every possible game one can play with a parachute.

When we get home, I tell Mom, "I feel sick. I'm going to lie down." Forgetting about my vow of silence.

She opens her mouth, prepared to act all motherly, but I wave her away. "Just stay with them," I say over my shoulder.

My camping cot never looked so good. I climb in and pull the covers over my head. I replay that moment in the cafeteria, a sick pit in my stomach. I'm never going back there again. I'll tell Mom I need to find a new school. Make up something—rampant drugs, a rat sighting, no running water. Something. She can't make me go back.

Will. The best and the worst all at once. To be humiliated so completely and then to sit there, so close to him. I'll probably never see him again.

I can't lift my head. Can't move from this bed. When Mom comes in to get dressed for work, I pretend to be asleep.

SIXTEEN

I lie low over the weekend, mostly on the sofa.

"Why don't you call Jacquie?" Mom says, searching my gray face. I shake my head.

I don't set the alarm on Sunday night. Mom gets up halfway through the day on Monday and finds Maisie cutting out a picture of a flower at the table. Evan is playing with the crooked dollhouse. Me, I'm watching daytime court shows.

"What's this?" she asks.

"I felt like throwing up." I pull a blanket up to my chin.

She mumbles something and disappears into the kitchen.

*   *   *

Tuesday morning, I take Evan to day care and Maisie to her school. I wait at the stop across the street to catch the bus back home, the wind churning up grit and tossing it in my eyes. I keep looking over my shoulder at the school doors, like Mr. Talmage might come bursting out and haul me back in. Or Will. Or anyone else in the school who knows my name and face, which is possibly everyone now. *My name's Isabelle, I'll make your life hell.*

Behind me the windows of the English classroom stare at me. If Will turns his head to the left, he'll see me standing here. What would he think? Or Celeste. Anger churns up at the thought of her, that sick charade. Better to take me in the hallway and knock me to the floor than to apologize, pretend to speak kind words. The most cruel thing of all. Now I know I underestimated them all, to think their payback would be insults and bruises.

And something else. It had hit me on Sunday afternoon, watching Chef Cathy make homemade pesto on TV. I'd been so busy feeling ruined about others learning the truth, I'd forgotten to ask myself how they knew it in the first place. How did Ainsley or Pole Dancer or one of their minions know that my mom is a drunk and I live in a dump? The question had been flitting around like a mosquito ever since. Who ratted me out?

I never told Will, Clara, Miss Yee, Mr. Talmage. Nobody. Jacquie's the only one who really knows my life. As I peek over my shoulder at my English classroom, I remember. Mr. Drummond. He's the only one. Who did he tell? In an instant, I hate him. Hate him for setting me up to come crashing down, for pretending to care. I can hardly breathe. I want to bang into his room, screaming. What have I got to lose?

Down the street, the bus rumbles toward me, a cloud of dust rising behind it. No, I'm going to walk away from this place and not look back. Will can find some other less-insane girl to like. His future children will thank me.

At home, I lock the apartment door behind me and jump. Mom's standing there, hair tangled. Pouches under her eyes.

"What's wrong?" I say, stepping close.

She studies my face and swallows. "Mr. Talmage called." He must have called about ten times in a row to get her out of bed this early. I know where this is going.

"I'm not going back!" I push past her, still wearing my shoes and coat.

"Isabelle—"

"No!"

I try to get away, but there's nowhere in this whole damn apartment that's my own. I march down the hall to our bedroom, kick off my shoes and climb into my cot with my coat on. Blanket over my head.

"Don't even try," I say. "You have no idea."

I hear the creak of her bedsprings beside me. She gives me a minute to sulk. "What happened?" she finally asks.

"Didn't he tell you?"

"He said some girls embarrassed you during a school event you were involved in. Why didn't you tell me you were doing that?"

She knows I was publicly humiliated and now she wants to know why I didn't tell her about my extracurricular activities? I'm glad Mr. Talmage didn't tell her more. How can I say that she was their weapon, that they attacked me with my own mother?

"They made up a stupid poem about me being a prostitute, and the whole school saw it." I choke on having to say the words out loud.

She peels back the blanket and rubs a tear off my cheek. Smooths my hair away from my face. I look up to see a glint in her eye, her jaw set. I don't often see her angry. Usually she's as soft as Play-doh.

"Mr. Talmage asked if you could come in tomorrow. Those girls received an in-school suspension for two days, and he wants them to apologize to you."

Not worth it. I'll get exactly the kind of apology I gave to Ainsley.

"Think about it," she adds.

"Okay," I say, to make her stop talking. Then I roll over and face the wall.

She doesn't move, lingering. "Isabelle," she says, "have you had boyfriends?"

Now she's wondering if I really *have* been whoring around the school. "Goodbye, Mother." Blanket back over the head. As if it wasn't enough with Jacquie always asking me.

*　　*　　*

The next morning, my arm stretches out to stop the angry beeping. Maisie or Evan is already moving next to me. I open one eye.

It's Mom, pulling on a pair of jeans.

I push myself up on my elbows. "What are you doing?"

"Going to the school with you," she says, doing up the jeans button and rummaging for a shirt.

"What?"

"I think you need some extra support through this, so I'm going with you."

The full meaning of this hits me all at once. Me, trotting up the front walk of the school with my mother—the very same mother from the poem. Sitting in Mr. Talmage's office with those three girls, my mother by my side. Not only do I need my hand held by mommy, but by my drunk mommy.

She pulls a sweater from the drawer and slips it over her head. "You need to get moving now."

"Mom, you don't have to go," I say. "I'm going to find a new school."

"No." She turns, jaw grinding again. "No, you're not."

"What are you talking about?" I sit up, wide awake.

"You are not going to let some bitches drive you away from your school." She wags her finger in my face.

She said *bitches*. Mom never swears, even if she's quoting someone. She'll say "the b-word" or "the s-word." Uncle Richie swears like a sailor after one beer, but Mom never does. I don't know what to say.

She looks like hell, dark circles under her eyes. Probably only had three hours of sleep.

"Why do I need to fight this fight? I don't even like that school."

"You fight the fight, Isabelle," she says, her voice rising, "because the very same thing may happen at your next school. And I don't want you running from these people."

I watch her pacing around in front of me. Is she drunk?

"That, my girl, is life," she goes on. "What do you think happens every day I go to work?"

To be honest, I never really think about what happens at Mom's work (besides getting pissed about her drinking with the bartender). I don't think about what people say to her, or if old perverts grab her butt and snot-nosed kids talk down to her. Maybe her boss is uptight.

She's not done yet. "We all have our"—she searches for the right word—"our stuff, but you can't just lie in bed and give up."

The devil on my shoulder whips up some choice words to throw at her now, but I'm too stunned to say them. And although I remember every time she's failed, she is still here every day. Not like Jacquie's mom. And I remind myself how hard she tried to quit drinking when she was pregnant with Maisie and Evan. I'll give her that.

"Now, get dressed," she says.

"Mom." I stand up. "I'll go. But let me go on my own." She narrows her eyes, like I'm trying to brush her off. "You can call Mr. Talmage to check if you want. I'll go."

"I'm dressed now. I'll come with you," she says.

"Mom, I think it's something I have to do by myself."

She considers this. "Okay, but let me know if you change your mind. You can call me."

"You'd better get some sleep," I tell her, but she comes out instead and helps pack lunches and get Maisie and Evan dressed. Evan asks to sit on her lap as he eats his cereal at the table. It's Christmas morning for them when she's around.

"Sorry about the swearing," she says as I step out the door. I try not to smile.

My return to school doesn't seem real as I drop off Evan at day care, Elaine's ugly mug at the front door. As the bus drags Maisie and me closer to school, I start to feel the nausea. And wish I hadn't eaten anything this morning. I take a deep breath and close my eyes, moving with the sway of the bus. Trying to keep it all down.

For once, though, I don't feel like one solitary person pushing on through. It's like Mom is standing beside me, not obliterated in some dark room.

I hug Maisie goodbye at the door of her school, her head at my belly. I wish I could bring her along and hide behind her hair when I needed to. Things couldn't be too bad if she were there, coloring butterflies.

As I walk down the front path of Glenn Eastbeck, a few heads turn my way, whispering. I think I hear my name. Head high. One foot in front of the other. I told her I would go. I carry Mom's words with me down the hall to Mr. Talmage's door and as I face those six wicked eyes. Her words make it all more bearable. Ainsley's shifty apology, the laughter in her eyes. Pole Dancer's mumbling, already plotting my death every time Mr. Talmage turns his head. Only Celeste seems upset. Her eyes are red, staring at the floor.

After all three say, "Sorry," Mr. Talmage says, "There's something else Celeste needs to tell you, Isabelle."

Celeste draws a deep breath, lip trembling. "I listened in on your conversation with Mr. Drummond," she says, "about your mother." My stomach drops to the floor. I remember then, the shuffle in the hall and Mr. Drummond getting up to close the door that day I fell apart in front of him.

"Then I told them"—she motions with her chin without making eye contact—"and they started making this plan."

"You did it too!" Pole Dancer says with a whine that could rival Evan's.

"I never wanted to!" she shouts at them. "I never wanted to be a part of this." She turns back to me. "I'm sorry for eavesdropping and spreading that around."

I have to ask now. "What about the rest of the poem?"

Apparently Celeste is the only one talking. She shrugs. "They just made it up." A lucky guess that I live in a dump. "Can I go now?" she says to Mr. Talmage. Looks like she's going to cry again.

"No." He pins her in place with a stare and hands me an envelope. "This is a letter from Seamus Holmes, who also played a part in this. Seamus is on the volleyball team. He'll have to sit out the next three games." I'd bet a million bucks that Seamus is that stupid blond from Social Studies. Hope he gets jock itch. I'll save his load of crap for later, when my stomach is better. Maybe never read it at all.

"I'll have you know"—Mr. Talmage looks at all of us now— "I take this very seriously, both the fighting and the bullying."

Celeste starts to cry into her hands. She probably has her university application already filled out. Mom and Dad certainly won't approve. "I encourage you to wipe the slate clean now and leave this nonsense behind you, or you won't remain at this school. Don't test me on that." He rubs his stubbly chin. Does the man ever shave?

We all nod back at him, except Celeste, who wipes her face on her sleeve. When he sends us back to class, Celeste bolts from her seat, the first through the door. Ainsley and Pole Dancer give each other looks like, *That was stupid.* I watch them disappear in the hallway before I move. Don't want some cozy scene with the three of us.

English has already started, and I don't have the heart to walk in late. All those eyes on me. I doubt Celeste went either. I go to the library instead. Ms. Hillary gives me a nod, a little softer than usual. I'm sure she knows. I have a feeling she's about to become my new best friend again.

I don't budge when the lunch bell rings. I wonder if it's possible to spend my entire high-school career in here. I have to go to the bathroom, but I'll wait until the dancing stage. I sign out another stack of books instead, to distract me.

The chair next to me slides back. Will.

"Mr. Drummond said you might be back today," he says. He fills me in on what happened. After the fiasco, Mr. Talmage asked students to come forward with information about the "incident" at Words on the Wall. People talked. "Janine and Seamus did the writing," Will says.

"Janine?" I ask.

"The tall one."

Right. Pole Dancer. I guess she has a name after all.

"But it didn't take long for her to rat out Ainsley. Celeste turned herself in. There's already a patch covering it on the scroll."

I don't think I want to see it.

Ms. Hillary's mouth starts to twitch, so I say, "Pull out a book."

After a minute, Will's hand slides over, entwining my fingers with his. Sparks fly up my arm. I move our hands under the table, motioning to Ms. Hillary at her desk. She doesn't tolerate any "hanky-panky."

We stay like that the whole lunch hour, as I read the same page over and over. He runs his thumb along my fingers, our hands resting on my knee. When the bell goes and he lets go, my palm feels cold.

When I walk into Biology, something's different. Eyes follow me. A head turns and whispers to the one behind. Too still. Too silent. It's a relief when Miss Dennhart gets started, pumped to show us a YouTube video of an experiment gone wrong.

"Isabelle!" Damien runs to me in Spanish, crushing me with a hug.

Daniela won't turn to face the front, won't leave me alone. "No one likes those girls," she tells me in a whisper the entire class hears. "I'm glad you came back." My face heats up.

She turns around every few minutes to give me bright, bucktoothed smiles.

No one's mean, but by the end of the day I feel like hiding in the prop room again. The eyes. The comments. The whispers. I know what I told Mom, but I don't want to live every day under a microscope. I'm starting to feel nostalgic for my old school, where I went for three months talking only to my lab partner and the librarian.

As I walk down the hall toward our apartment door, Maisie and Evan holding my hands, I start thinking of what I'll tell Mom. I can tell her everything that happened at the meeting except the part about her. She might want to read Seamus's letter or hear what Daniela said. As I swing the door open, I almost expect her to be standing there.

"Mom?" I call out. No sign of her.

Not in the kitchen. I hear a noise in the bathroom.

"Mom?" I tap on the door and listen.

"Come in!" She's in the bath, letting it all hang out.

I look at the toilet. "We're home now."

"Isabelle, will you get me another?" She waves the empty in my direction.

"No, Mom. I'm leaving for work now. You need to come out." I pull the plug and hand her a towel. Get her bathrobe. She leans against my shoulder on the way out to the living room.

"Maisie, you're just like a bunny rabbit in that pink shirt. Do you have a hug for Mom?"

She's gone, the mom I saw this morning. I close my eyes and take a picture of that memory. Tuck it away with Will's poem.

* * *

In English, Celeste doesn't look at me at all. She stares at her desk or talks to the girl in front of her until the bell rings. Never once turns toward the back half of the class. Fine by me. She started this whole mess by eavesdropping, but I believe she never wanted to do the poem thing. I guess if you actually have friends and some kind of status, you might fight to hold on to that. I'll never like her, but I've put away my plans to make a voodoo doll in her image.

Mr. Drummond catches me on the way out of class. "Isabelle," he says, "I trust yours was the Shakespeare. Good choice."

Right. My poem. "Yes, that was mine."

He cocks his head, sad smile. "I'm sorry about what happened."

I nod, looking down. Silently apologize for blaming him.

"Not only was it inappropriate," he says, "but it was a terrible poem. Really, really bad literature." I smile. "Don't let it get you down. There will always be some idiot."

As I walk out the door, he calls after me, "*From this time forth, my thoughts be bloody, or be nothing worth!*"

The rest of the week is more of the same. Looking over my shoulder as I walk, pretending I don't notice eyes on me. Random strangers telling me how wrong that was. Others hiding their mouths as they lean toward friends. I move around the school like a mouse, ducking into holes and shadows.

Still, there's Will, his feet against mine under our desks in English. His hand in mine in the library. I look for his face as soon as I pull open those school doors, and there he is.

On Friday he asks, "Can I see you outside of here? I have to go to my dad's on the weekends, but what about during the week?"

What, fugitive love in the library isn't enough? "I don't know," I say. "It's hard with me looking after my brother and sister."

"What about after school?"

"I pick up Maisie from school and Evan from day care."

"In the evening?"

"I'm with them when my mom goes to work."

"Does she get a night off?"

I'll give it to the boy—he is persistent.

"Sometimes, though she's not always in any shape to look after them." That's all I say about Mom. It's already too much. She's been pretty good lately, but it's hard to count on.

"You could bring them along," he suggests, and we start laughing. Ms. Hillary darts out from behind a shelf. Actually, there are worse things I can imagine than spending an evening with Will, Maisie and Evan.

"It's just hard," he says, looking down at the table. He's not used to darting for cover, hiding in a hole. For me, sneaky hand-holding in the library is living the good life. Again, fitting Will into my world seems impossible. Why do I tease myself? My usual high with him deflates, and I can't shake the feeling.

I run into Ainsley and Pole Dancer that same afternoon, moving from Biology to Spanish. They're never in that hallway, but *boom*. Face to face.

"Look, Janine," Ainsley says in a singsong voice, "*it's* still here."

Pole Dancer throws back her head and cackles, which probably cracks her three inches of foundation.

I pretend I haven't heard and step around them.

Ainsley calls after me, "Sorry for embarrassing you in front of the whole school with your little family secrets!"

"Sorry your mom is a drunk and dropped you on your head," Pole Dancer joins in.

"Or on your face!" Ainsley says, and they both snicker.

I will not give them the satisfaction of even missing a step.

*　　*　　*

It must be the day for awkward conversations, because Mom calls me into the bedroom as soon as I get home.

Bright face. Getting fixed up for work. She has me sit on the bed, which always makes me nervous. Is this about the boyfriends again? Is she going to give me "the sex talk"?

"Isabelle," she says, "I'm seeing someone new."

SEVENTEEN

"What?" is all I manage. Didn't see this coming.

"His name is Oliver." She says *Oliver* like it's something delicious. "I met him at work."

This is not good. Should I skip all the drama and just call Child and Family Services now?

"I know what you're thinking, but he's very different from"—she clears her throat—"Claude."

I stare in silence.

"You'll like him!" she says, cheery bright. Translation: *I want you to like him.* I hate it when people talk that way.

"I highly doubt that, Mother. Who is he?"

"Well, he has a job helping customers over the phone, and he takes care of his parents, who are getting older." Translation: *He works in a call center and lives with his parents.* Still, I'll take that over an alcoholic sociopath. "He comes to see me every night at the bar. Very sweet."

If all of this is true, the poor fool has no idea what he's getting himself into. "What about us?" I say. "Does he know you have kids?"

"Yes. He loves kids but hasn't had a chance to have any of his own—hasn't met the right girl yet." She gets a dreamy look when she says this and rummages for a pair of earrings. Of course he loves kids. And probably volunteers in soup kitchens and rescues orphaned puppies in his spare time.

"The best part is"—*wait, there's more?*—"he wants to stop by on Thanksgiving to meet you kids." *That's the best part?*

"I thought we couldn't afford a turkey this year." That's all I've got.

"Oh, it'll just be a little lunch. He's bringing some salads and cold cuts. I'm sure we could manage a pumpkin pie, right?" We purposely didn't make plans for Thanksgiving this year. Mom said it was because of money, and she's not wrong. I think it's more about Maisie's birthday fiasco, and letting things settle. We haven't heard from Uncle Richie since then.

I feel like saying, *Fine, then I'm bringing my boyfriend too.* Will would probably be thrilled to see me outside the library. But is he even my boyfriend? It would be a lot of weirdness all at once. I don't say anything.

*   *   *

On Monday the boyfriend stops by. *Oliver.* Exactly how I pictured him. A few years older than mom, a little doughy.

Hair thinning across the top. Wearing a striped button-up shirt. Wide smile, crooked teeth.

"You must be Isabelle," he says, shaking my hand.

He walks in and starts unloading a bag on the kitchen table. Mom walks by, and he catches her in his arms. "Hello, gorgeous." Gives her a kiss on the neck. I shudder.

"I brought corned beef. You like that, Isabelle? Potato salad, pasta salad. I bet those little ones like pasta salad," he goes on. I'm not sure what about *those little ones* gave him the impression they like pasta salad.

Maisie and Evan stand two feet away, completely silent, watching like it's a puppet show in the mall. I don't think Evan really remembers Claude, his dad. I know Maisie does, although she doesn't say much. Sometimes she asks me where he went, always afraid of him. Still, she's never seen another man touch her mother like this.

When he's done unpacking, Mom bustles off to get some plates. Oliver joins me on the sofa. "Your mom's so beautiful," he says, like he's paying me a compliment. I'm not sure why men tell me that. "The first time I saw her, I thought I was looking at an angel. Isn't that right, Marnie?"

"Oh, go on." She giggles. I definitely made a mistake not inviting Will. Or Jacquie. Someone I could escape with. Now I'm here, stuck in this middle-aged-love scene. At least we didn't cook a turkey. Those meals take hours.

As it turns out, Mom and Oliver possess the rare gift of stretching out sandwiches and potato salad to last for hours.

"Tell Isabelle about the time you tried to rent the car in Mexico," Mom says, patting his leg.

"So I was in Mexico—Puerta Vallarta, to be exact— and wanted to rent a car. Something nice, you know? And I wanted air-conditioning. You definitely need air-conditioning..." Here we go, another delightful tale from Oliver. Maisie and Evan have wandered off to their room very quietly. "...and he comes out with this Chevette. A Chevette! Have you ever driven one of those? Now I don't mean the ones built around 1979, 1980—those weren't too bad. Do you have a driver's license, Isabelle?" He rambles on without waiting for an answer.

Somebody kill me now. This is absolute torture. Then I remember Claude, squeezing Mom's wrist in his hand, and Oliver doesn't look so bad. Plus, she's only had one drink this whole afternoon—too busy hanging off his every word.

Oliver's visit is one fascinating story after another: the time he wrestled a policeman, got the chicken pox, threw up at his best friend's wedding, performed CPR on accident victims. I'm wondering if she gets any work done at all when he comes to see her.

He finally looks at his watch and jumps. "All this chatting has made me late," he says, like we were the ones keeping him here. "Mom needs her heart pills."

He gets out of his chair and stands close to me. I'm scared he's going to hug me, but he pats my shoulder instead. "You really are the special girl your mom talks about." He hollers down the hall, "Bye, kids!"

Mom walks him to the door, and I hear some loud smacking noises. I pretend to be somewhere else. Can't wait to tell Jacquie about this visit. I think it might be lost on Will—he's too nice.

Mom comes back all breathless. "You see what I mean?" she says. "Now there's a real gentleman."

When I don't say anything, she turns to me. "You didn't like him?"

"He's all right," I say. That's the best I can do. Mom once said about Claude, *A bird and a fish can fall in love, but where can they make their home?* Personally, I think they were both fish splashing around in the same dirty puddle. Two budgies fighting over one mirror. Now, her and Oliver—there's a bird and a fish. At least I have no illusions about my relationship actually functioning outside my head. "I just need to get used to you being with someone again," I add.

"Okay." She kisses the top of my head and goes to find Maisie and Evan.

*   *   *

On Tuesday I tell Will about my Thanksgiving. He gets a good laugh from my retelling of "Oliver Saves the Neighbor's Dog," in which Oliver claimed to have performed chest compressions on a golden retriever.

"I was at my mom's house this year," he says. "Nothing exciting. My aunt and uncle came over." Will's parents are divorced, but in a normal, shared-custody sort of way.

Not like my dad or Claude. Will lives with his mom and spends weekends with his dad. Has grandparents, uncles, aunts, cousins. A dog.

He points to a poster as we leave the library. It's for the Halloween Howler—the first dance of the year.

"Are you going to that?" he asks.

"I'm not sure." I don't know my life more than five minutes in advance. Why does he even ask?

"Maybe we can go together," he says.

"Maybe."

"And wear matching costumes," he says, "like Raggedy Ann and Andy."

I look up at him. "Shut up. Frankenstein and the Corpse Bride, more like."

We spend the next two days thinking up stupid couples costumes, somehow getting stuck on toiletries. *Shampoo and conditioner*, I scribble on a note to Will in English class.

"Dental floss and that gunk between your teeth," he suggests at lunchtime.

"Ew. You get to be the gunk."

"Leg hair and a razor," I say outside after school. It's sunny but crisp, trees half naked now. A few scrappy leaves still clinging on. Groups milling, cars honking for rides.

Will laughs and pulls me toward him, my chest against his. I stiffen, pushing back until we're side by side again. I look toward the girls sitting on the grass in front of us. He stops.

"You're embarrassed to be seen with me," he says.

Now they look up. I take his arm and drag him over to the hedge by the school.

"What are you talking about? Of course I'm not." The sweetness of the moment is gone. If anyone's embarrassed, it should be him—hooking up with the drunk-spawned, dump-living whore.

"You don't mind me touching you when we're in the library or the prop room, where no one else can see," he says, running his fingers through his hair. "Not anywhere else."

"It's not what you think." *Excellent cliché, Isabelle.* Next I'll be telling him, *It's not you—it's me.*

"You're embarrassed." A crease in his forehead. That crumpled look on his face. I did that. Sick sinking in my gut.

"It's just—" How can I possibly explain it, that I can never bring him home to Crazyland? That I'll have to pack up and leave any day now? Here, then gone. That life with me is not knowing what's going to happen from one day to the next, one moment to the next. It's changing wet beds and trying to feed mouths and running. How can Will—who explained to me the properties of cadmium—possibly fit into that world?

He waits for me to finish, his face a cloud.

"I don't think this is going to work," I say. Which says nothing. Which are stupid words that hold the lid on a big fat mess. I open my mouth to say more, to explain, but nothing comes.

He nods, staring at his feet now. His boat-size runners with the red stripes. Hands in the pockets of his slouchy jeans. "Okay, I get it." He turns and walks away, stooped.

I've lost him in two break-up clichés. There is a special hell reserved for people like me.

Don't move, Isabelle. Don't chase after that blue T-shirt weaving through the crowd. Because I've always known. I let it go too far, as if being with him in dark places didn't count. But here, in the light of the sun, in the eyes of everyone—then we'd be official. Then we'd be something. And to lose that something, that would hurt. Even more than this hurts now.

I hold my breath to push down the rising knot. Turn and walk down the path, across the street, through the doors. Walk on.

Maisie looks at my face. "Did that girl hurt you again?"

"No, let's go."

I turn away from her on the bus, my forehead against the tinted window.

*　　*　　*

Days lose their color, like oatmeal left on the counter overnight. Bland. Crusty. One congealed mass. School is a crowd of muffled voices at the end of a tunnel. Every eye on me pricks my skin.

In English class, Will always glances up as I sit down, says, "Hey." I'll give him that. Then he goes back to his book. It's the best and worst part of the day. When I swing my backpack to the floor, the second before I slide into my seat, I see the arch of hair that ends below his eye. Long fingers along the spine of the book. But I'm in my compartment, and he's in his. No gangly feet under my desk.

Why did I say anything? I had to. Then I'm angry at Will for pushing me, making that happen when things were fine the way they were. Stupid. Like I could ask him to go on forever in an ambiguous blob of a relationship. I should say something to him, but what? It all sounds like excuses. *It's not you, it's me.*

Mr. Drummond gives up on calling on either one of us— an exercise in painful silence. *Hamlet* finished, he reads Kate Chopin's "The Story of an Hour" aloud, moving between pensive whispers and a booming voice when the wife realizes her husband's death means her freedom.

He pauses to scan our faces. "*What could love, the unsolved mystery, count for in the face of this possession of self-assertion which she suddenly recognized as the strongest impulse of her being! 'Free! Body and soul free!' she kept whispering.*"

I think of Maisie and Evan—even Mom. What could love count for in the face of freedom? Apparently a lot. Or I wouldn't still be here, in this hellhole, playing mommy around the clock. Spending my paychecks on bread and coins for the laundry. Take that, Kate Chopin.

* * *

It's even worse since Mom started seeing Oliver. Better and worse. She's sober a lot more and actually goes to work. Giddy, tickling us, swatting bums. Making plans.

"Maybe we could get one of those dividers for the bedroom, Isabelle," she says, "so you have a little more privacy. I'm going to start putting aside some tip money." I hope that doesn't mean Oliver will be staying overnight. Instantly I banish the image. Not fast enough.

He takes her out on her nights off, which pisses me off. She might be more sober now, but she's never actually around anymore.

"Good thing I like you, kid," I tell Maisie, who smiles, touching her now-loose bottom tooth.

"What would happen if you didn't like Maisie?" Evan says, who asks a lot of "why" and "what if" questions lately.

"Then I'd leave her in the lobby for the guy in the bathrobe to look after." They both squeal, Evan clambering onto my lap.

Oliver usually wants to come up and say hello before they go out. I try not to roll my eyes. Sometimes I succeed. Mom catches me tonight and says, "Why that face? Oliver likes you." When that doesn't impress much, she adds, "Would you rather I was still with Claude?" I've got nothing to say to that.

"Isabelle, Isabelle!" Oliver bursts in like there's a matter of national security. "I was by the motor vehicles branch today and picked up this booklet for your learner's test."

Because we have a car?

"Oh, thanks," I say. Mom beams.

"Everything you need to know is in here." He flips through the pages. "Signs…right of way…" He's going to read me the whole pamphlet. "…pedestrians…"

"Great. I'll have a look." I try to take it from his hand.

"School zones…speed limits…"

I'm starting to wonder if life was better when Mom was passed out silently in another room.

"And a whole little index at the back. Hi, kids!" He takes a break to wave at Maisie and Evan, sitting on the sofa, staring. He turns back to the pamphlet.

"You guys better get going," I say. "You don't want to be late." For what, I have no idea. Mom shoots me a look when Oliver turns his back.

I call Jacquie when they leave. "He's killing me," I say. "They're killing me."

"At least he can't stay overnight there," she says. "You should've seen what crawled out of Dad's room last weekend. The type who'll steal your deodorant. Seriously."

She has a point.

"How's our apartment looking now?" she asks.

"Don't tempt me. I'm weak. Oliver just read me an entire booklet about driving."

We make plans for her to come over on Friday night and keep me company when Mom goes out with him again.

I start taking out my notebook at night. I don't even have to hide it from Mom; she's gone all the time. It's mostly poetry lately: *No butterfly sleeps inside this cocoon, only binding layers that suffocate.* I write until my eyes feel heavy enough to sleep.

*　*　*

Cold dread fills my stomach at the sound of the alarm. I linger with Maisie at her school and walk her to her classroom. Say hello to Mrs. Williams. Slip into English just before the bell. Will doesn't have a chance to say hello before Mr. Drummond starts. Did he even try? The worst will be that day when there's nothing—that little "hey" is barely keeping me from falling somewhere dark.

It's getting harder to put one foot in front of the other, to keep my chin up. I give up on chin up and settle for one foot in front of the other. With those little bursts gone— those pockets of warmth with Will—the hallways seem long, voices echoing. Rooms too big. My library, my refuge, feels like an empty house the day after a party. Only pizza crusts left, broken streamers, tipped bottles. I start going to the computer lab instead.

One day I see Nimra in the cafeteria, her back to me. She's sitting in a small circle of friends. What would they say if I sat there too? If Amanda, Damien or even Zara was with her, I'd go. I don't recognize any of the other faces. Can't bear that awkward pause, eyes darting, too polite to send me away.

"Whatever happened with you and that Will guy?" Damien asks in Spanish.

I pretend not to hear him—two feet away from me—and keep writing. *How much does the fruit cost? Cuesta veinte dólares.*

The next day, darting between classes, I see them. Will and Amanda. Two figures disappearing down the hall, his thin line next to her sturdy frame. He leans in to hear something she says and laughs. The good laugh. My chest shrivels. Mouth is sucked dry.

What right do I have to feel this way? I sent him away. They make a good couple, actually. Both a little weird and reclusive. And he could probably even hold her hand in the light of day. Go on a date. Visit her family without risking his life. If I really care about Will, I'll want him to be happy, right?

I spend all of Biology in a bathroom stall.

Walking to Spanish, a coin brushes my leg and hits a locker.

"Hey, Isabelle. I got a dollar," someone calls behind me. Chorus of laughter.

I'll have a go for a dollar or so.

"I don't mind the smell!" he shouts to my back.

Walk on. I'm already far away.

* * *

I have to pick the right time to tell Mom about John E. Hartwell High School, only ten minutes from Maisie's school. If I drop Maisie off and get the right bus connection, I might slip in on time. Maybe two minutes late. Still. Coming back should be the same. Maisie could wait in the office for a couple of minutes if she had to.

I'll tell Mom before she goes out with Oliver. She'll be excited, a bit distracted. No, dismissive maybe. After?

Maybe on Sunday afternoon, if I can keep that idiot away for more than an hour. I'll make her understand somehow. It isn't only about Ainsley and Pole Dancer, and strangers throwing coins at me. Maybe I should tell her about Will. Even worse— running from a boy. I don't know exactly what's dragging me down, just that my feet feel heavier every day. And someday soon they'll stop.

On Friday I walk into English, head down. As always, I find my desk, drop my bag, look for him.

But something's different. Before I even drop my bag, I hear his voice already talking. I snap my head up without thinking.

Turned in his desk, elbow resting on the top, legs taking up the aisle. He chats with Amanda, smiling. Like how he smiled when he teased me. *Raggedy Ann and Andy.*

In that split second between dropping my bag and sliding into my seat, nothing. Not a glance. Not a nod.

This is the day.

EIGHTEEN

"Have you seen my green dress?" Mom says. "The one with the little flowers?"

I trail after her, clipping her heels. "No, Mom."

"How many places could it be?" She digs through a drawer, tossing clothes over the side.

"Mom, do you remember me saying I wasn't happy at this school?"

"Oh, it has a stain," she says, pulling it from a basket of dirty clothes. "That ruins everything. What was that, Isabelle?" She drops the dress back in the basket and starts to rifle through hangers in the closet. "Too bad you're such a Skinny Minnie. I could borrow your stuff." Her voice sounds muffled through the clothes. All of my clothes are hand-me-downs from Jacquie, fairly decent.

She emerges with a black velvet skirt that strains as she zips it up. "Well, it'll do." Goes to find a blouse. I give up and look for Maisie and Evan.

They're in their bedroom, making a road on the floor out of Popsicle sticks and Hot Wheels. Barely look up as I walk in.

I wander out to the living room, toss some crayons back into their container. Check the sink for dirty dishes—none. Pick up and put down a newspaper Mom brought from the bus stop. *Jacquie, when are you coming?*

After a few minutes, Mom comes out, all ready. Makeup, little hoop earrings. She has found a purple sweater—which gives her great cleavage—to go with her skirt.

"Which shoes do you think?" she asks, slipping one foot into a black flat and another into a four-inch heel.

"I hope you guys are using protection," I say. "The last thing I need is another mouth to feed."

"Isabelle!" She's speechless.

I know I should apologize, but I stick out my chin instead and stare her down. Saved by the buzzer. Mom trots to the intercom and presses the button.

"It's me!" Oliver. "Can I come up and say hello?"

I'm in the shower, I mouth, pointing toward the bathroom.

She shakes her head at me, annoyed. "Isabelle's in the shower. I'll meet you downstairs."

"Would it be too much—" she starts to say as she gathers her jacket, but I walk to the bathroom and lock the door. If she tries to talk to me, I'll run the shower. I hear her say goodbye to Maisie and Evan before she leaves.

I know I do this with her—take these jabs. I should feel guilty. I don't. It isn't just that she's dating the most annoying man in the city, or that she subjects us all to his cleverness every night of the week. To be fair, he could be worse. But this hopeless Prince Charming dream. Has she thought past this week? Can she really see us all living with Oliver, eating pasta salad with his aging parents? Will he pick up the pieces when she loses her job or can't get out of bed to look after her own kids? I know exactly who'll pick up the pieces. I feel like running after her now, hurling more words at her back.

Buzzer again. Jacquie.

"I'm freezing my butt off," she says through the intercom.

Evan and Maisie come out when they hear her voice in the living room. "Monkey one," she says to Maisie, scooping her up in one arm. "Monkey two," to Evan in the other. "I think it's time for monkeys to go to bed."

They protest, but she promises them two stories each and no tooth-brushing. It's a better deal than they'd get from me. After they're settled in, pretending to sleep, Jacquie wanders into the kitchen and pulls a beer from Mom's case.

"She'll notice it's missing, you know," I say.

"So?"

Right. What's she going to do? Miss Knocked-Up-at-Sixteen-and-Drunk-for-the-Rest-of-It.

We stretch out on the floor, head to head. Jacquie tells me about her dad getting an eviction notice after not paying rent for two months, a new guy from her apartment building, a fight with her science teacher.

I tell her about Words on the Wall and the poem, skipping the part about Will. I cut straight to the lame apology, going to a new school, and Oliver and Mom.

Jacquie can't find enough swears for Ainsley, Celeste and Pole Dancer. "You should've let me beat them up when I offered," she says. "Wait, you actually call her Pole Dancer?"

"Well, not to her face."

Jacquie rolls on her back and laughs, her belly jumping.

"If you saw her makeup, you'd understand." My laugh fizzles out. "Bet they're all there tonight, at the dance." I've been trying to forget all week. *Frankenstein and the Corpse Bride*.

"Your school's having a dance?"

"Some Halloween thing."

She rolls over, gripping my wrist. "We should go."

"Did you hear anything I just said? Besides, I can't leave Maisie and Evan."

"Right." She rolls onto her back again, hands behind her head. "Too bad." Jacquie was banned from dances at her own school after instigating a brawl and holding some girl hostage in a bathroom stall.

We're making stove-top popcorn in the kitchen when something appears beside us. Jacquie yelps. It's Mom. Hair slipping down, cheeks drooping. Sad flower.

"Mom, what are you doing here?"

"Oliver's mom had a fall. He had to rush home," she says, her voice flat. How inconvenient of his mother. I hope her hip surgery doesn't interfere with their next date.

"Mind if I join you girls?" She reaches into the fridge and pulls out a beer. Jacquie sneaks another and gives Mom a wink.

"Actually, Aunt Marnie," she says, twisting off the cap, "Isabelle's school is having a dance tonight. Do you think she should go?"

Mom blinks. "You should've told me, Isabelle. Oliver and I could've stayed in."

"It's okay." I glare at Jacquie. "I didn't want to go."

"She's been a bit down lately, hasn't she?" Jacquie continues. "Maybe a night out is just the thing?"

"She has been down lately," Mom murmurs. They're both carrying on like I'm not standing right there. "Why don't you go, love? I'm sure Jacquie could come along, right? I'll just stay and read my book," she says, loading a few more beers in the crook of her arm and shuffling toward the bedroom.

Great. Now I get to hang out with Jacquie while Mom gets quietly hammered in the next room.

"Look." Jacquie pulls me close. "You said you're leaving anyway. Why don't we just go together and have a good time? Screw everyone else." I haven't danced with Jacquie since she came to my grade-nine graduation. The only family member who came. "We'll dress up, do our own thing, and people won't even recognize you." She's pushing hard now.

Maybe she's right. What do I care? In another week or two, I'll never see those people again.

"Fine. But you have to behave yourself," I say. "No locking anyone in the bathroom."

"She deserved it!" She laughs. "But yes, best behavior. Pinky promise."

"And no more of this." I take her bottle and put it by the sink. "They'll be checking at the door."

"Yes, sir."

While Mom's buried in her book, stretched out on the bed behind us, Jacquie and I rummage through the closet, looking for something to make into costumes. Jacquie slips a sequined tank top, one Mom wears to work sometimes, off a hanger.

Then she rifles through my clothes—her old clothes—throwing most of them in a pile. "Ah, I remember this one," she says, handing me a stretchy black top with a V neckline. I've never worn it. "Go try it on."

I take it to the bathroom, Jacquie a step behind me. I tug it over me and turn toward the mirror. White bra poking out of the V. It's tight.

"I don't know." I swivel to check from the side.

"It looks good! For once in your life, Isabelle—" She cuts herself off. "Do you have a push-up bra?"

I shake my head. "I do have a black bra though."

"Anything to help these little bee stings." She motions toward my chest.

"Shut up." I slap her hands away.

Jacquie talks me into my tightest black jeans—ones I already put in the give-away pile. Smoky eyes. I won't be able to make fun of Pole Dancer's makeup tonight. I cut out some black paper triangles and tape them to one of Maisie's headbands while Jacquie gets herself ready. She ends up in a sequined tank top, black leggings, fairy wings from Maisie's toy box and sparkly makeup. We stand side by side in front of the mirror.

"We're definitely the hottest cat and fairy," she says.

I feel like Maisie, clomping around the house in Mom's heels, makeup like a clown. But somehow, behind all this black and mascara, I get to be someone else for the night. This Isabelle would never run and hide in a hole. This one would do three backflips and land on her feet, machine gun poised. Karate chop to the throat and leave with the guy.

"Let's go!" I say. We sneak out before Mom can see me dressed like a feline hooker and Jacquie wearing Mom's good shirt.

We walk on the road. Holler at cars. Every seat around us empty on the bus as we fall against each other, laughing.

"This is it," I say, motioning to the bright windows against the night sky. Strange to see it like this, the vibration of music thumping across the lawn.

"Wait a sec," Jacquie says halfway up the school path. She looks around. "Wait here." She heads toward the cars along the curb. This better not be a dealer.

I stand there for a minute, squinting in her direction. Goose bumps through my thin sweater. Two shadows emerge on either side of her.

Jacquie and two guys. Two months at this school and I don't have a single friend. Less than ten seconds, Jacquie's got a guy on each arm.

"Surprise!" she says. "I got us dates."

I stare. They smile, eyes glassy. Probably clam-baking in the car.

"Can I talk to you for a second?" I take her arm and steer her onto the lawn. "Who are those guys?"

"Relax. Nick's the taller one—he's with me. I asked him to bring a friend for you. Jamie, I think. I texted them back at your place."

"What happened to *just you and me*?"

"I thought you'd be happy," she says, taking a step back. "He's pretty cute, actually. Not as tall as Nick, but you're a small fry. Give him a chance." She walks away. This is what I get for not telling her about Will.

I look back at them, giggling, hands shoved in their pockets. Technically, he's not ugly. Blond hair, baseball cap, athletic.

Then he opens his mouth. "I gotta take a piss," he says. Nick snorts. Jamie wanders over to some bushes—not far from where I stood with Will—and turns his back to us. I swivel around, checking for teachers. *Thanks a lot, Jacquie.*

While we're waiting, Nick and Jacquie start making out, tongues all over the place. I feel like catching the next bus home. *Catwoman, Isabelle. You're Catwoman tonight.*

Jamie strolls back and tells them, "Get a room." He looks me up and down now, making a face like he got stuck with the ugly sister. Like he's some prize.

"Let's go," I say, and we head for the door.

Mr. Talmage. Of course. He shifts as we approach: Isabelle the thug, some other girl who's falling out of her clothes, and two clowns tripping over each other.

"Hi there!" I start with an optimistic smile.

"Brought some guests?" he says, peering down.

"This is my cousin Jacquie"—I grab her arm and drag her next to me—"and her boyfriend." I point to Nick. Jamie sidles next to me, looping his arm through mine. "And this is my… boyfriend." I throw up a little in my mouth.

Mr. Talmage looks from face to face. Probably wondering if he should go against his better judgment. Chewing on a mint, he leans close to our faces. Everyone's standing upright.

"I don't want any trouble tonight," he says. "Is that clear?"

We nod dumbly. He takes our money and stamps our hands. I feel his eyes on our backs as we head in. I'd hoped he would say no and spare me this "date."

Dark gym. Pounding music. There are a few circles of girls jumping around together in the center of the gym. Shadows in dark corners. Always that one couple slow-dancing to a fast song. Flashing lights. A string of chaperones slump against the wall, their arms crossed. The DJ moves at a black-covered table on the stage.

It's hard to make out faces—it's dim and smoky. There must be a dry-ice machine somewhere. Jacquie was already dancing as we came through the door. She pulls Nick onto the dance floor, his hands on her swaying hips. Jamie and I shuffle behind. While I barely move, Jamie dances in his own world, putting on a show for an invisible audience.

I'm looking over heads, past heads, around heads. *Stop, Isabelle.* Checking for Ainsley and Pole Dancer, right? *Liar.* I spy a tall head bobbing in the corner but can't make out the face. The song finishes, and I'm still craning my neck, trying to catch a better look.

"What are you doing?" Jacquie shouts, pulling my arm.

On the edge of the dance floor, Nick leans over and whispers to Jamie, then Jacquie. She nods. They turn and disappear.

"They just went to do…something," she says in my ear. She takes a breath to explain. I wave my hand like, *I don't want to know.*

Now that they're gone, I drag her back out to the middle of the gym floor, bodies pressing all around us. Maybe they won't see us right away. A new song's already starting, pounding. We jump, sing to each other, arms in the air. Now I'm Catwoman, light in my black suit. For three and a half minutes I don't care about that tall head or Jamie pissing in the bushes or Ainsley or Pole Dancer. I sweat, heart pounding.

Between songs, Jacquie puffs, "Okay. Let's go find our boys."

We see them huddled by the wall, laughing. Jacquie takes Nick's hand, and we go back out on the dance floor again. Whatever that "something" was, Jamie's loving me now. Hands on my waist as I move, running his fingers down my arms. I try to back away from him and bump into a girl behind me. No escape. It's not even a slow song.

"What's your name again?" he says in my ear. Really knows how to make a girl feel special, this one.

While I'm evasive-dancing with Jamie, I turn my head to the left. My chest squeezes tight. There he is. Will as Waldo, in a red-striped T-shirt, red-and-white hat, blue jeans.

Who's he dancing with? Amanda. A sick wave washes through me. Has he seen me? As I turn away, I think his head flicks in my direction.

I understand now why Mom drinks when she thinks of Claude. The impulse to fight against that helpless sting, to wash it away with something, water it down. To be somewhere else, something else. If only I were stumbling drunk or had some of what Jamie had. Maybe I'd want Jamie smelling my hair or might not notice Will smiling down at Amanda.

I slow, almost stop. Jamie hasn't noticed. I lean in to tell him I have to use the bathroom when the song ends.

"Let's slow things down..." The DJ's voice over the mic. Panic. Jamie presses up against me before the music even starts. Over his shoulder, Jacquie gives me a thumbs-up. *Go, Will. Don't make me watch you swaying close with Amanda. Don't want you to witness Jamie and his many hands.* I close my eyes for a second and order Will away. Open.

His back's to me, Amanda's arms around his waist. Her pale fingers against his red-striped shirt. I can't stay here and watch this.

"I think I'll sit this one out," I say to Jamie, who doesn't hear me at all.

Eyes closed, he strokes my hair down my back and slides a hand onto my butt. I pull it up. We move in a slow circle. I smell his sweat, his body pressed against mine. Stretch to keep my face away from his. Over his shoulder, I see Jacquie and Nick practically having sex.

As we move back into sight of Will and Amanda, I look in his direction. Shouldn't have. For one horrid moment our eyes meet. He holds Amanda in his arms, her head on his chest. On cue, Jamie runs his hand down my body, tongue on my neck. Shell shock in our eyes. Something snaps.

"Get off!" I shout, pushing Jamie away. He stumbles back, dazed.

I don't wait to hear what he says. I force my way through the swaying shoulders, couples pressed together. I didn't volunteer for this—to be a warm body for some total moron. To watch Will hold someone else like he held me. Did he wait a whole week before moving on? Why did I ever feel guilty about rejecting him? Obviously it meant nothing. I should go back and make out with Jamie. *See how that feels, Will.* Knowing I can't.

My old friend, the bathroom stall.

A minute later Jacquie bangs on the door. "Open up, Isabelle!"

I turn the lock, and the door falls open. Then I perch on the edge of the toilet seat again.

"What's wrong with you?" Her eyes are on fire.

"I don't like that guy," I say.

"You don't like any guy." She leans in close, says in almost a whisper, "Are you a lesbian?"

Jacquie drags in some total stranger off the street and wonders why I don't want to get it on? Obviously I'm a lesbian.

"No, and stop trying to set me up."

Her chest swells, and she opens her mouth to come down on me like an anvil in Bugs Bunny. I hear voices behind her, on the other side of the door. I raise my finger to her lips, pull her all the way into the stall, shut the door and turn the lock. She looks at me like I'm officially insane.

I motion toward the girls talking on the other side and mouth, *That's them*. Her eyes light up, and I lower my hand. She twists back the lock and peeks out.

"I told her not to..." Snatches of conversation. Pole Dancer.

"...supposed to get a ride with her," Ainsley says.

Jacquie watches them at the sink counter. I can only see the back of her head.

Low giggling—the cackle of witches. A tap runs. Then paper towels are pulled from the dispenser.

"Fix my tail," Ainsley says.

They stay for another minute, fiddling with costumes. I pull Jacquie behind me and peek out. Ainsley is squeezed into a gray unitard with a tail pinned to the back, and she has mouse ears. Pole Dancer is some kind of '80s rocker. More makeup than usual and a skirt that's more like a belt.

They wander out, their voices disappearing as the bathroom door swings shut. Jacquie pulls open the stall and pushes past me. Halfway to the door, she turns. Cheeks flushed.

"I'm going to catch me a mouse tonight," she says.

NINETEEN

"Jacquie!" I stumble after her, the door already swinging shut between us.

I've lost her in the crowd of people, my eyes straining in the dark again. Scanning. There. I see her wings pop up through the bodies. She moves low and fast, barely making a ripple.

I trip over feet, bump shoulders. Push. This can't happen. Even if I pretend not to know her, Mr. Talmage saw who she came with. Ainsley and Jacquie together—this is bad. Through the pulsing light show, I almost lose her again. She moves toward the middle of the gym—the thickest crush of bodies.

I can't hear the music over the pounding in my ears. A flash of Ainsley's blond head. Jacquie closing in.

"Hey!" a girl squeals as I cut between her and her partner.

"Jacquie!" I scream after her, my voice swallowed by the noise.

Almost there. I reach out to grab her wrist. As my fingers close around her, Jacquie's other arm darts out—the flick of a snake's tongue—and rips off Ainsley's tail. The fabric tears, a pink patch of skin showing through.

Ainsley's jaw drops as she twists her head. There's Jacquie, savage eyes, dangling a tail in Ainsley's face. Me hanging on her other arm. Pole Dancer opens her mouth and raises a finger to point at the tear. We run. Jacquie drags me, her swift legs dodging bodies. Back, back toward the far door.

We hit the double doors at the same time, one on each side. *Bang.* Once we're through, Jacquie turns toward the hallway to the library.

"No, this way!" I swing her in the opposite direction. There's a back door at the far end of the school, the one I used once to get Maisie. We dodge a twisting line at the concession.

"Slow down, you girls!" someone hollers from the counter as we tear by.

The beat of footsteps behind us. I clutch Jacquie's shirt and pull her through another set of doors, into the dark hall. An eerie glow shines from the Exit sign. Every doorway's a black gap.

"Is one of these open?" Jacquie pants, pointing to the classrooms.

"This way!" I charge ahead. "There's an exit down this hall!"

She laughs as she runs, hair streaming behind her. White teeth in the dark. The hall doors open and close behind us, followed by pounding footsteps.

Ainsley shouts after us, cursing, her voice raw.

Jacquie cackles and waves the mouse tail in the air, her legs pumping faster.

We hit the exit doors at the same time. *Bang.* Locked. I dart over and try the third one. Shut tight. Ainsley laughs, her voice moving closer. Plan B. We turn and dash for the stairs behind us, the only escape from the two shadows closing in.

Up the stairs, two or three at a time. On the landing and up the next flight. I don't know yet how we'll get out. We just need to get away. Or something bad will happen. Feet on the stairs below us. Into another dark hall, the moonlight from the staircase windows mapping a path. Ahead, a set of double doors. Okay, from there we can loop back down through the cafeteria and out the main doors. *Mr. Talmage, please be gone.* A sharp pain spreads in my chest. My feet barely touch the floor as I head for those squares of light.

We slam the handles at the same time and bounce back. Locked. We try again, fumbling for the locks. Can't see. Rattling the door. Jacquie turns first. Flight done, ready for fight.

I turn, my heart splitting my throat. Two shadows closing in. Jacquie springs, not waiting to be cornered. With a guttural scream, she lunges at Ainsley, shoving her back into a locker. Her body slams the metal.

"Why don't you pick on someone your own size?" Jacquie growls, already pulling up Ainsley's shoulders to fling her again.

Pole Dancer shrinks back away from the beast. Ainsley picks herself up and tackles Jacquie's belly, both of them falling to the floor. Tries to punch her face. Jacquie dodges fists, grabbing a wrist in each hand. She twists Ainsley onto her back, pinning her.

"Who's tough now?" Jacquie breathes in her face.

I have a feeling the floor's about to give way under my feet. She'll kill her. Jacquie moves like a whip of fury. Ainsley's roped like an animal.

"Jacquie, stop! Enough now!" I shout. She grips Ainsley's wrists in one hand and squeezes her cheeks in the other, puckering Ainsley's lips.

"Say sorry to Isabelle for what you did," Jacquie says.

Ainsley makes a kind of choking sound, like a sob.

"Apologize to her, or I'll wrap your little mousey tail around your neck." She pushes her face closer to Ainsley's, knees crushing her chest.

"Jacquie!" I want to pull her off now, but I'm afraid to touch her.

"What's going on?" Another voice from the dark. We jump, Jacquie dropping Ainsley's head to the floor. She gasps for breath.

Will. There's a split second of shifting. Eyes back and forth on each other. Reassessing. Jacquie poised to spring again.

"I'm going to get Mr. Talmage," he says, his voice quiet through the roar of adrenaline. A snort from Pole Dancer. *Way to be the tough guy, Will.*

Ainsley shoves Jacquie off her and rubs the finger marks on her cheeks. She wipes away tears with her sleeve.

"Who the hell are you?" Jacquie spits at him, on her feet again. Ready to take him on.

I step in front of him. "This is Will," I say. "He's…" He's what—a friend, an almost ex-boyfriend? Someone who used to hold my hand? "He's with me." Whatever that means.

Now that nobody's getting killed, Pole Dancer finds her voice. "Well, if it isn't Beauty and the Beast." I wonder who's Beauty and who's the Beast.

"Shut your mouth," Jacquie says, stepping toward her. Pole Dancer stumbles back into a locker. To me, Jacquie says, "This must be the one you call Pole Dancer." Laughs.

Thanks, Jacquie. As if there wasn't already a bounty on my head at this school.

Ainsley pulls herself off the floor and shoots a look of pure hatred at Jacquie. Then she turns to me. "You won't always have your bodyguard here to fight your battles. You know what's coming, princess."

"Leave her alone." Will's voice erupts behind me, hard. Startles me. I've never heard him angry before. Jacquie shifts toward Ainsley, ready to pounce again.

"Why are we still fighting?" I say to Ainsley. "Can't you see you've already won?" Jacquie and Ainsley turn to me, wary. "That poem—it doesn't get any worse than that. The battle's over."

Ainsley stares at me like I've started speaking Cantonese. "Let's go, Janine." They move slowly, Ainsley holding Jacquie in place with one eye.

As they turn away, Jacquie's voice follows them in the dark. "If you ever go near my girl Isabelle, she's going to tell everyone how you got your butts kicked tonight. And there was a witness." She pauses to let the words sink in. "And I already broke into the school office. I know where you both live." Her words echo down the hall. Footsteps quicken.

She holds her tough-girl pose until we hear the footsteps pattering on the stairs. "Ha!" She turns to me. "Problem solved."

Everything in the last fifteen minutes rushes at me, sucking my breath away. I turn to her. "Are you insane?"

"What?"

"I thought you were going to kill her!"

"*I* thought I was going to kill her," Jacquie says, laughing.

"Why'd you go after her in the first place?" My voice climbs. Will disappears into the shadows near the stairs.

"Trying to save you!" she shouts back.

"I didn't ask you to save me!" Right in her face.

"You don't ask for a lot of things you need."

"Like bringing Tweedledee and Tweedledum with you tonight, with their combined IQ of fifty?"

"What, compared to your wussy boyfriend? Who here saved your sorry butt tonight?" she roars.

"Leave him out of this!"

Red faces, arms waving. Jacquie and I have never fought like this. The anger of the whole night rushes from my mouth. I take a step away, trying to disengage from the torrent between us.

She swallows, voice low. "Look, Isabelle. I've only ever tried to help you. You have a sad life, watching it all go by from the sidelines."

Every word stings, truth and hurt mixed into one. She has always tried to help me—like running in the night with Evan on one hip. She's the only person who understands my life. At the same time, there are all those moments when she becomes someone else I look after. Trying to hide her from the flashing lights and sirens that come when she smashes bottles on cars. Dragging her home from parties in the middle of the night when she's too drunk to stand. Stopping her from shoplifting or beating someone to death.

A sad life. The words sink in, cutting a bloody groove. All true. But even in an ideal world, maybe the life I'd choose would never measure up. Hers would be full of police chases and explosions, kinky sex in moving vehicles—like some James Bond movie. Mine would be more like an episode of *Barney*, baking cookies and picking flowers in the garden.

"I don't think it'll work, us moving in together." The words fall from my lips before I can stop them. Before I really know what they mean.

She stands still in the dark. I can't read her expression. Then she throws her hands up like, *I surrender.* "You know what?" She backs away from me. "From now on, you can live your own pathetic life. Keep me out of it."

"Jacquie—"

"And fight your own battles." She turns, walking toward the stairs. "See how that goes for you."

"Jacquie, wait!" I call to her. I can't bring myself to chase her, stand in her path.

"Because I'm done!" Her silhouette moves past the windows, then onto the stairs. Footsteps descend, and then she's gone.

And there's just me. In the dark. Every part of me trembling. I lean against a locker and slide down, the metal cold against my back. I put my head on my knees and try to breathe. What just happened?

A noise. I look up but don't see anything. Probably Ainsley and Pole Dancer coming back to find me alone. I don't even care anymore. Let them beat me up. Then Mom will let me change schools. I put my head back down and wait for them.

Footsteps come toward me. I have no more run in me. Can't move at all.

Something nudges my feet. I lift my head. Size 12 runners with red stripes.

"You do have a knack for finding me in dark places, Will."

He crouches and lowers himself next to me, his back against the next locker. Touches my hand for a second. "You're shaking," he says, pulling his hand away again. Me in my compartment, he in his.

I lift my head and lean it back against the locker. Glance over at him. He looks how I feel tonight—heart ripped from my chest and pounded back in with a meat mallet.

"You heard all that?" I say.

He nods. There's something different about Will tonight—a little unbalanced, dark around the eyes. Unfair of me to think of him as an unending sea of calm.

"Do you want to come downstairs?" he asks.

I shake my head. "Can't move." We sit in silence, a little warmer now that he's here. "Will, I'm sorry." I close my eyes to make the words easier. "I have to explain, about what I said."

Now he pulls his knees up and rests his head on his arms. Face away from me.

"I did like you." Take a breath to keep going. "I still like you. It—" I swallow. "It hurts to see you with Amanda." The words limp out. He doesn't say anything. "I have a complicated life. Maybe you'll believe that now. I didn't know how to fit you in. Was afraid, I guess."

"You didn't even give me a chance," he says.

"I know. Sorry." I try to see his expression in the dark. "I don't want you to think it was you, or that I was embarrassed."

"Well, that explains the mixed signals."

"Yup."

He leans his head back against the locker, staring into the fuzzy gray. We sit for a minute, my words floating between us. Neither of us sure what to do with them.

"Anyway, you don't have to worry about rescuing me in dark places anymore," I say. His head rolls toward me. "I'm transferring to John E. Hartwell in a week, as soon as I can convince my mom. Then you can get on with things." Amanda's head on his chest.

"Why?"

Stupid question. "Because." I feel like leaving it there. "Because everything about this school hurts." *Including you.*

He doesn't respond. I try not to look at him. Tapping his thumbs together, he says, "You know, Amanda and I aren't together. Not like that."

"Didn't look that way to me."

"We're just friends."

"Uh-huh."

"I've talked to her about you and me," he says.

"What?" Elation and fury all at once. There was a "you and me" to talk about, and he talked about it with someone else. What did he tell her?

"She noticed things were weird and asked what was going on. We started talking more."

"Why didn't she come to me?" I drop my legs and sit up.

"You can be a little intimidating, Isabelle," he says.

I hate that he's right. Hate their cozy little friendship. Hate him for holding her while looking at me.

"Well, I'm sure you'll be very happy." I spring to my feet, a new energy pulsing through me. I wish I'd punched somebody when I had the chance.

"Wait." He scrambles up, grabbing my arm as I turn to go. "There's more." I don't want to hear any more. I snatch my wrist from his hand. "I found you on the dance floor because I was curious about who you were with," he says, "and maybe wanted to make you a little jealous." He looks at the floor.

"Why are you telling me this?" Didn't I just say it hurt seeing him with Amanda?

"Let me finish, please."

I'll give him another ten seconds before I call back Jacquie to whale on him too.

"But it backfired," he says, "because then I saw what happened with *him*." He swallows hard, like he's about to throw up. "I hated seeing him touch you like that." He closes his eyes and shakes the picture from his head. "I guess I deserved that. Sorry."

So Amanda was his "warm body." I hurt you, you hurt me. I never thought that would be Will and me. He looks back at the floor again, hands jammed in his pockets. Reaches up and pulls off the goofy hat.

"If it makes you feel any better, *I* hated him touching me like that," I say. Dry laugh from Will. "I left."

He nods. "I saw."

We stand there looking at each other. Him, hair flat from the hat. Me, vampy Catwoman costume, makeup running.

"You'd better go," I say. "Amanda's probably waiting." *Insert knife. Twist.* He looks like I just kicked him where it counts. Guilt nips at me. What if that's the last thing I say to him?

"Goodbye, Will." I reach up to give him a hug—the backslapping sort that men give each other. He doesn't move, stiff. Doesn't matter. I give him a quick squeeze on the shoulders and let go.

As I move away, he wakes up. His hands come out of his pockets, and his arms wrap around me, pulling me close.

My cheek presses against his cotton shirt. I feel his breath on me, his heartbeat at my ear. I wait for him to drop his arms, let go. He doesn't move. I close my eyes, warmth trickling through me.

Not fair at all, Will. I raise my fingers to his chest. So tired of fighting this. Tired of being practical, giving up things I want because of everybody else. Tired. Can't I have something—somebody—I want? I don't want to know the ending anymore.

I reach up, hand behind his neck, and pull his mouth down to mine. Soft. All thoughts leave. Then I stand close to him, fingers entwined, until I start to remember where we are again.

"It's getting late," I say. "We'd better go back."

As I turn, he tugs at my arm and pulls me close again. This time I stay.

* * *

Later that night, I stand over Mom. Her mouth hangs open, a nasal squeak every time she exhales. Tipped bottles beside the bed. Still in her dress. I pull up the blanket and take back a few of the words I threw at her earlier.

TWENTY

I wake up slowly, a memory nudging me awake. Kissing Will in the dark hallway. That was real. I lie in bed, smiling, until Maisie and Evan stumble in, arguing over the last clean spoon.

"Shh, Mom's asleep." I wave them out. Like they could possibly wake her.

In the kitchen, I pull out the eggs I bought with my last paycheck and start to make French toast. Evan stabs the yolks with a fork.

We eat on the sofa, watching cartoons, Evan dribbling syrup on the cushions.

I float, my head only half with them. Then I deflate at the memory of Ainsley pinned to the floor, her choking sob. And Jacquie and me screaming at each other. I'm not even sure I meant what I said. I have to call her today and set things straight. Right or wrong, I can't leave it like this.

I'm getting out of the shower when Mom pokes her head in, the phone pressed to her chest. "Richie wants to know where Jacquie is," she says. Smeary clown face, tangled hair.

"I don't know." I wrap the towel around me and turn from her. "Isn't she at home?"

"No." Her face pinches together. "He thought she was here. She didn't come home last night and isn't answering her cell."

I almost drop the towel. An avalanche of guilt cascades over me.

Mom pulls her head out and shuts the door, her voice muffled. I follow her, clutching the towel around me, water dripping in my eyes. She places the phone back in the cradle.

"What did he say?" I ask.

"He's going to call her friends. It's not the first time she's done this."

No, but it's the first time I feel responsible. I stand there, waiting for her to say more. She's about to brush by me when she stops, looks at my face.

"What is it? What do you know?"

"I don't know anything. It's just"—I chew on my lip—"we got into an argument last night, and she left the school. I don't know where she went."

"An argument? About what?"

Does it matter? "She picked a fight with this girl, and I got mad at her for it." I leave out the part about the idiot she set me up with, her death threat to Ainsley, my words.

"Well," she says, "let's see if she turns up at a friend's house."

I have a hollow feeling for the rest of the day, knowing she won't. Every time I start to think about Will, an image of Jacquie takes over—hitchhiking, trapped, bloated in a ditch. I can't eat anything.

Sunday—Halloween—still nothing.

I take Maisie and Evan to the park, trying to distract myself. Watch them duck under trees and follow each other up the climber. When we get back, Mom meets me at the door and pulls me into our bedroom. I feel dread in every limb.

"Jacquie called her dad from a pay phone," she begins.

Jacquie called. Alive. So relieved I can't respond.

"She said she's not coming back—wants to live on her own. She won't tell him where she is." She pauses, leaning toward me, her eyes drilling. "If you have anything else to tell me, Isabelle, now's the time."

I'm trapped by her stare. I guess now *is* the time, with Jacquie gone AWOL.

"Jacquie and I planned on moving out together... eventually," I say. Mom shifts away, her face blank. "When we argued, I told her I didn't think it was a good idea. She got mad and left." That's about as much as I'm willing to share.

Mom looks down for a second, scratching the back of her neck. "When were you going to tell me this, about your plan?"

I shrug. "I didn't think it was an issue right now." *Seeing as we're so happy at home and all.*

"Okay." She drops her hands in her lap. "I think I understand better now. I'll have to tell Richie."

I nod. "And something else." This is going to be painful. "Jacquie brought two guys with her—Nick and Jamie. I don't know if she left with them or not, but they might know something."

"How can you not know if she left with them?"

"They weren't with us when we had the argument." *Lost them when I was hiding in a bathroom stall. Then stalking and beating up Ainsley.* "I didn't see if she found them before she left." *Too busy kissing Will in a dark hallway.*

"Well, who are they? How do we reach them?" she asks.

"No idea, Mom. They weren't friends of mine." She watches me get up, take clothes from a laundry basket and fold them into the dresser. I see about twenty more questions on her lips about Nick and Jamie. Her eyes follow me around the bedroom.

"Isabelle, do you know where she is?"

"No."

She watches me another minute, then says, "Richie called the police, but they don't have much to go on. They'd need her location or something. Can you tell me if she contacts you at all?"

"Yes."

"Promise?"

"Yes, Mom! I said yes." It's not fair to be annoyed with her actually acting like a parent for once. Not fair when it's Jacquie I'm angry with. Taking off without a word, like she's trying to punish me. Doesn't she know people say stupid things when they're angry? Didn't I have the right to be?

*　　*　　*

I take Maisie and Evan out trick-or-treating that night, reviving their old clown and pirate costumes from last year. Maisie's clown pants rest two inches above her ankles.

"I want to be a princess next year," she says, staring at her crumpled mask in the mirror.

We make it an hour before Evan complains about being cold and drags his striped pillowcase on the sidewalk. I take them by the store on the way back, and Rupa gives them each a big chocolate bar. I can't stop thinking about Jacquie, wondering if she's cold in her sequined tank top and fairy wings.

*　　*　　*

I'm happy to see Monday for once, a welcome distraction from the anger-guilt-worry cycle that I've been spinning around Jacquie. The school looks less like the prison camp it was before Friday, the brick less dull. The lights seem a little brighter.

I march straight to my locker first thing. No more hiding. No more dragging around this fifty-pound backpack. I peel off the old princess sticker, a relic of Ainsley. It leaves a gummy residue. Try to remember my lock combination.

In English, Will's enormous feet are under my desk again. The world is as it should be. Amanda looks over and gives us a smile. It's hard to say what's in her head, whether she also thought they were "just friends." I still want to be mad but can't. What if she feels what I did before, that ugly sting?

Will and I spend another lunch hour in the library before he says, "Why don't we eat in the cafeteria like everyone else?"

I open my mouth to respond, but the words don't make sense anymore. "Less chance of getting killed in here, I guess?"

"In case you haven't noticed," Will says, "I'm kind of a big guy." I try not to smile. There's no question, between the two of us, who could bench-press more. But has Will ever had to make a fist and punch somebody in the face? Claw, twist, choke someone to get away? I doubt it. Escape from getting licked to death by his dog, more like.

Still, I don't want to hide anymore. I know he'd stand up for me, if it came to that. Two of us against them now.

"Okay. Tomorrow the cafeteria."

* * *

The next day we find a table near the wall, empty at one end. He sits beside me, and we both look around. People wandering, throwing food, playing on their phones. Okay, I can do this.

After a few minutes Amanda joins us. Damien stops by to say hello, smiling at Will's arm around the back of my chair. I pretend not to notice his smug expression.

I tense as Ainsley walks by, not with Pole Dancer this time. Her eyes flick in my direction and pretend not to see me. Will feels me stiffen and squeezes my shoulder when she passes, like, *See?* I guess the threat of Jacquie showing up on her doorstep made an impression.

When the bell rings, Will walks me back to my locker. "You know," he says, "this Friday is a professional-development day for teachers. There's no school."

"Yeah?"

"Well," he says, "your brother can go to day care. Your sister probably has school. You can come to my house." He smiles, proud of himself.

I think about what he said. True. Mom at home. Maisie and Evan spoken for. That's seven free hours.

"You're right. Okay." I have a silly happy buzz for the rest of the afternoon.

* * *

Friday, I leave the house just like usual, without saying anything to Mom about where I'm going. Every time I think of telling her about Will, the words won't come. She's either gushing about Oliver or having an anxiety attack over Oliver or just plain passed out. I've never had a boyfriend before, so I don't know what she'll say or do. She'll definitely want to meet him, and then what? I play Russian roulette on what kind of Mom I get that day? Anything involving her becomes more complicated.

Will meets me at the bus stop in front of the school, which is dark and lonely today. A light burns in one classroom. Patchy lawn deserted.

We stroll along, hours open in front of us. The day is damp and overcast. Chill stings our fingers—no snow yet. Will curls my hand inside his.

He points out his house as we get closer. It's olive green with chipped white trim. The porch is a little crooked, with wilted potted plants resting on each step. There's a tidy hedge in the front and a black Lab barking wildly against the fence in the back.

"That's Sadie," he says.

Once inside the front door, he takes my coat. We look at each other, not sure how to be in this place.

"I'll show you around?" he says. I guess that's what you do when someone visits.

In the living room, a large window overlooks the front lawn. Hardwood floors. Pushed against one wall is a sofa with worn scarlet cushions. A stumpy television sits on a stand too big for it.

"My mom doesn't like me watching much TV," he says, pointing to it.

The kitchen's basically a box. No table, but there's an island with stools in the middle of the room. Utensils hang overhead, threatening to skewer Will, and a fern droops above the microwave.

He takes me to his room upstairs, one of two doors. The roof slopes in one place, making him duck his head. I note an attempt at making the bed—a wrinkled blanket pulled over the sheet. There's a basket of clean folded laundry at my feet (his mom, I bet). Cluttered desk with a laptop wedged on it. In the corner, a set of weights and a bench.

"You work out?"

"Sometimes." He shrugs, face red.

We face each other, eyes looking everywhere else. The poster over his bed is peeling away in one corner. Plaid curtains dangle from a thin rod.

"My mom's still sleeping," he finally says. "We should probably go downstairs." Will's mom is a nurse. She works mostly nights.

"Okay." I'm the first out the door.

Last stop, the basement. The floor is covered in gaudy patterned carpet, and there are tiny windows above us.

Brown wallpaper. Will ducks his head. "The basement needs some work." He folds a blanket left on the floor and looks over a few beanbag chairs and boxes in the corner. Taps his fingers against his leg. It's funny to see him embarrassed about this. He should see some places I've lived.

"It's a nice house, Will," I say.

"Yeah, it's okay."

We go back upstairs. Still no sound from his mom. We end up taking the dog for a walk. As we head back toward the school, we find our voices again. Will lets Sadie off her leash in the football field, and we throw sticks to her and watch her run around. Huddle on the damp bleachers.

After a while, we head back. Will makes grilled-cheese sandwiches for lunch. I watch his hands move in the kitchen, this new place. While he's pouring milk, there's a shuffling sound behind us. I turn.

His mom in a pink bathrobe and long wet hair. Dark, tight eyes. I see where Will gets it—the unruly black mane. He must get his height from his dad. She's not much taller than me. Slim.

She looks at us both without saying anything, and I feel my gut shrink. Then she smiles, like an afterthought. "Hi, I'm Nancy." She shakes my hand. "William…" She sighs and darts over to him, slipping a plate under the bread on the bare counter. The she disappears up the stairs again.

"Will," I whisper, "did you tell her I was coming?"

"Of course." He carries on.

We watch a horror movie after lunch, taking bets on the next person to be picked off and how.

"The blond, in the garden shed. Hedge clippers," I say.

"Ha! Lawn mower!"

"Cheater. You've seen this before."

I tuck my legs up on the sofa and lean into him. His arm around me. Nancy pokes her head in, looks around with eagle eyes. I fight the impulse to leap to the other side of the sofa and deny all contact. She checks in twice more before the end of the movie.

"Your mom seems a little worried about you having a girlfriend," I say, the word still strange in my mouth.

"She'll get used to it." He shrugs. "She's paranoid about me getting someone pregnant and not going to university. She's been talking about it since I was twelve." Yes, Will the Womanizer.

Then I think of my mom, how different her life would have been without having me so young. Or maybe not.

"Well," I say, "I am pretty irresistible."

He laughs. "True."

I feel like telling his mom not to worry—just sitting close to Will makes me feel like I've won the lottery. When he tries to pull me closer, brings his lips by my ear, I pull away.

"Are you crazy?" I hiss, checking the doorway. He laughs again.

I keep my eye on the clock. Maisie's still getting out at the same time. Fifteen minutes before her school day ends,

Will walks back with me. On the elementary-school side of the street, cars are pulling in, parents getting out.

He stops me half a block away and pulls me in as I start to shiver. "When can we do this again?" His chin on my head.

"I don't know," I say. "When's the next PD day?"

"Too far."

I don't know what to tell him. He kisses me goodbye—fifty onlookers not as terrifying as his mother.

Maisie chatters as I watch the blur of cars through the bus window.

Jacquie, disappeared. Mom, caught up with Oliver. No one to tell about the best day of my life.

TWENTY-ONE

As we leave Evan's day care, white flakes drift down.

"It's snowing!" he and Maisie both squeal, holding their hands in the air and chasing each other around. I hope their boots weren't left at Mom's friend's place too. I should have checked already. We stomp slushy shoes in the lobby.

Mom is at the table, reading a newspaper. This is new.

"What are you doing?" I ask.

"Checking jobs in the classifieds," she says.

Okay... I don't have time to ask her more—off to work. Through my shift, her words pick at me. Why is she looking for work? Did she lose her job? I didn't hear about any big scene or drunken breakdown. Maybe her boss doesn't like Oliver hanging around, chatting her up at work.

Hasan tries to talk to me, asks me how Jacquie's doing. I volunteer to clean the bathrooms, scrubbing the urinals to a shiny white.

I press back home through the wet flakes and corner Mom in the bathroom as soon as I get in.

"Why are you looking for work? Something happen with your job?" I start in before even saying hello.

She pulls down on an eyelid, adding a curve of black liner. Blinks at a lash in her eye and dabs the eyeliner with toilet paper.

"No, nothing happened. Oliver wants me to look for a different kind of work."

I sit down on the edge of the tub. "Why?"

"Well"—she starts on the other eye—"he doesn't like the"—she pauses—"attention from the other men there."

It takes me a second. He's jealous. Mom has to find another job because Oliver is jealous.

"That doesn't seem quite fair to me," I say. "You were doing that job when he met you."

She puts down the eyeliner, inspecting each eye in the mirror. "I don't expect you to understand, Isabelle. Someday you will."

I imagine Will telling me to quit a job or drop a class because other guys might pay attention to me. No, I think I understand now. Oliver's a prick.

"So what kind of job are you thinking of?" Something in a convent, I think.

"Maybe working in an office?" She moves on to the hair straightener now. Working in an office? Mom left school after grade eleven and has worked in bars forever. Who will give her a chance? I'm not crazy about her job either, but having Oliver call the shots makes something flare in me.

"What next? Oliver's going to dress you, tell you how to be a mother?" I say.

"Relationships are all about compromise," she says, probably quoting Oliver.

I shake my head and go scrub dishes in the sink. An uneasy feeling moves through me. It was hard enough keeping things together before, when it was just the four of us. At least I know Mom's crap. Now there's Oliver, pushing and pulling from the sidelines. I don't know what I'm dealing with.

When she leaves for work, I wish I could call Will. I actually have his phone number now. Knowing my luck, Nancy would answer and want to have a conversation about birth control or abstinence. What would I say to him anyway? I've done my best to shield him from all of this.

Thinking about Will gives me another idea though. After I get Maisie and Evan to bed, I pull out my homework in the living room. Will asked when we could get together again. Here I am, sitting by myself in an empty room night after night. Maisie and Evan are out cold until morning. Mom's at work until three or four. Why couldn't Will be here with me for an hour or two? Besides the fact that he'd see our really ugly sofa.

No. Is even seeing this apartment too much? The camp cot in the bedroom. Bathrobe guy wandering the halls. Fridge stocked with beer and not much else. But he already knows my mom is a drunk and I live in a dump. He seems okay with that. Every time I talk myself out of asking him over, the idea pops back again. When else am I going to see him, especially with Mom out with Oliver all the time? At this rate, we'll have a date when all the planets align and world peace is achieved.

I go back and forth about it until English the next morning, when his foot against mine gives me a boost of courage. While Mr. Drummond writes the elements of a short story on the board, I scratch a note on a piece of paper: *Talk after class.* Drop it over my shoulder. For some reason, my stomach flutters. Afraid he won't think it's a good idea, that he'll see too much if he comes, that he'll think it's too much effort for an hour or two with me.

Mr. Drummond gives us an assignment: write a short story, due in a week. I think of my notebook with my tale of the twins and their suicide pact, or the story I wrote about the bullied nutjob. I think I'll start something new.

At the end of class, I pull Will down the hall a bit, away from Mr. Drummond's door, and tell him about my idea. He stands there, smiling like an idiot. "Of course I'll come."

I try to explain the timing, how it'll have to work. How he'll have to bus to me, all the details. He's not really listening—he's smiling, jittery.

When I stop talking, he stoops to kiss me. There's a shuffling noise off to the side, and I pull away. Mr. Drummond turns on his heel to go back into the classroom. My face is on fire.

"Okay, you're late for Chemistry," I say, shoving Will in that general direction.

We work out some details at lunch, like what day would be the best. I tell him which bus to catch from the school and when it runs. When Maisie and Evan will be asleep.

"You haven't told your family about me, have you?" he says.

I shake my head, watching his reaction. "I'm not embarrassed, Will. I don't trust my mom with a lot of things."

He nods.

"I will eventually, when I know she can handle it."

"Okay."

*   *   *

That night, lying in my cot, I think about the story I'll write for English. I know exactly what it'll be: a girl who runs away from home and, using her street smarts, manages to eat and find a place to stay every night. She dodges seedy pimps. Outsmarts dealers. Does some wrestler moves on the guy who thinks he'll have his way with her. Returns home with a new respect for life.

Where are you, Jacquie, and how do you survive? Because I don't think it's a part-time job at Safeway. My mind wanders to dark places. I try to steer it back. Almost succeed.

I'm still awake when Mom comes home from her date with Oliver. She leaves the hall light on, opening the door a crack to see her way into the bedroom. I hear her drop her clothes on the floor, the clink of earrings in a dish.

"You're home early," I say.

"Isabelle. You startled me."

I lie in the dark and hear her sniff.

"Are you okay?" I ask.

"Yes, yes. Fine." Knowing I know better. "Just working through some stuff with Oliver."

She pads around the room for another minute before shutting the door behind her, leaving me in the dark again. I hear the refrigerator door open, the clink of bottles.

I stay awake a long time.

*　　*　　*

Thursday, the temperature drops, and there's an icy wind.

"Do you still want to come over tonight?" I ask Will. "We could pick another day."

"No, I'll come."

Evan starts to cry on the way home from day care, getting a full blast of it in the face. I pick him up, his back to the wind, and carry him the rest of the way.

At home a few empties dot the table. I drop Evan and search for Mom, my snowy shoes leaving tracks across the carpet. I find her stretched out on the bed. My heart sinks. The plan won't work if she doesn't leave tonight.

I tap on her feet. "Mom. Mom, wake up."

She cracks open an eye and lifts her neck off the pillow. Okay, not too far gone. "Hi, love. Just having a little nap before work." She rolls onto her back and stares at the ceiling. Puffy eyes.

I sit next to her, the springs creaking. "What is it?"

She closes her eyes and shakes her head. "Just being sensitive."

"What?"

"Oh, something Oliver said hurt my feelings." She stops. I think she's finished. "He said I have 'baggage.' I took it badly."

Something twinges in me. How would I feel if Will said those words to me? Even if they were true. Especially because they are true. "I'm sorry." What a joke, him saying that to her. A forty-year-old compulsive talker who lives with his parents, and she's the one with baggage. I consider hiring a hit man.

"We're just going through a bumpy patch. All relationships have them," she says, pulling herself up.

"I'll make supper," I tell her, trying to help. Possibly feeling a tiny bit guilty about sneaking Will in later.

She has a double rum and Coke with her tuna sandwich. Cheeks low, eyes flat. I can see we're going to skip the giggly stage tonight and go straight to weepy.

When she reaches for a refill, I put my hand on hers. "Wait until after work, okay?"

She nods, knowing I'm right.

I offer her some of my money to take a taxi tonight rather than the bus. She uses her tip money to catch a taxi home each night, but we can't normally afford it both ways. "No, no. I'll just bundle up," she says. And she's gone, right on schedule.

I straighten up and give Maisie and Evan a quick bath. Wash the dishes. Rush through bedtime stories to have them in bed ten minutes early. I want them out cold when Will comes. I get a little panicky when Evan gets up twice to pee.

"Enough," I tell him, "or I'll skip stories tomorrow night." That seems to work.

A couple of minutes to fix myself up, and then there's a quiet tap on the door. Someone else must have buzzed him in.

I open the door and there he is, ears bright red. Snowflakes in his hair. I reach up and put a warm palm on each cheek, then tiptoe to Maisie and Evan's room to see if they're still awake. Sound asleep. I ease their door shut behind me.

"Okay, we're good."

I know I should be embarrassed about everything— the mismatched dining set, fraying flowered sofa. Hideous shag carpet. He probably already saw the guy in the bathrobe. Definitely rode in the pissy elevator. I'm so happy he's here, though, I don't even care. It's like being in the prop room again.

I kiss his cold mouth and press his ear against my cheek to warm it. "I can't believe you took the bus in this." I ask him how long he can stay, and we work out the bus schedule.

"My mom's working tonight," he says, "but she usually calls around 11:00 on the home phone."

"She doesn't know you're here, does she?" He shakes his head. So I'm not the only one sneaking around. "Well, I'll try not to get pregnant," I tell him. He laughs, and I worry Maisie and Evan might wake up.

We sit on the sofa and pull out our English stories, which was the plan. We don't get too far.

"What's yours about?" I ask.

"It's science fiction. About a guy who discovers a new planet."

"Is that what you read?"

"Mostly," he says.

"Who's your favorite author?" I ask.

"Ray Bradbury."

Then it turns into a sort of question-and-answer session, with me asking all the questions. "Favorite food?" I ask.

"Lasagna."

I try not to cringe. "Favorite color?"

"Anything but orange."

I go on for a while, then make it more complicated. "Favorite moment?"

He thinks for a second, tapping his pen against the page. "The first time you kissed me. I thought you were leaving."

That's a personal favorite of mine too. I smile.

"How about you?" he says.

"I'm not done yet. Worst moment?"

His face falls thinking about this one. I'm almost sorry I asked. "There are a few—my parents' divorce, losing you before, and seeing you with that guy at the dance."

Jamie. Will still thinks about that? At this point, I know the Q-and-A can't ever get to me. Worst moment? How would I choose? Any one of a thousand bad days with Mom. Seeing Claude hurt her. The time I hit her. Watching Maisie crumble on her birthday. And also Will, holding Amanda, smiling down at her. I understand why he deflated when I asked him this one.

But he's here now. I take his hand in mine and run my thumb along his palm. Love these hands, these long fingers.

I can't stop now. "What are you most afraid of?"

He doesn't take long to answer. "Failing." He looks away. "And this ending." I envy him, that he can say the words I can't say out loud. To his list I silently add: foster care, losing Maisie and Evan.

"Will," I say, trying to pick the right words, "when did you start to like me more than as a friend?" What I really want to ask is, *Why do you like me?* Sounds too desperate.

The gray leaves his face. "I think I always liked you. I used to watch you in English."

"Why?" My alluring beauty? Animal magnetism?

"I guess I felt like I already knew you," he says. That's pretty good too. "What about you?"

I can handle this one. "In the prop room. I thought you were a little weird before then." I regret the words as soon as I say them. Watch his face to see how he takes it.

He laughs. We're okay.

"Well, you were reading a thesaurus the first time I saw you," I add.

"I'm glad you gave me a chance." He slides our books to the floor and pulls me close, my face in the curve of his neck. My heart beats faster, floating. Everything disappears. He runs a finger up and down my arm, and his mouth finds mine. Slow, every move slow. A hand on my thigh. On the small of my back, his fingers against my bare skin. Breath on my neck. I'm falling somewhere warm, dark.

"What is this?"

Crashing back. Ice cold. Mom.

We're on our feet in less than two seconds, not touching. Gasping like fish.

"Who the hell are you?" Eyes wild, she leans against the wall and swings an arm toward Will. His mouth opens but doesn't make a sound. She's already turned back to me. Stumbles forward.

I tap my hand against him. "Go."

"You slut," she spits. Words like a punch in the gut.

"Go." I push against Will again. Instead, he edges in front of me, protecting me from this.

"You little whore. Always so anxious to get me off to work. Now I see why." She charges forward, tumbling against me. Will grabs my shoulders to stop me from falling backward.

"Go, Will! Leave!" I shout at him. I can handle her, this. Can't handle him seeing it.

She raises her hand to me in a clumsy slap. I catch her wrist and push her away. She falls to the floor.

"Get out of here!" I shove Will toward the door, still open to the hallway. He stands between Mom and me. Hands out, like he can hold us in place.

"Will, please." I'm pleading now. He looks at me, something set in his face, and dashes for the door as Mom pushes herself up. He's gone when she comes at me again.

"You and your secrets. How many have there been?" Ugly words, face twisted. I don't want to hit her again. When she grabs me, hands pinching my shoulders, I push her away. Her knees buckle.

"Stop it, Mom!"

"So much to say about my life. Sneaking around like a tramp—" She looks around, her eyes frantic. Picks up Will's binder and hurls it at me. I dodge. It bursts against the back of a chair, papers raining.

I back toward the bedrooms as she pulls herself up and staggers after me. Maisie and Evan. I dodge into their room. A crack of moonlight through the blind. I hold myself against their door. *Wham.* Her body slams it. Doorknob fighting against my hand.

"Open this door!" she screams, cursing.

Shadows move in their beds. Evan starts to cry. What was I thinking, coming in here? I wanted to protect them but led her straight to them.

"It's okay, Evan. Maisie, it's me!" I shout over her voice. Maisie squeals, terrified.

Bang against the door, something hard. "You think you know it all. Whadda you know?"

"Stop, Mom!"

Evan clings to my leg, wailing. Mom goes on slamming things against the door, hurling words at me.

It's quiet for a second. Then, "Isabelle, it's me!" *Will?*

"Get out of here! What are you doing?"

"Out of my way!" Mom's hoarse voice. There's a scuffle, then a thud and a cry from Will. She hit him with something?

The door gives a crack, and I slam it shut again. It's harder with Evan hanging on me. I try to pull my thoughts together, form a plan. If I can hold her off in the hallway, Will could get Maisie and Evan out the door and down to the lobby. I might have to push her down to make a break for it myself. Then where?

Now I hear them, the sirens. *No!*

"Go to Maisie!" I holler at Evan. Maisie cowers in the corner of her bed.

Will is shouting to me. Mom is screaming at him. The door bangs back and forth between us. Then come the loud voices, the knob suddenly quiet in my hands. I step back as they push through the door, the uniforms. Mom, restrained by strong arms, thrashes, swears. Will is pushed back. One of them flicks on the light, stinging our eyes. Evan and Maisie are wild, clinging to me.

"Are you okay?" someone asks. I can't answer.

The uniforms move in, dragging Mom away, then reach for Maisie and Evan. I turn and see him, standing on the edge of it all. It was him.

"You did this!" I shout.

Will's face is white. I lunge at him and scream every curse word I can think of. Arms hold me back, their voices in my ear. Maisie and Evan are hysterical behind me. Uniforms guide Will out the door, out of sight.

It all disintegrates before my eyes. Everything shatters.

TWENTY-TWO

I stare at the dark wall of Jacquie's room, my arm stretched across Evan and Maisie. Evan is sleeping now. Maisie is still shifting next to me. It's a narrow bed—no one can roll over tonight.

I'm numb. Every thought jumbled together. A vibration runs through me and overpowers every feeling. Just one survives—the feeling that something has been broken. Irreparably. I can hold on to the pieces, but it'll never be whole again. I wish I could sleep, or at least forget for a few hours. Will's face as I flew at him. Mom. I never expected those words from her, even during the worst of it.

After Will was escorted out, Maisie, Evan and I huddled together on the sofa. Evan curled up in my lap, Maisie glued to my side. The officer who came to talk to me said, "Can you tell me what happened here? Your boyfriend didn't say much." Will, still trying to edge in front, protect me.

I lied. Lied like our lives depended on it. Because they did. I found the words to mix truth and fiction, to spin it better, and fought to keep those small people by me.

I told him about Mom being stressed at work and with her boyfriend lately, probably had a bit too much to drink. How she came home to find me with my boyfriend, who she had never met before. She wanted to know what was going on.

"I was pretty rude to her," I told him. "I said some awful things. She got mad." He waited for me to go on. "She wanted to keep talking, but I told her to leave me alone. I closed the bedroom door and wouldn't let her in. I guess Will got nervous and called the police."

"Was anyone hurt?" he asked, watching my face.

"No, just yelling."

"Has this happened before?"

"No." I shrugged. "She's usually an awesome mom." I cringed inwardly—maybe *awesome* was overkill.

His eyes swept the burst binder, the papers all over the floor. "My homework," I said. "I threw it when she wouldn't stop talking to me." Basically, I'm a jerk.

"What did you mean when you said *You did this* to your boyfriend?" he asked.

I thought fast. "I didn't think it was a good idea for him to come over in the first place, but he kind of talked me into it. Turns out I was right." *Sorry, Will.*

He asked if we had any relatives to stay with that night, with Mom in the drunk tank. Which was pretty funny.

We'd have been better off if I'd just stayed with Maisie and Evan myself, but I couldn't say it.

"We have an uncle," I said.

I called Uncle Richie to come and pick us up—luckily caught him at the beginning of a binge, so he'd only had a few. Still, I clutched the door the whole ride to his place and wouldn't let him go over thirty kilometers an hour. He showed us to Jacquie's empty room, still just as she had left it. Rumpled clothes on the floor. Unmade bed. Makeup still open on her vanity. One last blow at the end of it all.

*　　*　　*

Every time I drift off, my body jerks awake, ready to run again. I sleep sometime after the sun comes through the curtains. Maisie and Evan are still sound asleep after last night.

Evan wakes me up in the late morning to go pee. When I take him out, I find Uncle Richie at a table ridged with brown coffee rings. He's holding a newspaper, a box of donuts at his elbow.

He pulls me aside while Evan's in the bathroom. We whisper in the kitchen, the counters heaped with crusty dishes.

"I talked to your mom this morning. Her man, he broke up with her at work last night. She had a bit too much to drink." He swallows, rubbing at his charcoal stubble. "It got kind of ugly. She lost her job." As an afterthought, he says, "I'm sorry you kids had a rough night."

Had a rough night.

He must see my nostrils flare, because he adds, "I'm going to pick her up this morning. Just try and go easy. She's had a rough life."

Compared to our walk in the park? I can't even speak.

He drives us home first.

A patchwork of papers over the carpet. A gash in Maisie and Evan's door. It *did* happen. I gather the remnants of Will's binder and run a finger over his black, scratchy writing. A bruise in my chest.

They still won't leave me, Maisie and Evan. But when Mom comes through the door, Evan runs to her. Kisses and apologies. Maisie stays next to me on the sofa, her eyes cold. The first crack in my frost, first pang in that numbness. Not because she rejected Mom, but because I see myself. I see it all starting again, no matter how hard I try to make it different for her. Broken pieces in my hands.

We pass, two silent bodies moving around each other. Mom waits until later in the day, when I go to our bedroom to get the laundry basket.

"Isabelle, I'm sorry." Her voice breaks like a twelve-year-old boy's.

"Don't talk to me." I push past her back into the hall. "Don't ever talk to me."

I want to run far away from this place, but Jacquie's gone. Will's gone. Nowhere in this world for me. I drag my cot out of her room and jam it into Maisie and Evan's.

"Like a sleepover!" Maisie says, and Evan hops back and forth between my bed and his.

Later, when they're asleep and snoring, I let myself think the thought. Let myself admit it wasn't just her. I relive the moment when I flew at Will and said those unthinkable words. *No, Isabelle, that wasn't Mom. You lost Will all on your own.* Then I cry.

*   *   *

Over the weekend—strange, disjointed days—a plan takes shape. A vague plan. Saturday, I take a bus to the mall and buy a new binder for Will, the best one I can find. Evan and Maisie tag along, and I spend a buck on the kiddie rides for them.

Then I park myself in their room, papers spread across all three beds, and try to piece things together. Check dates. Put the pages in order, which is an accomplishment. Will is a prolific note taker. In the end, it looks pretty good. I stick a new piece of loose-leaf in the front and sit there with a pen for a long time. What can I possibly say after all that happened? I end up writing *Sorry, Will* across the top line, knowing it's not nearly enough.

Monday morning I hang out at Maisie's school until I know I'm late. Hallways empty. I sneak into the library. Ms. Hillary watches me unload my books but doesn't say anything as I disappear in a copy of *The Catcher in the Rye.*

The bell rings after the first period. I wait. Then a little more. Now everyone must be gone. I can't face those people right now, especially him.

Mr. Drummond is at his desk, wiry hair going in all directions, scribbling away at something. He looks up at me. "Isabelle." Drops his pen. "We missed you this morning."

I go to the door and ask if I can close it. He nods. I pull up a chair without being asked. "Mr. Drummond, I have a request," I say. He waits for me to continue. "Something happened at home this weekend, something bad. And Will was there." He cocks his head, probably wondering why I'm telling him this. "I'd like your permission to transfer out of this class and finish the term in another English class."

His bushy eyebrows jump. "I—well—should I ask?"

I shake my head.

"It's highly unusual, Isabelle."

"Please. It's the only way I'll finish."

He leans back in his chair, round belly up, and exhales. Watches me as if I'm a specimen in a petri dish. "And what about next term, and in the cafeteria and hallways and everywhere else?"

"I'm moving out on my own at the end of this term. I'll have to work and finish school part-time."

Slow shake of his head.

"I'd leave now, but I don't want to redo these courses." When he doesn't answer, I say, "I can't live there anymore." Clear my throat to steady my voice.

"Okay." He nods. Sighs. "Okay. Let me see what I can do. Ms. Furbank might have a spot, but not at the same time as my class. Hers is in the second period."

"I have a spare. That'll work."

"I'll talk to her today."

As I push back my chair to leave, he says, "Isabelle— two things." I sit back down. "One, I want you to finish the short-story assignment I gave you. After that, Ms. Furbank can have you."

The story. I forgot about it. *It's science fiction. About a guy who discovers a new planet.* I hate the story assignment and everything connected to that night.

"Second—think about something for me."

I nod, folding my hands in my lap.

"When you come from a difficult family, like you do—like I do—remember to put yourself at the top of the list once in a while. Your life can't always be a reaction to somebody or something else."

I nod dumbly. What is he talking about?

"Maybe you won't really hear me right now, but think about it, will you?"

"Okay."

"Otherwise, you'll wake up one day in your forties and find you've lived your entire life as a character in someone else's bad screenplay."

"Hmmm."

"Okay." He gives me a firm nod. Now we're done.

I'm so distracted by his pep talk, I reach the hallway before I remember Will's binder and have to run it back to him.

I spend the rest of my spare and lunch hour writing the story for Mr. Drummond, pulling it out in Biology and Spanish when I'm supposed to be working on projects. At the end of the day, I slide it under his closed door. *Goodbye, Mr. Drummond. Goodbye, Will.*

* * *

At home, I find Mom passed out on the sofa, an empty mickey by her dangling fingers. Doesn't matter. No job to wake her up for. I think of pulling a blanket over her but don't.

"Why is Mom sleeping on the sofa?" Evan asks. Maisie stands by me, watching.

"She must be tired, Evan." It's painful to talk this much crap.

When they're in bed, I start pulling out boxes, the same ones I use for every move. I start with the summer clothes, things they don't need right now. In an hour I've already done three. The same old routine. I hope the eviction notice doesn't come until I finish my classes.

I'll start riding her soon to find another job. I just need to get through this term first, because who knows where we'll end up after that. Different part of the city. Maybe even a different city. Doesn't matter. I'll have my own place then, with a lock and key. Maisie and Evan can come over every night. They'll know how to phone me. She can leave them with me when she goes to work. They can sleep at my place. I'll take care of them. And there won't be anyone banging in, throwing words, books, bottles. No more running. I'm putting myself at the top of the list, like Mr. Drummond said.

* * *

I show up at Ms. Furbank's class the next day, Damien waving wildly from the back. Those pink streaks make all the eyes on me a little more bearable. I find an empty desk near the front and face forward.

Ms. Furbank introduces me before she gets started. Tight smile from Zara in the next row. She probably thinks I'm here to challenge her position as Reigning Queen and Champion of the World.

Ms. Furbank is different than Mr. Drummond—more worksheets and notes. She starts the short-story unit today, which I take as permission to zone out entirely.

Jacquie, how can you disappear at the exact moment I'm ready to move out? I didn't even ask Uncle Richie if he'd heard anything—he probably hasn't.

At the end of class, Ms. Furbank waves me over. "Mr. Drummond wants to see you. He's in his room."

Okay. I round the corner, expecting Will, my mom, Mr. Talmage. One big therapy session. I'm relieved he's alone, shuffling papers.

"Mr. Drummond?" I say, startling him.

"Isabelle! Sit down, please." I know the drill by now. "How was your new class?" He doesn't wait for the answer. Instead he digs in a pile and pulls out my story. Flicks through the pages. I wasn't expecting this.

"I read your story. It's quite good."

I don't know what to say. "Thanks?"

"A little dark, with the poisoning of the mother. Should I be worried?"

I smile and shake my head.

"Good. Okay. I'm going to suggest one of two things here. One, therapy." He winks. "Or two, you consider writing a one-act play for the drama festival in March." Always knocking me off-balance, this man.

I give him a long look. Has he already forgotten the Words on the Wall fiasco? "I don't know. Remember last time?"

"You're the writer! No one would even see you. You could adapt this story. They'd love it. Half the drama department would fight over something this creepy."

I suddenly remember. "I won't be here."

"Well, you could write it before you leave, or if you change your mind…"

So that's what this is about. Throw me a bone so I'll stick around. "I'll think about it," I say, knowing I won't.

Still, as I leave, the old warmth rises up again. I try to crush it flat—no good ever came of it.

* * *

I move between the library, the computer lab, my classes. A drone. Waiting to see him but terrified. Crippling shame— what he saw, what I did. I search for and duck away from every tall head. He knows where I am and doesn't come, so there's my answer. What right do I have to cry? I knew from the first day how this would end. I knew.

I finally finish the story in my notebook about Abby, scribbling away whenever I have the chance, filling my head with that family, their doom. The mother gets married. The sisters die. The end.

*   *   *

Mom is barely conscious while we're awake, worse than she's been other times. How can I push her to find a job? She can't even brush her teeth or make a sandwich.

Friday, I come home, Maisie and Evan fighting over who gets to be first through the door. "Stop it, you two. It's not a race," I say.

Empty sofa today. The usual bottle carnage spread through the apartment, across the table, by the sink. I check the bathroom—not in the tub.

In the dim bedroom, I see the outline of her bare feet when I open the door. There, in bed. I pull the door shut. Something in me starts to buzz, that old vibration. I open the door again. Sour smell. Dread rising in my throat. What's wrong with me? I flick on the light.

She's sprawled across the bed with a trail of vomit from her mouth. White face, still chest. I open my mouth to scream—don't know if any sound comes out.

Then flashing lights and uniforms fill this space again. Small hands claw at my neck. Uncle Richie frantic over the phone. Everywhere, that high-pitched vibration, like breaking glass.

TWENTY-THREE

We wait, Evan wilting against my neck. I perch on the edge of the plastic chair, Maisie at my arm. Uncle Richie, eyes like pouches, stares at nothing. His coffee grows cold in his hand.

Colors come and go. Blobs of people. Voices talking about change for the parking meter. Scrubs wheeling things back and forth. All outside our bubble of silence. Even one word will burst it, and all of this will be real.

Evan slumps against me now, his soft hair at my jaw. Slow breath. Maisie gets up to find the bathroom and wanders in the hall, her coat a red dot weaving around wheels and brisk legs. I'm frozen to this spot.

Until the woman in the white coat comes. I can barely turn my head. Wait as she opens her mouth.

"She's alive…" I don't hear anything else she says.

Some time passes (A minute? An hour?), and then we pile into the back of Uncle Richie's car, nobody buckled in.

Wait as he sobs like a baby against the steering wheel. Then we drive through the city, Evan in my lap and Maisie falling asleep against my shoulder.

Uncle Richie carries Maisie up, Evan still in my arms. We lower them into their beds, my muscles numb.

Collapse.

*   *   *

A gray form takes shape in my mind, nudging me awake.

I blink. It's still dark through the window, but the noises of morning traffic drift up. I remember. As though every day of our lives was leading up to yesterday. Now what?

I slip from my cot and ease the door shut behind me. They're still quiet in their beds. Mom's door hangs open. I close that one too, turning my head away. My feet step silently on the carpet as I head to the living room. There's a hint of dawn through the kitchen window, still dim. I freeze at the creak of sofa springs.

He stayed. Uncle Richie's dark head bobs up, his leather jacket slipping from his arms. I sit next to him as he rubs his face, stubble chafing his fingers.

"Did you sleep?" I ask.

He shakes his head.

We sit in silence for a minute, watching the room grow lighter. He gets up and flicks on the television. The morning news: an apartment fire, a petition to save a local duck pond, another homicide.

Within an hour Maisie and Evan wander out, two pale ghosts.

"Where's Mom?" Evan says.

Maisie whispers in my ear, "Did Mom die?"

"No," I say. "Mom's in the hospital, getting better."

"Why is she sick?" Evan asks, brown eyes on my face.

I get up to make them breakfast. Can't answer their questions yet. Another memory for them to pull out later—the day Mom almost died. This just gets better and better.

We cuddle under a blanket, watching cartoons. Uncle Richie sits at the table and knocks back cup after cup of coffee. His eyes on the TV but not really seeing.

He phones the hospital midmorning, shutting himself in the bedroom to talk. His voice rumbles through the closed door. Then he comes out and stands in front of us, Evan craning his neck to see the TV. "Your mom's awake, doing okay." He says to me, "She wants to see you."

Me. Do I want to see her? My world turned on its head and shaken. Still holding those broken pieces in my hand. What can Mom possibly say or not say at this point that would make any difference?

"I don't know," I say.

"Go see her." Not a request. When I turn my head away, trying to ignore him, he says, "I'll drive you."

"Fine." I wear the same clothes I slept in. Skip the shower. Skip breakfast. Whatever.

In the hospital parking lot, I slam the car door behind me, Maisie and Evan's small faces in the backseat. The electric window lowers as I walk away. "Call me when you want me to pick you up," he says. I keep walking.

I retrace my steps from last night, which happened a long, long time ago. Up to the nurses' station. I try not to look at the plastic chairs.

"I'm here to see Marnie Bennett," I say to a nurse in pink scrubs. "I'm her daughter." She nods and points me in the right direction.

Outside the door, I take a deep breath. Now I feel it: the pounding. That vibration starting up again. I remember the white face, the still chest. I'm suddenly sweating, shivering. Should I knock?

I throw open the door and stand in the doorway.

Greasy hair limp against her head. Thin arms in a bland hospital gown. She puts a drink back on a tray over the bed, smiling. Like we're going out for lunch or something.

"Isabelle, I'm glad you came." She can't stop smiling at me.

I close the door and lean against it, arms crossed. What do I have to say to her?

"I need to talk to you." She waits for me to say something, which I don't. Now she wants to talk? Kill herself first, talk later?

"I know you're angry." She looks down at her tray. "You have every right." Silence. "It's just—after what happened, I'm glad to be alive. Isabelle, I didn't try to—I think you should know—well, it wasn't on purpose," she stammers.

A hot coal ignites in my gut, spreading fire through me. "Maisie asked me this morning if you were dead." I spit out the words.

"I know. I'm sorry." Cheeks flushed.

"Stop saying you're sorry. It means nothing."

She blinks back tears. "Okay. You're right." She takes another drink, clearing her throat. "I think I need to explain some things to you. Things I should have told you a long time ago."

Great. Here come the excuses. I walk to a window overlooking a food court and turn my back to her. She must know this is as good as it gets, because she keeps going. "My family had a lot of problems growing up." *Had* problems? "You know I haven't been in touch with my mom or stepdad."

Below me an endless line shifts, people loading up on pasta, apple juice, pie. One man sits alone with a book, his back to the crowd.

"My stepfather, Everett, he was an angry man. He used to hit me and Richie." She takes a shaky breath and moves the tray aside. I close my eyes and see her shielding her head in her hands, Claude coming at her.

"*Hit* might not be the right word—more like *hurt*, in every way imaginable," she continues. "This scar is from his cigarette." I picture the small white circle near her wrist, where I've seen her fingers rest a million times. "You should see Richie's back."

I lean against the window, wanting to be somewhere else. I can't turn and face her. Don't want that picture in my head.

"I know you thought Claude was bad. He did have a temper." She shakes her head. "But Everett, he was different. I think he waited for us every day after school, almost like clockwork. And if we didn't come straight home—knowing what would happen next—it was so much worse later. That leather belt. Richie's arm still isn't right. Everett pushed him down the stairs, but they waited too long to get it looked at, afraid people would ask questions."

"Didn't they?" I squeak.

"It was a small town—half of them related. I think everyone tried not to notice. We looked forward to the times he drank himself to sleep before we got home. But the next day, when he woke up hungover, it was twice as bad. Richie and me," she says, "we tried to take the worst of it, to protect Laina." I think of my life, huddled in dark places with Maisie and Evan, running, running. So Mom did that too. "I knew if I left, he'd come after her." Only, she wasn't running. Worse, much worse.

"Richie left when he was eighteen. Couldn't take it anymore. Then I met your father, Cliff. Practically tried to get pregnant. I knew Mom would kick me out. She did." She draws a slow breath into her chest. "Called me a whore."

"And then"—behind me a cry, inhuman—"I left. I left her," she sobs. Her body is shaking. I turn to watch her but can't reach her. She's gone somewhere else, a place of pain where I can't follow. When she finds her voice again, she says, "Laina was only eleven. Eleven years old."

I imagine leaving Maisie in the hands of someone like that—like Everett. I sink to the ground. My legs won't hold me anymore.

"When she was sixteen, she came to live with me for a while. You were four. Do you remember?" I shake my head. "I was pretty messed up. Wasn't much help to her, already drinking." Her voice steadies. "I think you know the rest." She tries to smile—a grimace in the bloated red.

I can't speak or I might be sick.

"When I saw you the other night with that boy, something snapped. Like history repeating itself." She looks away, can't meet my eye. "I was in a bad state after Oliver dumped me and I lost my job. I can't remember everything, but I think I said and did some awful things. I hope someday you can forgive me."

History repeating itself. How often do I live the same day over and over? Try to fight against this inevitable path and always lose? I don't want that history.

That boy. "Will. He's—" I start again. "Will was my boyfriend. It was the first time he came over. What you saw"—*don't make me spell it out*—"was where things were at. I didn't tell you about him because you always mess things up."

She nods. "I'm so sorry, Isabelle." A tear slides slowly down her cheek. I hide my face from her, wiping my eyes on my sleeve.

"I'm going to change," she says.

"Stop."

"I'm going to get help."

"What do you mean?"

"They've told me about a program for women like me, with"—she clears her throat—"addictions." It's the first time I've ever heard her say the word. In sixteen years. "There's a place outside the city. Isabelle, I'll have to be away for three months."

My head snaps up. "Three months? What about us?" I always knew it would come to this. Uncle Richie couldn't handle it. We're lucky he made it through a day. They won't let me keep Maisie and Evan on my own. The best I can hope for is the same foster home.

"I'm working on that," she says, leaning back on her pillow. "Richie said he'd stay in the meantime." Eyes closed now, dark circles against her face. Her strength gone.

*　*　*

Uncle Richie comes when I call him and motions for me to climb in the front seat. His eyes dart to me as he drives, skidding on the icy streets. A pine-tree air freshener wags back and forth between us.

"So, she told you about going away?" he says.

I nod. I wonder if he knew she was going to tell me everything else too. I don't have the guts to ask.

"It'll be okay," he says—the other drunk who can't take care of his one kid.

He drops us off at the front door of our building and calls, "I'll be back later!" as he drives away. He doesn't come back.

I had a feeling twenty-four hours was about his maximum. That's okay. It's better with just me, Maisie and Evan anyway.

I make canned soup and toast for supper and try to explain things in a way they might understand. Watch for Maisie's face closing up.

"Mom has a sickness that makes her drink too much," I say. Evan leans in, gnawing toast. "She's going away for a while, to a place like a hospital, to get better." Maisie stops eating and lowers her spoon. "When she comes back, she'll be better." *Don't make a liar out of me, Mom.*

"Is she coming home today?" Evan asks.

"No, Evan."

I open my mouth to say we might have to live in a different house for a while, with a different mom, but I don't have the heart. Wasn't this enough to dump on them for one day? And it's not only the house. Schools will change. It'll all change. So much for finishing my classes. It doesn't matter. When the social worker comes, every word, every thought, every part of me will be about keeping us together. I think of Mom, repeatedly beaten by her stepfather, and Jacquie, too, in that foster home before. I won't let it happen.

The phone rings as we're finishing. Rupa. I've never heard her voice over the phone before. She wonders why I didn't come in to work tonight. Work. Another world away. A lifetime ago.

I apologize and explain that my mom's in the hospital. Fortunately, she doesn't ask why. I tell her I'll be away for a week (and don't say *probably forever*).

* * *

I take Maisie and Evan to the mall the next day and buy them ice-cream cones with the last of my money. They play with the toys in the toy store. Sit on the kiddie rides with no money to put in them.

Evan wants a piggyback ride the last block home, still tired from the other night. *The* night. As I slide my key into the lock, it turns too easily in my hands. Not locked. I locked it. I know I did.

On the other side, a thief, a rapist, a social worker. Does Uncle Richie have a key? No. Not from me.

I lower Evan to the red-checked carpet, pushing him and Maisie back into the hallway, away from the door. "Wait here. Don't move. If I yell, you run back to the elevator and go downstairs, all right?" Maisie nods, taking Evan's hand.

I push the door open a crack. Nothing. Grab an umbrella propped by the closet and hold it above my head. I creep into the living room, checking every direction. No sign of anyone.

A creak from the kitchen. I'm ready to spring, skewer him with an umbrella.

Then a head pokes around the corner. "Hello, Isabelle."

TWENTY-FOUR

She smiles—familiar eyes. Dirty blond hair in a long braid down her back. She wipes her fingers on an apron.

"I'm sorry. You don't remember me, do you?" Her eyes rest on the umbrella poised to whack her.

I don't say anything, still on the balls of my feet.

"It's been a long time. You were just little. I'm Laina, your aunt."

Laina. Does Mom know she's here? Good thing Uncle Richie's not around. Fifty questions hit me at once, mostly about what she's doing here and how she got in.

I lower the umbrella, feeling a bit stupid now. Not stupid enough to drop it. Whispers in the hallway. I call in Maisie and Evan, fairly sure Laina's not going to jump us. They stand on either side of me, peering around my arms.

"This is Mom's sister. Her name is Laina," I tell them.

"Mom doesn't have a sister," Maisie pipes. "Only Uncle Richie."

Thanks, Maisie. I'm sure that felt nice. Laina pretends not to hear, folding the apron into a tidy square on the table.

"Why are you here?" I say. Can't hold that one back anymore.

"Your mom sent me. Didn't she tell you?"

I shake my head.

"Well, come sit down." She motions to the table and pulls out a chair. I stay standing.

"Go play in your room," I say to Evan and Maisie, giving them a little shove. They shuffle down the hall, looking back over their shoulders. "How did you get in?" I say to Laina.

"I stopped by the hospital today. Your mom gave me a key. She said you might not remember me." She smiles down at her hands. The same look as Mom as she turns her head. But younger. And something else—less trampled by life.

"Look," I say, "I don't mean to be rude, but I don't get what's going on here."

"Your mom will be gone for a few months, and you need an adult around, right?" *Okay. Yes.* "I made a promise to your mom, a long time ago, that if she wanted to sober up and get help, I would help her. So, here I am."

I watch her for a minute, turning over their agreement in my mind.

She smiles, raising her eyebrows. Waits for me to respond.

"Better late than never," I say before I walk to the bedroom and close the door.

* * *

Monday morning, I find her up, already buttering toast for Evan and Maisie, lunches lined up on the counter. I snatch the toast from her hand. "I usually get them breakfast."

"Oh, okay." She moves on to washing dishes. Helps Maisie and Evan get dressed while I'm in the shower. I end up being five minutes early for the bus.

Is this what it's like having a parent around? I know I should be grateful. I am grateful. I was preparing to be shipped off somewhere when she showed up on our doorstep. So why do I feel like putting her braid in the blender?

On the bus, Maisie pulls a cinnamon bun from her lunch bag and waves it under my nose. "Look what Auntie Laina made." I shrink from it like it's toenail clippings.

Why do I hate her for buttering toast, making cinnamon buns? Nothing but sweetness so far, kind words. Endless patience toward me being a jerk.

Maybe that's it. She pulled out, got away from all this. Then she shows up at the last minute like the good guy. *Where were you, Laina, when we lived in that shelter for a month? When Evan was born early after Claude beat Mom? When we moved from house to basement to shelter to apartment, chasing one crap job after another? Where was Super Laina then?* I know where she can shove her cinnamon buns.

The question eats at me all day and through a quiet dinner. Homemade clam chowder and fresh buns.

"What does a clam do on his birthday?" she says to Evan and Maisie.

"What?" Maisie asks.

"He shellabrates!"

They giggle and pull out all the knock-knock jokes they know.

I wait until Maisie and Evan are in bed, then confront her in the kitchen as she kneads bread dough. Who is she, Betty Crocker?

"I need to know why you came back now," I say, backing her into a corner.

"Your mom—"

"No, not because my mom asked. Where were you all those years? Why are you here now, really?"

She peels the dough from her fingers and runs them under the tap. "Come sit down with me, Isabelle." This again? Don't adults ever speak standing up?

Fine. I sit at the table, right on the edge of my chair.

When she's settled, she says, "Did your mom tell you anything about our family growing up?"

I nod.

"When I finally left home, I went to stay with your mom for a while. Did she tell you that?"

Nod again.

"We all had a lot of hurt, a lot of pain. We dealt with it in different ways." She stops to see if I'm following her. I don't say anything.

"After I left," she says, "I started seeing a counselor, looking for healing. It took a while." She gets up to move her dough to a bowl on the back of the stove and covers it with a tea towel. "It's ongoing.

"Your mom and Richie, they drank a lot. After a few years, I found those relationships so hard, so volatile. I felt like I was being hurt by them when I was trying to move on." I think of Mom and Uncle Richie together, their sadness and anger, hurling words and bottles. Hurting those they love, those who love them.

"So"—she studies the tabletop—"I told them both I couldn't be in their lives like that. If they ever wanted help moving on, I'd be there in an instant."

She left. The only sane one. What would've it been like to have Aunt Laina to call when times were bad, when I was scared? Someone to bake buns with, like she does with Evan and Maisie.

"You left us," I say.

"I know things were hard—"

"You know nothing!" I shove back my chair, towering over her.

On her face, the first wince of pain since she came. I remember what Mom told me about Laina. Eleven years old. Not fair of me. Of course she knows something of this life. Here I am, mad at her for not staying in hell with the rest of us.

"I'm sorry. I shouldn't have said that," I say.

"It's okay, Isabelle. I can only imagine what you've been through." She blinks back tears. I feel my eyes stinging. *No. I won't.*

"I'm moving out at the end of this term," I say. See what she does with that.

"Okay. I can help you, if you like."

"Or I might switch schools."

"It's up to you," she says.

"Okay." I turn and disappear into Maisie and Evan's room, my cot still wedged between their beds.

* * *

The next week, she goes back to work. I go back to work and school.

Laina runs her own cake-and-cupcake business, which Maisie and Evan think is pretty cool. She brings home all sorts of fancy cupcakes and desserts and writes their names on top. She leaves during the day to use her own kitchen and comes back in the evening to stay over. She sleeps on the sofa, and does a few minutes of yoga in the morning. I'd need yoga too if I slept on that sofa.

"I cleaned up that room," she says, meaning the mess that Mom left. "You can sleep in there if you want. It's yours."

I tell her she should sleep in there. Neither of us sleeps in there.

My first shift back at work, Rupa hugs me. Arif manages a smile. I'd probably get a kiss from Hasan if he were here.

Rupa drags me into the back room again and shows me another box stacked with stuff. "We saved this for you." It takes me two trips to get it all home.

*   *   *

Friday, I drop in to see Mr. Drummond over the lunch hour.

"Isabelle!" Like he's seeing a long-lost friend. He wipes mustard from his cheek. "How are things?"

"Good." I pull a chair from a random desk and drag it over to him. "I have a question," I say. "How many more characters do you think I should add to convert that story into a play?"

He smiles.

I start writing that night.

*   *   *

Life falls into a routine with Laina—a new routine. When I get up, she's finishing yoga, lunches already made. She leaves breakfast to me, after I practically ripped it from her hands that first day. I get Evan and Maisie off to day care and school, like always, though if I'm running late, she takes Evan herself. I pick them up after school, and she's there within half an hour, making supper. Always some treat tucked away.

"How did you get into this?" I ask one night, watching her knead bread dough.

She laughs. "It's very therapeutic. Try it."

I roll up my sleeves, and she shows me how to press the dough with the heel of my hand, pull it back and start again. Spongy mass in my hands. That warm yeasty smell.

Maisie and Evan do yoga with her on Saturday mornings, their short legs in the air, bodies wobbling. One of these days I'll try it with them.

They always ask about Mom, if this is the week she'll come home. Laina explains, over and over, how Mom needs time by herself to get better. She started a box for Mom, where Maisie and Evan put drawings, cards, schoolwork—things they want to show her when she gets home. I used Laina's phone to take a picture of them making cinnamon twists with her.

I still get stuck cleaning bathrooms at work, but I get a small raise after passing my probationary period. And there's the extra food. And them.

One night at the beginning of December, I wave goodbye to Rupa. A blast of icy air in my face as I push the door open.

She is on the sidewalk, her back to me. Long dark hair over a wool coat. Tight jeans. I stop.

TWENTY-FIVE

She turns, red scarf streaming behind her, and crushes me in her arms. My feet off the ground. I must be dreaming. The smell of perfume and cigarettes.

I push her away. "Don't ever take off like that again."

She laughs, pulling me into a headlock. Jacquie. I don't know where to start.

"I stopped by your place," she says, "but some lady said you were at work."

"Laina."

She curses, then gives a low whistle. "I really have missed a lot."

We go to a nearby diner, where they still have a jukebox, and order fries and Cokes. I call Laina to tell her I'm with a friend.

"Okay, you first," I say, eyeing the inky tattoo on her wrist and twisting her arm to see it better.

"Don't ask." She shakes her head. She tells me about the night she left, calling up some guy who was always chasing her.

"A real grown-up. He's twenty-two," she says. "Thought I was ready for that. Turns out I'm not wife material." She laughs and pulls out a cigarette. "Already trying to quit.

"I lived with him for almost a month," she says. "Tried some new things." I'm afraid to ask. "Then just ended up on couches for a while, which sucked." She blows smoke into a nearby table until the manager comes and tells her to put it out.

"So are you back home now?" I ask.

"I'm going home tonight. Thought I would see you on my way." She taps her nails against the table. "I needed a little boost first. Dad's going to freak out."

Probably. I haven't seen him since that night, with Mom. "He'll be happy though."

She nods. "Okay, your turn."

I tell her about Ainsley and Pole Dancer leaving me alone. ("See?" she says.) A few vague things about Will. Mom walking in when he was over and losing her mind.

"Wait," Jacquie interrupts. "You got busted by your mom, on the couch with a guy."

"Yeah."

She laughs, slapping her hand against the tabletop. "There's some hope for you yet, Bee Stings."

I kill her with my eyes. She doesn't seem to notice. "Can I go on now?" I talk about the police hauling Mom off. Staying with Jacquie's dad for the night. Mom's alcohol poisoning and rehab. Laina coming.

I don't know if I should tell her what Mom told me, about Everett and all of that. I watch her while I talk and think how she is part of that history too. Her entire life shaped by something she never knew about.

"There's something else Mom told me, something you should probably know." I tell her about Everett beating her dad and my mom on a daily basis, the leather belt and cigarette burns. I tell her about the other stuff—how Mom protected Laina, then left. How Laina was only eleven years old. Then how Laina walked away and why they hated her.

She doesn't say a word the whole time I talk. Not one stupid comment.

When I'm finished, she shakes her head. "Well, that explains a lot." We sit in silence. "Quite the family, eh?" After a minute she says, "Have Dad and Laina made up?"

"I don't think so. I haven't seen them talk."

She slides from the booth, her coat on in two seconds. "Well, time to face the music."

As she starts to walk away, I say, "Jacquie, I'm glad you're back."

"I know." She winks. Then she's gone.

Maybe we'll never live together. I don't know. Either way, I think I need a few of her explosions in my life. And she needs a little of my quiet reading in a coffee shop.

* * *

School falls into a routine too—a mix of new and old. Spare. English with Ms. Furbank. Zara waving her hand in the air anytime the teacher looks my way. That's okay. Invisibility has always been my main goal.

Lunch in the library, like old times. Biology, where everyone's gone back to ignoring me again. Spanish with Daniela and Damien.

"It didn't work out with you and the big guy, did it?" Damien says.

I shake my head. "A bird and a fish."

He looks confused, about to say something else, when Mr. Dent chews him out for talking.

I do see Will one day as I'm walking by the cafeteria doors—a snatch through the glass window. He's sitting with a short pimply guy. Amanda's at the same table, and another girl I don't recognize. I stand near the edge of the glass, peeking in like a CIA agent. He leans across the table to hear the short guy better and smiles.

I remember for a second what it was like to be on the receiving end of that smile, to touch that face. *Will.* Then the door swings open, and I'm standing there like a stalker without his hedge. I back away out of sight. Did he see me?

I run into Ainsley and Pole Dancer the same day at my locker. Acid voices behind me.

"Watch out for that one, Janine. She'll sic her pit bull on you," Ainsley says. Pole Dancer sniggers.

Without turning around, I say, "How'd that floor taste, Ainsley?" Then nothing. It doesn't matter, them or anyone else. This is my school too. I picked it.

* * *

A week later I'm in the library, my biology textbook in front of me. Thinking about Mom, wondering what she's doing.

A swish next to me and the scrape of a chair. I look up, the air all gone.

"Will." I didn't actually mean to say it out loud. I smile at him—can't help it. He's in some tacky sweater his mom probably bought him.

He smiles back. He's here.

"What are you doing?" What am I saying?

"I thought it was time to say hello," he says. "It's been a while."

"It has." I think of the last words I said to him—and what happened right before that.

We talk about exams, holidays. When things get quiet, he says, "I've missed you." I nod. Don't trust my voice. "Why'd you drop English?"

"Ashamed," I say. What's the point in lying now? "What you saw. What I said to you. Especially what I said to you."

He shrugs. "You did try to warn me, didn't you?"

"I did."

"I think I understand," he says. Quiet. I'm afraid he's going to get up and leave now.

"What did your mom say about that night?" I ask. Never thought about it before.

"She doesn't know. I was a little late getting back, so I told her I fell asleep watching TV and didn't hear the phone."

"Very devious, Will," I say. "I think I'm rubbing off on you."

He laughs. The good laugh. "Well, I just wanted to say hi." Then he's gone, leaving a draft like someone left the door open.

* * *

The next day I pretend not to be checking every thirty seconds for his head ducking through the library doorway. And there he is.

My stupid smile. *Keep it together, Isabelle.*

He pulls out homework today. I try not to watch his fingers grasp the pen, his messy scrawl across the page. The dip in his collarbone through his T-shirt. Tiny scar by his eyebrow.

He looks up and catches me staring. My cheeks prickle.

After a few minutes he says, "You seem different, you know? More calm."

I tell him about my aunt staying with us while my mom gets help. "She almost died."

His face falls. "Why didn't you tell me?"

"Well, we weren't really…together. I mean, I'd just cussed you out and had you interrogated by the police."

He shakes his head. "You don't think I can handle this stuff."

"Can you?" He makes a face like I just waxed his eyebrows. "Our lives are very different, Will. You have no idea."

He looks at me, his eyes clouding over. A vein pops in his neck.

He drops his pen in his bag and closes his books. Starts to pull his hoodie from the back of the chair.

"Will, wait." It's true I never gave him the chance, never thought he could handle it. In his world of walking the dog, refrigerator full of food, helicopter mom with her university agenda. Maybe it's time to find out what he's made of. "You want to know?"

He nods, jaw still out. Big baby.

"Fine. Don't say I didn't warn you." I look around. Ms. Hillary's hammering away at a keyboard on her desk, already giving us the stinkeye. "But not here."

I take his arm—not gently—and drag him through the halls, bumping shoulders, stepping on feet. Down to where it's quiet. Through one door, then another. He flicks on the light. I turn it off. These aren't things I can say in fluorescent light, with go-go boots and pom-poms in my face.

"Sit down," I say. Him against one wall. Me against the other.

I start with the stuff about Mom, taking care of her, Maisie and Evan. Calling in to work, cleaning up, the humiliation. All the lies. Living in shelters, basements. Going hungry. Claude, seeing him beat her. The names he called me, locking me in rooms, getting caught in the crossfire. The time I slapped Mom. Maisie's birthday and every other special day that never was. Uncle Richie. The time I had a great boyfriend until my mom humiliated me and I screamed at him because

I got scared. Then when she almost died, walking in to see that. Facing foster care.

I don't soften anything. Blunt words. Full details, all repulsive and in-your-face. When I finish, voice grating, I say, "There, Will. That's my life. Can you handle that?" Hurling words through the darkness. Absolute silence. Through all my stories, through every word. Silence. "I didn't think so."

I push myself up from the wall, knocking shirts off a rack. Angry tremor in every vein. I'm at the door in less than a second.

As I twist the knob, the door's stuck tight. An arm above my shoulder—his arm holding it closed.

"Move," I say, bumping against him.

"Wait."

"Move!"

His free arm pulls me to him, then the other one. I want to push him away, knee him. Scratch. I can't leave that warm circle, his ribs under my fingers. Are his cheeks wet?

I stop fighting and lean into him. "It won't always be like that," he says. Then it's my turn to cry.

I don't know how much time passes. Bells ring. A class actually comes in to use the drama room, a crack of light under the door. If they need their prop room, they'll find two bodies huddled in the corner. Probably drag us to Mr. Talmage. Then it's quiet again.

"I feel like I've lived my whole life as some kind of a rodent," I say. "Running from hole to hole. Picking up scraps to survive."

Will listens, twirling my hair in his fingers. "Think of this," he says. "Rodents are very resilient. They survive when nothing else can—even become immune to poisons. Did you know a rat can tread water for days?"

"No, I didn't." I laugh.

"Survive being flushed down a toilet?"

"No."

"So if you're a rodent," he says, "you'll probably outlive us all."

When it's time to get Maisie, this time I pull him to me. It's been too long. Then I ask, "Will, how come you keep coming back?"

"Haven't you figured that out yet?" He steps into the drama room, pulling my hand behind him.

TWENTY-SIX

The Tuesday before winter break, Mr. Drummond stops me as I leave Ms. Furbank's class. "The deadline for play submissions is at the end of this week," he says. "Have you finished yours yet?"

Finished it? I wrote a few pages in November, when I told him I'd stay, and nothing since. "You said it was in March," I say, blocking the doorway and making everyone else move around me.

"The plays are performed in March, but they need time to judge submissions and prepare the plays. It's a competition, for both the playwrights and the actors."

I'll be competing with other students? Mr. Drummond made it sound like the drama department would just fall all over anything I wrote. I blink. "I don't think I can do it." I've missed my chance.

Seeing my face, Mr. Drummond says, "Why don't you come by my classroom over the lunch hour? I'll help you get started." When I stand there, looking blank, he adds, "You have a few days. It's enough."

He's wrong, but I follow him anyway.

We sit with some lined paper on the desk between us, and Mr. Drummond shows me how to properly format a play. I tell him what I've written so far, and we decide on three more characters: another sibling and two friends. There are five characters in total, including the original daughter and the mother. Mr. Drummond helps me decide on the role of each character and the basic plot line. By the end of the lunch hour, we have a sibling who doesn't know anything about the poisoning, one who planned the murder, two evil friends and a dead mother. It's a start.

"Now," Mr. Drummond says, as the bell rings and students file in, "go home and write it." Just like that.

"Thanks," I say, gathering the sheets. If I don't get it in on time, I'll fail him too. I don't know why I care about the stupid play at all, but I do. Maybe because I know I could actually write something good, something to be proud of. And Mom might even see it, if she's back by then.

Will's waiting at my locker after school. "What?" he says when he sees me. I guess I have my pre-Laina, I'm-about-to-whack-someone face.

I tell him about the play competition and how I have four days to finish writing a play and submit it.

He shrugs. "You can do it." What's wrong with these people? Do I look like I can pull a five-character play out of nowhere?

"Actually, I don't think I can."

He turns my shoulders to face him. "You can. Do you want me to come over tonight and help?"

A feeling of horror fills me, and then I take a deep breath. It's different now. Mom's gone. No sneaking around.

"I think you should tell your mom," I say.

He nods, probably remembering the last time too.

"And I'll have to ask Laina." I've never had anyone over since she's been there, since *that* night.

He walks me to Maisie's school before turning toward his house. "Call me," he says over his shoulder. I stand for a minute and watch him go through the drifting snow. We can do these things—call each other, make plans to get together. So simple. So impossible.

As soon as Laina gets home, I ask her about having Will over to help me with the play. She gets really excited and gives me these little smiles. Which makes me want to disappear into the bedroom.

"Why doesn't he come for dinner?" she asks, already a blur of movement in the kitchen.

"Well…" I'm about to say no. Then: "I'll ask him." Maybe it is time for him to meet Maisie and Evan too. No more treading water by myself.

Will does come for dinner, which isn't as weird as I thought it would be. Probably because Mom isn't around to call me names or throw binders at anyone. And no police are involved. Laina makes this delicious tortilla soup and her signature buns. Maisie's a little shy with him, but Evan wants to show him every toy he owns—which isn't very many—and even climbs in his lap after supper. Will and Laina have a conversation about the chemistry of bread dough.

After we've finished cleaning up, Laina offers to take Maisie and Evan to one of those indoor playgrounds at McDonald's. She's right; we wouldn't get much done with Evan climbing Will like a monkey or Maisie drawing all over my stuff.

I sit Will on one side of the sofa and me on the other, with a bunch of papers between us—all business tonight. I read him what I've written so far, and the new pages as I write them. He's actually pretty good at giving feedback, and I try not to be defensive when he suggests changes. When Laina, Maisie and Evan come back after two hours, I'm about a third of the way through.

I walk Will down to the door of the apartment building so I can say goodbye without Maisie and Evan staring. The bathrobe guy must be giving the lobby a break tonight.

"Why don't you ask Damien and Amanda to help too?" he asks, finally allowed to pull me close. "Between the four of us, we could read the parts before you hand it in. Then you'd get an idea of what it looks and sounds like."

That's possible. I see Damien in English every day. Will sees Amanda in his class. "Okay. I'll ask Damien tomorrow. You ask Amanda. Maybe we could borrow the drama room at lunch on Thursday." Not like we ever really ask.

I keep working on my play after Will leaves and long after Maisie and Evan fall asleep. Laina takes a bath, then stands behind me before going to bed. When she doesn't say anything, I turn to look at her.

"I talked to your mom today," Laina says.

"You did?" I almost drop my pen.

She nods. "She's doing well. She misses you guys."

Her words squeeze my chest. I haven't really let myself think about it, but sometimes I miss her too—at least the good days.

Laina watches my face.

"I'm glad she's okay." I swallow.

As I turn back to the pages in front of me, Laina touches my elbow. "Isabelle, you should know that when she comes back, that may not be the end of it."

I don't know whether I should laugh or roll my eyes. Here's Laina, trying to prepare me for the possibility my mother might drink again. As if I didn't live that story for sixteen years. "Yeah, I know."

She looks relieved. "I just don't want you to be disappointed if…well, you know. These things take time."

I nod. Before, the best I got from Mom was a cheap promise at the end of a binge. At least she's trying now.

I expect Laina to put her blankets on the sofa, but she stays behind me. "I won't leave you again, Isabelle, even if your mom relapses. I'll be around."

I nod again. "Thanks." I try to finish writing a sentence but am too distracted by an odd feeling moving through me: an incredible lightness.

She settles on the sofa, shifting on the flat cushions. Then, from under a blanket, Laina calls, "Will seems nice."

I smile.

* * *

I wave Damien over before Ms. Furbank starts. "I need to ask you a favor," I say, motioning him closer. He rests his elbows on my desk and leans in. Zara cranes her neck to stare at us. "I'm entering a play in the drama competition, and it's due on Friday. I'm going to try to finish it tonight." I swallow. *Try* is the operative word.

He nods, his eyes on mine.

"Can you meet with me, Will and Amanda to read it through at lunchtime tomorrow?" One of us will have to read two parts.

His eyes light up. "I'll supply the props too." He slides back to his desk before I can tell him what kinds of props we need. Not that Damien's props would likely correspond anyway. I suspect I'll be poisoning the mother while wearing a tutu and a shark-tooth necklace.

At lunch, Amanda comes to sit with Will and me in the cafeteria. It's nice, having two people to sit with, out in the open. Amanda tells me she's in too.

When Laina gets home that evening, I tell her about the rehearsal with Will, Damien and Amanda. She gets that excited look again, probably at the prospect I might actually have friends.

"If you have something left over, can I bring them some cupcakes or something?" I say. I don't know why, but asking her makes me shy. Maisie and Evan practically dive-bomb her, checking for desserts, as soon as she walks in the door. Now I'm doing the same.

"Leftovers? I think I can do better than that."

"Don't go to any trouble…"

She's already pushing me out of the kitchen.

"Only" —I feel bad for saying it—"I don't think names should be written on them." I picture handing out special cupcakes for everyone with their names written in fancy pink gel.

Laina laughs. "I was sixteen once too, Isabelle." Then she gets to work, hands and measuring cups flying.

I finish the first draft of the play just before midnight. Laina insisted the light over the table didn't bother her and pulled a blanket over her head on the sofa. Both of us still avoid Mom's old room. For one second I contemplated working in there, but I knew my brain would stop functioning for sure.

On my way out the door the next morning, Laina hands me a white box, taped shut. I don't know when she had time to finish whatever this is. The apartment smelled good when I woke up.

"Try not to tip it," she tells me. I'm curious, but I'm too busy chasing Evan and Maisie to peek.

I catch Mr. Drummond before his class starts. "First draft done," I say, waving the papers in the air.

"Never doubted it," he says. From his face, I can tell he means it. He actually believed I could pull it off.

I ask him if I can use the photocopier in the office to make copies for the rehearsal today and also if I can borrow the staff fridge for this white box I'm carting around. I don't think it'll survive my locker. I already see some oily-looking marks on the cardboard.

He's on the phone to the office before I'm out the door. The admin assistant looks only mildly annoyed at having to help me with the photocopier. Then she guides me to the staff room, which has two couches uglier than ours, and shows me an empty shelf in the fridge.

When the lunch bell rings, Damien and I leave Ms. Furbank's class and meet Will and Amanda in the hallway. As we're turning toward the drama room, another body joins us. Nimra.

"Hey." I smile. "You're coming too?"

"Damien asked me," she says, falling in step with the rest of us.

"The old crew." Damien shrugs. "I didn't think you'd mind."

"I don't." It feels right, all of us together, heading to the drama room again. Now there are enough readers for every part too.

"What are you guys doing?" a voice calls behind us. We stop and turn. Zara. She probably sensed an unauthorized gathering of two or more people and came to crack down.

Everyone shifts, staring at me or at the floor. Zara and I lock eyes. I don't know what to tell her other than the truth.

"We're going to practice a play I wrote," I finally say.

"Oh."

When it doesn't look like she's going to raise hell, the rest of the group turns and starts to walk away. I watch her, noticing that her jaw and shoulders look stiff but her eyes are different. A little sad.

"Do you want to come too?" I ask. I'm probably going to regret this.

"Yes," she says, striding to catch up. "I mean, I should probably be there. I've had lots of experience organizing things."

There it is: the regret.

The drama room is, of course, unlocked and empty. This time we meet near the stage, and I hand out a copy of the play to everyone.

"This is a first draft," I explain. "I'll probably have to make some changes before I hand it in tomorrow. Feel free to offer suggestions." I say the last part more quietly, hoping Zara misses it.

Before I have a chance to assign parts, Zara asks, "Which is the main character?" She scans the pages.

"You should be the mother." I smile.

Everyone else picks a character. Will ends up as the sibling who plots the murder, which is pretty funny. While they're reading through their parts, and Damien's looking for props, I jog down to the staff room to pick up my white box. No one even turns to look at me as I slip in and out.

Now that there are five readers, I can just watch and listen. I make notes on my copy as they go through it, underlining parts to change, parts to keep. The others make some suggestions too. Once, Nimra stops us and says, "That line isn't very clear. Does my character know what's going on or not?"

Zara takes that as her cue to critique every second sentence. I manage to keep from tackling her and only snap two pencil leads against the page before switching to a pen.

Damien—playing an evil friend—reads all of his lines in an accent that's somewhere between English and Australian. "I'm probably an exchange student from the UK," he explains.

I was right about the props being unrelated. Zara actually agrees to wear a pilling bathrobe, which kind of works. Will ends up holding a light saber, and Amanda has what looks like a fox tail pinned to her jeans. Damien's wearing the Stetson this time, and Nimra nearly kills herself in a pair of four-inch platform shoes. The poison itself is in some kind of plastic gourd. It's all good.

When we get to the end, Nimra, Zara and Amanda make a few more suggestions—most of them good.

"You should have the mother come back from the dead," Damien says. "Kind of a zombie twist."

I laugh. "I'll think about it."

While they're putting the props away, I pull the tape off Laina's white box and lift the lid. It's one of those cakes made out of cupcakes, in the shape of a comedy and tragedy mask. Most of the icing is chocolate, with the exaggerated expressions done in white icing.

"Wow," Amanda says. "Where'd you get that?"

"My aunt made it for us." In that moment I see all of the people who came together for me, who helped me pull this off. Mr. Drummond, who pushed me forward and saw things in me that I didn't see. Will, who was always there when

I needed him. Laina, who put her life on hold to look after us, so I could actually do things normal teenagers do. And this fabulous cake. Then Amanda, Damien, Nimra and even Zara, who showed up without a second thought. Even the admin assistant, who helped with the photocopies and showed me where to store the cake.

We're finishing our cupcakes, licking icing off our fingers, when the drama teacher comes in. "What's all of this?" she asks Damien, probably the only face she recognizes.

"Hi, Mrs. Murphy," Damien says. He has a chocolate smear on his cheek. "We were just practicing a play for Isabelle." He points at me. "She'll be handing it in tomorrow."

"Wonderful!" Mrs. Murphy smiles over at me. "Actually, Mr. Drummond told me about you. I look forward to reading it." She has this great bohemian look to her, like all her clothes came from a market in Mexico.

I silently add her to the list. *Thank you, Mrs. Murphy, for (unknowingly) lending us the drama room on many occasions.* I leave a cupcake on her desk.

"Let's bring one to Mr. Drummond too," I say to Will. He's standing at the door and reaches for my hand as I join him.

It doesn't matter if the drama department picks my play or not. I've already won.

ACKNOWLEDGMENTS

I would like to thank Jocelyn Brown and Marina Endicott for their mentorship and for telling me to keep writing. Their advice and encouragement were invaluable to me. Thanks also to Sarah Harvey for her guidance and direction as an editor and for seeing something special in Isabelle.

Many thanks to Alissa Takahashi and Jenna Hardy, my then-teenage consultants, for answering a string of bizarre questions! Thanks also to Calvin Takahashi for humoring me with his police-related advice.

Thank you to Mike, Liam, Maia and Anna for the daily adventures and ongoing support.

LISA J. LAWRENCE grew up in small towns in British
Columbia and Alberta. She could often be found in the
library during summer vacations or hammering away at an
old typewriter. She graduated from the University of Alberta
with a BA in Romance Languages, an MA in Italian Studies
and a BEd in Secondary Education. Since then she has taught
preschool, post-secondary Italian, and Spanish as a second
language. Lisa lives in Edmonton, Alberta, with her husband
and three children. *Rodent* is her first novel.